MW01138160

ISBN: 1-4196-9561-4
ISBN-13: 9781419695612
LCCN: 2008910917

Visit www.booksurge.com to order additional copies.

UNBRIDLED

A TALE
of a
DIVORCE RANCH

A NOVEL BY

MARILU NORDEN

*"To my darling Thomas (in memoriam)
and progeny Philip, Kristin, Michael, Christopher and Nick
for gifts of love and encouragement and for
the freedom to create."*

CHAPTER 1

Swift as a shadow, short as any dream.
—— *William Shakespeare*, A Midsummer Night's Dream

Lara Treadwell shivered. "We don't usually go home this way," she said as raindrops splattered hard against the station wagon's windshield. "This road is so dark, even with our headlights on."

"Better let Billy stay on at Mom and Pop's for tonight, too," her husband Rick said, turning on the Ford's wipers as he drove. "It'll be late when we get in. Got to get my sleep. Bad enough I have to catch that early morning train into New York."

Lara missed three-year-old Billy this October weekend in 1950. She and Rick often took their son with them, employing a hotel babysitter to watch over the boy while Mommy and Daddy conducted ballroom dance workshops, plus Rick's magic show. This weekend's gig featuring "The Talented Treadwells" was at a resort in the Berkshires, however, so Billy was being cared for by Rick's parents in their Carleton, Connecticut home.

"What time do you need to get up tomorrow?" Lara asked her husband, thinking to herself how chilly and light-headed she felt. "God, this rain is really coming down. It's freezing, too. Is the heater working?" She pulled the collar of her black lambswool coat closer around her neck.

"If we turn it on the windows'll mist up. Damn. They're doing it anyway." Rick whipped off his wool scarf and flung it at Lara. "Wipe the inside of the windshield every once in a while so we can see where we're going, okay? If this keeps up there's no way I'll be in shape to make tomorrow's meeting with Sinatra's TV people. This weather's the pits."

"Maybe we ought to stop 'til it blows over." She gave the inside of the glass a swipe.

"I would if there were a safe place to stop. These country roads have no shoulder, in case you didn't notice."

"Oh. Sorry. I just thought…"

"Yeah." Rick squashed his cigarette out in the car's ashtray. "You're always sorry for something. Every time you goof up a step in the routine, every time."

"Oh, Rick. Did I do that tonight? I'm sorry." *Oops,* she thought, *Rick is right. I say "sorry" too often.* She glanced at her husband, his face illuminated by the light from the dashboard. A prominent nose kept him from being Hollywood-handsome, but she admired his chiseled features, light brown hair, and gray eyes.

She resolved, as she had in the past, to work harder as Rick's dance partner. From compliments they received after a show, she realized that small blunders she knew she'd made usually went unnoticed by the audience. But Rick was a tough taskmaster. She often felt she could never please him despite her having heard a former dance instructor say that when couples danced there were no mistakes made by the women, only mistakes caused by the man leading them. This didn't seem to apply to Rick. He was talented in so many ways; he couldn't help being a perfectionist. Lara was in awe of that in her husband; it was something to which she could never aspire.

"Oh my God!" Rick yelled.

"What?" Lara lurched forward, her head almost hitting the windshield as Rick stomped on the brake pedal and the car skidded to a stop.

"There! Oh God, it's not stopping. Shit!" He flashed the headlights on and off in warning.

"Rick, it's a *horse!* Oh my God."

Lara froze, fearing the creature would slam straight into their car and onto the hood. Mercifully, the horse stopped, reared up on its hind legs and gave a loud whinny, coming down with a thud inches from the hood, its large, luminous eyes filled with a wild, fearless expression, exulting in its freedom.

For one crazy moment, Lara felt those equine eyes connect with hers. Could it be her imagination? Even through the watery windshield she felt the animal's proud, magnetic power, felt its spirit. The horse "spoke" to her. What it "said" was not known to her, not then, on that rain-slicked country road.

Turning quickly, the creature flicked its tail, tossed its mane, and disappeared at a canter into a clump of trees off the passenger's side of the car, a white, dream-like horse-figure fading into the rainy night. *Could it be real*, thought Lara, *or a trick of the eye, similar to Rick's magic machinations onstage?*

"Thank God I didn't hit the thing. They warned me about hitting a cow or a deer on this road. But a damn horse?" said Rick, shaking his head in disbelief as he revved up the engine.

"Wait a minute, Rick, I have to, uh-oh." A wave of nausea seized Lara. She opened the car door and vomited onto the roadway. "Oh God, I'm sorry. How disgusting." Trembling, she fished a handkerchief from her purse and wiped her mouth.

Rick sighed. "Maybe you're getting that bug that's going around. Shut the door, will you?"

Oh dear, thought Lara, *with all the performing, I haven't been keeping track.* She slumped down in her seat, suddenly pierced with the possibility that she might be pregnant and what this would mean professionally for her and Rick.

Staring into the night as they drove, Lara wondered: could the horse's unexpected, dramatic appearance be a sign of some kind?

Eight months later, ripe with child, Lara sat on a chair in the small master bedroom of her and Rick's newly built house on the outskirts of Carleton. Rick sat on the bed, his back to her as he smoked a Lucky Strike.

"Is something wrong, Rick?" she finally asked.

No answer.

She tried again, aware of a spring breeze ruffling the curtains at the half-open window and muffled sounds coming from the TV in the living room.

"Rick? Honey?"

She watched him tap the ashes from his cigarette in the bedside ashtray, take a slow drag, then exhale.

"I just don't love you anymore," he said.

The baby kicked. Lara remembered her doctor's admonition to keep calm since being bedridden for a month due to a near miscarriage.

Laying one hand on her smock-covered stomach, she told herself she wouldn't cry. She watched the blue-white smoke of her husband's cigarette curl lazily toward the window and wished she could float away like those acrid-scented wisps of smoke, float away on the breeze and escape the magnitude of this moment.

Throat tightening, she managed a faint, "But why, Rick? Why now when we're having another child?" How dare he? She felt her face flush hot, then hotter.

Rick drew deeply on his cigarette. "Because," he said, exhaling, "when we have this kid and we break up I could have one and you the other." He took another drag, gray eyes fastened on the floor. "Especially if we have another boy. But if it's a girl, I'll take Billy and you can have her."

Lara felt her heart pound with the sonorous beat of a drum-roll preceding an execution. The child within her kicked again, innocent, unaware.

I know Rick well enough, she thought, *to realize his mind is not going to be changed by arguments of any kind. Once he makes up his mind, that's it, like a tombstone-cutter's drill on a slab of marble. In a way, I've always been in awe of him, even afraid.*

Focusing on the floral wallpaper on the bedroom wall, Lara asked herself, *how is it possible for me to believe everything's hunky-dory when it's crumbling into total shit? I feel so stupid.* She hadn't heard Rick object to the coming baby, not in so many words. But he wasn't home much, being busy training his new assistant, Eve O'Brian, a young high school junior whose talent stood out from all the other girls Rick and Lara had auditioned to take Lara's place when she became too pregnant to perform.

A tentative knock broke the silence behind the closed door.

"I'm hungry, Mommy. *Howdy Doody's* not on anymore."

"I'll be right there, Billy," Lara said, hoisting herself up with effort to open the door.

Rick stubbed out his cigarette and strode past his wife and son. "I'll catch a snack at Mom's. Have to be at the Center early tonight. Should be a late one. Don't wait up."

Numb, Lara watched as Rick went through his "Daddy" routine, tossing a delighted Billy up in the air a few times and catching the boy in a quick hug. Without glancing at her, Rick dashed through the front door and drove off with a screech of their station wagon's tires.

Rooted like a tree in the living room, Lara gazed out the picture window. Beyond the stone wall across the road from the house was a field, stretching green, dotted here and there with a proliferation of white mustard blossoms. Usually this cheered her. Not today. She felt dead. Dead in her soul. But not in her body. The baby gave another strong kick, a small mustard seed of hope.

Slowly she became aware of her young son's questioning eyes peering up at her.

"Mommy? Mommy, what's the matter?"

"Nothing, Billy." She shuffled like a sleepwalker into the kitchen. "Mommy's going to make us something to eat."

As Billy ran off to the corner of the room to play with his blocks, she told herself, *Somehow I'll get through tonight, the next day, and the next.* Switching to autopilot, she fixed a supper of macaroni and cheese, green beans, and a Waldorf salad.

Later, washing the dishes, Lara remembered that tonight was an important rehearsal for Rick's upcoming appearance on the Frank Sinatra TV show in New York City. She admired her husband's ability to garner spots on TV shows such as those of Ed Sullivan and others. *Amazing,* she mused, *how well Rick's built up his dance and magic act with nothing but talent and perseverance when returning from serving in the Air Force. Now that effort's beginning to pay off. I'm happy for him. For me, too, although I miss being his performance partner.*

Tonight, she knew Rick was rehearsing with Eve, perfecting an Apache-style dance-and-magic routine. But Lara couldn't help feeling a twinge of jealousy towards Eve. The girl seemed so sure of herself and her new status as partner to Rick. *Of course,* she thought, *everything will return to normal as soon as I get back on my feet...*

But... what if? Lara removed the plug in the kitchen sink. As the soapy water spiraled down the drain she comforted herself with the thought that, after all, Eve was only a teenager and Rick was twenty-seven. Besides, he was so aware of his reputation as an upstanding citizen of Carleton that he would never... or would he?

"Mommy!" Billy, dressed in his blue, red, and yellow Superman pajamas, came running into the kitchen waving his favorite storybook. "I want 'The Tin Soldier' tonight. Okay, Mommy? I brushed my teeth. See?" He gave her a wide, comical grin, revealing his white baby teeth with a space between the two front ones and a telltale glob of toothpaste in the corner of his mouth.

"Only the first part for now. Okay, Billy? Mommy's tired."

The little boy snuggled close to her as they sat on his bed, his blonde, crew-cut head leaning against her arm, small hands folded in his lap in quiet anticipation.

Lara opened the colorfully illustrated Hans Christian Andersen book and started reading aloud. Soon her voice caught on every sentence and each page became so blurry she could hardly see.

God, I'm a mess, she thought. Sobs rose in her throat and threatened to turn into an avalanche of tears. *Dear God, what am I going to do? What to do? What to do? I feel like I'm drowning, can't breathe, going down for the third time.*

"Don't be sad, Mommy." Billy looked up into her tear-stained face. "I love you." He nestled close to her and patted her arm with one warm little hand.

Oh no. What if he'd heard her and Rick's earlier conversation? Lara hugged him. "I love you, too, baby."

"I'm not a baby. I'm a big boy. Daddy said so."

"Of course you are, Billy. I'm sorry. I forgot. I'll leave the door open for you, sweetheart. Okay?"

He gave her a sleepy smile. She tucked him into bed and turned out the light. *What a great kid he is,* she told herself. *I owe it to him and the coming baby to keep as calm as possible.*

But what do you do when your husband of five years says—as though he were commenting on the state of the weather—that he no longer loves you? What do you do when you are carrying his baby, a new life conceived—as you believe—in love, God's handiwork; what do you do when your spouse tosses a bomb, blasting everything to smithereens? As part of the flight crew on bombing raids during the war, Rick's task in the plane's belly was to help drop missiles on

Germany. He was good at hitting the target… like he had today. *I can't wrap my mind around the fact that Rick might actually mean what he said. It hurts too damn much, like being betrayed, stabbed by someone in whose hands you had placed your sacred trust.*

Undressing in the small, maroon-tiled bathroom, she ran water in the tub and added some gardenia bath salts. *Maybe if I relax, I can think more clearly,* she told herself. *Uh, oh. Damn. The phone.* She turned off the faucet and, wrapping a large terrycloth bath towel around her swollen middle, padded barefoot to answer the wall phone in the kitchen.

"Larie? It's Janelle." The animated voice sounded far away and there was static on the line.

"My God! I can't believe it! Janelle!" How unexpected it was to be talking to her only sibling. "This is a treat. Where the hell are you?"

"Right now I'm in my dorm in Beirut, talking to my big sister a million miles away. Can you hear me okay?"

Janelle had sailed to Europe recently, along with their parents, U.S. Army Chaplain and Mrs. Grant Shepard. The Shepards were now stationed in Ankara, Turkey, while Janelle studied English literature at the American University in Lebanon.

Janelle continued, "Actually, Larie, I'm calling for Mother and Dad. They wanted me to contact you 'cause they're worried about you."

"Why? I'm fine," Lara lied. "Aside from being bloated beyond belief." She gave a nervous laugh. "Got a good reason for that, y'know." With her free hand, she moved the towel up to cover her breasts, tucking in the towel's top end to hold it in place.

"Right. Seriously, Larie, we all noticed how quiet you were when you and Rick came down to the dock in New York to see us off. Don't get me wrong. You looked terrific. But Mother and Dad thought…"

Lara plunked herself down on a chair by the kitchen counter and tried to recall the day at the dock. Had something been brewing between her and Rick about which she was unaware? And her parents picked it up? "Tell 'em I'm okay, Janelle. At the time I just wanted to get on that ship and sail away with all of you. But of course I couldn't in the shape I'm in. I might've sunk the boat!" She managed a chuckle and changed the subject. "How're Mother and Dad, otherwise?"

"Great. They're getting settled in their house outside of Ankara. Dad's busy with his chaplain duties and Mother's making friends with the army wives. Oh, did you know that Dad is organizing the first American church in Ankara? Really important work." The static on the line worsened. "We'll all write and keep you posted, Larie. Glad all's well. Gotta go. This is costing a fortune." Janelle sent breezy hugs to all, wished Lara good luck with the new baby, and broke the connection.

Lara sat holding the phone, reluctant to hang up. *Here I am,* she thought, *big and pregnant, confused, hurt, and trapped, while my nearest kin are halfway 'round the world. If only I had a close female pal to talk to, like my friend Leah Stein from art class at Syracuse. All Rick's and my acquaintances are people in the theatre who see us as a professional couple. I don't dare talk to any of them.*

She replaced the receiver in its cradle, feeling isolated. *I should have learned to drive by now,* she thought. *But with one car and Rick's always using it for work… Of course, he promised to teach me, but he never gets around to it. And I let it pass. In a way it's my own fault. Why don't I initiate things more often? Is it because it's easier to go along with Rick's way all the time?*

After her bath, Lara donned a clean nightgown, slipped into bed, and sobbed silently to herself 'til she could cry no more.

Around midnight, she checked the bedside clock and heard the box springs squeak as Rick got into bed. Her back to him, she pretended to be asleep, barely breathing. A forceful resolve rose from deep within her. *I must be brave in the coming days,* she told herself, *for my unborn baby's sake and Billy's. But how?*

Then it came to her: the image of the horse who'd almost rammed into her and Rick's car on that rainy night in October. *That horse's freedom of spirit inspired me,* she thought. *Can it serve as a beacon to light my way in the days ahead? God willing, I hope so.*

She fell asleep and dreamt she was astride a white horse cantering by rows of tombstones while countless couples tried to learn a dance routine taught by a man in a black top hat, wielding a whip.

CHAPTER 2

All the king's horses and all the king's men
Couldn't put Humpty together again.
— Humpty Dumpty, *anonymous*

One month later, doing the breathing her doctor taught her and timing her contractions, Lara decided to head to the hospital. She gave last-minute instructions to Reg, Rick's brother, and Reg's wife Gladys, who were watching over Billy.

"Can I come, too, Mommy?" asked Billy plaintively.

Lara hugged him. "No, honey, but I'll bring you back a brand new baby brother or sister. Be good for Aunt Gladys and Uncle Reg. Okay?"

With Rick's assistance, Lara made it to the car and settled herself in the front seat. She blew a kiss to Billy as he stood by the front door of the house with his aunt and uncle, all waving and smiling as Rick eased the station wagon out of the driveway.

It was a sunny, humid afternoon in June. Even with the car windows open, Lara felt warm and sweaty. The contractions were getting stronger and closer together. She tried to relax, tried to concentrate instead on the pattern of light and shadow cast by the trees lining the country road. But the pain proved all consuming.

Soon she and Rick were traveling on the main highway into Carleton at a fairly rapid pace, Rick making an effort to hurry but still keep under the speed limit. Her pain increasing, Lara cradled her stomach with two shaky hands. *Guess I forgot how intense labor can be,* she told herself. *If women remembered that fact more often there'd definitely be a decrease in world population. Ha.* She glanced at her husband, glued to the steering wheel, one eye on the road, the other on the speedometer. The significance of the moment swept over her in a tumultuous rush of feeling.

"I love you, Rick," she said softly.

Rick stared straight ahead, his face a mask, hands rigid as he gripped the wheel. "I love you, too, Lara," he muttered.

Another fierce contraction seized her, but all she felt was overwhelming joy. *He loves me!* Such magical words! The past month of tense coolness and lack of affection from Rick faded away. With a fresh burst of confidence, Lara felt instantly empowered and ready for the task ahead of her, like someone crippled who could now dance and leap. *Well, not quite yet*, she told herself.

She and Rick pulled up to the hospital's entrance and, after being quickly admitted, Lara was wheeled up to the maternity floor, while her husband went to park the car. Dr. Collins—Lara's young obstetrician, recently trained in the Reed Method of Natural Childbirth—appeared in a jocular mood as he entered the labor room. "You owe me one, Lara," he said.

"Oh?" She winced while puffing through yet another contraction. "What d'ya mean?"

"When you called, my wife and I were about to leave for an evening at the home of Josh Logan. You know, the Broadway producer? My wife went on alone, but now you and your hubby owe us a private exhibition dance performance." He smiled at Lara and laid a hand on her stomach.

"Uh ... oh, ow! Okay. But only if you promise to have Mr. Logan there so we can audition for him." She tried to laugh, but all she could do was huff and puff her brains out like the Big Bad Wolf in "The Three Little Pigs," a story she'd read to Billy the night before. "This is hard, Dr. Collins," she gasped.

"I know, but you're doing beautifully, Lara." Timing her every contraction, Collins held her hand as he stroked her brow. "Just remember to relax with each breath. Go *with* the pain, not against it. Good. It won't be long now."

Thank God, Lara told herself. *Maybe I should've opted for anesthesia, put out in Never-Never Land as I did with Billy's birth. I missed the whole experience. Don't want to repeat that so here I am, going with the pain. But, damn! I feel like cursing it at the same time.* "Huff-puff-huff-puff, huff, ... oh, ow!"

She heard a familiar voice say, "How're you doing?" It was Rick, standing close by.

Smiling weakly at him, Lara thought, *How great! He actually seems interested in what's going on.* She hoped it wasn't because Dr. Collins was there but because her mate was truly involved. She held out her hand. Rick took it and quietly held on until Dr. Collins gave the nurse an order and Lara found herself whisked away to the delivery room.

"Congratulations, Lara. You have a beautiful baby girl!"

She heard Dr. Collin's voice as through a misty veil. A shot of Demerol had helped make her job easier towards the end of delivery, but she still felt a tremendous elation and sense of personal accomplishment. *If only Rick and I can be a team again, like Dr. Collins and myself,* she thought. Surely Rick would be happy and proud of her. After all, he'd said he loved her. And she certainly loved him.

Later, in her hospital room, Lara's heart swelled when she saw her husband. "Have you seen our baby yet, Rick?"

"Yeah, she's a beauty," he said, standing at the foot of her bed. Lara wondered why he didn't come closer. But he did seem pleased. "The nurse told me she'll be bringing her in in a minute. I sent a telegram to your parents. My folks will be here shortly."

Lara nodded. *Why doesn't he show a little more enthusiasm? I'm hungry for a hug. More like* starved *for one,* she thought. But she didn't want to grovel. Not from a hospital bed. Not ever.

Her mood changed when she saw her baby girl being carried into the room by a cheerful young nurse who handed the infant, wrapped in a pink receiving blanket, into Lara's eager arms.

"Oh, Rick. She's perfect!" With tear-filled eyes Lara drank in the marvel of this gift from heaven. She nuzzled the baby's button nose, kissed the warm, rosy cheeks, and smelled the sweet newness of her. "I'm so happy, aren't you? Look. She has blonde hair, well, almost. Just like Billy."

All Lara's prior concerns melted away as Rick bent over for a close look at his daughter. The young nurse picked up the newborn and placed her in her father's arms.

Surely everything will be fine now, Lara assured herself. *With such blessings, how could things be otherwise?*

On the advice of her mother-in-law, Lara decided not to breast-feed Candace Ann. *Perhaps it's better I don't,* she thought, *in view of the emotional climate between Rick and me. Since I came home from the hospital he's been so distant. Polite, but cold and preoccupied. How can he be like that, with no let-up? Maybe I should ...*

One night, after tucking Billy in bed and feeding the baby, Lara determined to let her husband know how much she missed their former closeness. With guarded anticipation and a quickened heartbeat she approached him as he reclined on the living room sofa, smoking a cigarette and watching television.

"Rick, ... uh, it's been two weeks since I got home from the hospital and I wonder why you're sleeping on the couch every night. I mean, you were sleeping in our bedroom before the baby came and you'd be so much more comfortable there. Candace only wakes up for the two o'clock. She's so good, Rick."

"No," he said. "I don't want to." He sat up, stubbed his cigarette out in the coffee table ashtray, and lit another one. "I don't love you anymore, and, what's more, I don't want to have anything to do with you." His icy look of hate aimed directly at her made Lara feel faint.

Pulse racing, she leaned against the television console for support, thinking, *this isn't real. This can't be happening. It feels as though Rick's placed a bomb under me, lit the fuse, and blown me into a thousand pieces, never to be put together again, like Humpty Dumpty in Billy's nursery rhyme book. "All the king's horses, and all the king's men, couldn't put Mommy together again."*

Lara tried to steady herself. Then ... slowly, carefully, her breath coming in short gasps, she turned from Rick without speaking, ... for what was there to say?

Dazed, she stumbled into the bedroom, feeling stabbed, violated. But there was no blood, only a hole where her heart used to be. Blinded by tears, she fell into bed, pulled the sheet over her head, and lay like a stone, internalizing her sobs so as not to wake her baby sleeping peacefully in the bassinet beside her.

Had she heard Rick correctly? Yes. Sadly, shockingly, she had. But, did he really *mean* what he said? *Maybe*, she thought, *maybe tomorrow I can ...*

It was a long night.

The next week dragged on. Lara felt so isolated. She couldn't stop crying and burst into tears when least expected. She feared she would lose her sanity. With great effort, she tried to fulfill her obligations to the children without falling apart.

It occurred to Lara that Rick might be cold toward her due to a lack of sex lately. When she'd almost lost Candace at five months of pregnancy her doctor had prescribed total bed rest for a month and ordered her not to engage in any sexual activity until after the baby's birth. Rick had trouble with this, though he'd grudgingly put up with it. Determined to somehow remedy things sexual with her husband, Lara knew she couldn't go all the way just yet, but perhaps she could ...

Late one night she crept quietly into the living room and knelt by him as he slept on the couch. She pulled back the light blanket covering him, reached inside his shorts and gently massaged him. He groaned softly in his sleep. Encouraged, she touched him with her tongue where she knew he would be pleased.

"What th'... ?" Rick sat up and roughly pushed her to the floor. "Get the hell out of here and leave me alone. You're making a fool of yourself, Lara. I told you I don't love you. Go back to bed, dammit."

Oh God, she thought, *how humiliating. Why does Rick hate me so? Is there someone else? How stupid I am to think I can stroke him into loving me again.*

She stood up, fighting off feelings of revulsion, disgust. At him? At herself? Her voice sounded far off, as in a dream.

"I ... oh, Rick. Have you been ... is there someone else? I ... I can't believe that you ..."

"Go to bed, Lara," he mumbled. He lit a cigarette and lay back on the couch, smoking and staring at the ceiling.

Tears stung her eyes. An overwhelming rush of weariness and defeat propelled her into the bedroom. Silently she crawled under the covers and flopped face down in the bed. Waves of anger at Rick and remorse at herself for what she'd just tried to do washed over her as, with clenched fists, she beat on the mattress in frustration, sighed, then rolled over and sat up, hugging her knees tightly to her chest.

Dammit, she muttered to herself, *I shouldn't have done that. I feel like a fool. Rick is right. But what is happening? I used to feel so close to Rick, so loved by him, and, at first, seemingly adored by him.*

She lay back, pulled the covers up to her chin and closed her eyes, recalling how they'd met five years before. Eager to restart his dancer/magician career after a long stint overseas for Uncle Sam, Rick had tried to track down Lara. He'd met her one year before at a dance when she was visiting Carleton and he was on leave. He and his mother finally found her in New York, where, after spending two years as an art major at Syracuse University, nineteen-year-old Lara had moved to the city to try to get a job as an illustrator in an advertising agency.

Lara recalled how she failed to land the art job and ended up working at Saks, living in a seven-dollar-a-week walkup while sharing a bathroom down the hall with some grubby residents and lots of cockroaches.

Rick had showed up out of the blue one day when she was home from work and sick with the flu. He'd invited her to his parent's home in Carleton to help her recuperate. Once there, Lara was treated like a princess. Before she knew it, she'd agreed to marry the prince and live happily ever after. Her dad stopped by during a tour of chaplain duty. He'd wanted to make sure his daughter knew what she was doing and tried to persuade her to give it more thought. When Lara convinced her father that she truly loved Rick, and Rick pledged to Lara's father that there would never be such a thing as divorce, the chaplain gave his blessing. Lara never went back to New York, stayed on in Rick's parent's home and married their son one month after meeting him.

We probably shouldn't have lived with Rick's folks for four years after our wedding, thought Lara. *But I'm glad we finally have our own home,* even though I had to fight for it, getting Rick to move and all. Now, if only ...

Exhausted, she fell asleep.

The opportunity for possible dialogue with Rick presented itself one Sunday when Mom and Pop Treadwell picked up Billy for an outing and the baby napped outside in her carriage.

"Please, Rick, we have to talk." Lara followed her spouse into the kitchen and stood by as he grabbed a Coke from the refrigerator. "I have to tell you, Rick. I can't go on like this," she said. "I mean, I don't understand why you're so cold to me. If I did something to offend you, please forgive me. I certainly didn't mean to." *God*, she thought, *it's so hard getting through to him.*

She followed him into the living room. He stood with his back to her, looking out the picture window while taking quick sips from the bottle of cola.

Lara took a deep breath. "All I know is, Rick, I can't cope with something I don't understand. I mean, what do people do when they have problems and can't talk to each other? Get help? Get a divorce? What?"

Rick turned toward her quickly, plunking the soda bottle down on the coffee table. He pointed an accusing finger at Lara. "That's it! You're right." His tone was menacing, triumphant. "You said it. You put it into words. Divorce."

Dumbstruck, Lara felt tears sting her eyes. "You mean, oh, I *did* say it, but I didn't mean ... I only said it because I was asking a question about something I wasn't clear about, and I thought ...." Her heart was beating so fast she feared it would burst.

A new excitement appeared to surface in Rick as Lara watched him pace the room, energized, like a tiger about to spring.

"Okay. Okay." He lit a cigarette as he paced, took a drag, and gesticulated for emphasis as he spoke. "Since you can't go out yet, I'll go downtown tomorrow and arrange things with my attorney, Jack

Grossman. Jack's very understanding and can get you the best lawyer in Reno."

"Reno?" Lara's heart somersaulted. "What are you talking about, Rick? All I said was ... I didn't mean we ..." She stared at him in disbelief. "I mean, I don't want a ... oh no." She felt her breath come in short spurts.

"I don't see any point in dragging things out. You know the laws here. Too slow. Reno is quick. Jack can get you the dean of lawyers out there. I had a long talk with him already and he's really impressed. Says it's the first time in his law practice he's heard of such a friendly divorce."

Lara felt so shocked she had trouble speaking. "But I've never even met Jack Grossman."

"You don't need to. It's better if I work it out with him."

"Wait a minute. I know you said you don't love me, but, Rick, what about our beautiful two-week-old daughter and our darling Billy? Aren't they worth our trying to work things out?" She paused, thinking of her dad's family, long steeped in ministerial and mission-ary work. "And, Rick, according to the Bible, wouldn't it be wrong? I mean, you went to your Episcopal service this morning with your parents. Don't you think ...?"

"So? I don't need you to preach to me. You and your damn Pres-byterianism," he hissed, head held high as he stared her down with a cold, dismissive air and took a deep drag on his cigarette. He stood so close to Lara that when he exhaled, the resulting stream of smoke made her recoil.

Recovering, Lara tried to soften her voice. "But, maybe we ... Rick, would you go and talk to a counselor with me?" She didn't know who that might be, but she felt sure they could find a compe-tent therapist.

"Yeah? Just who did you have in mind? Don't give me that shrink stuff. Besides, everybody in town knows me. My reputation would suffer if people heard I had to go to a 'head shrinker.' They'd think I was mentally shot, which I'm not, thank you. So forget it. Just forget it."

Lara looked down at her hands shaking uncontrollably in her lap. In fact, her whole body was shaking so drastically that she lowered herself to the edge of the couch to keep from falling. "I wish I could talk to someone. There must be something to therapy or it wouldn't exist. We could call Dr. Collins. Maybe he knows somebody we could go to."

"No," Rick cautioned her. He stopped pacing and pointed a finger at her. "I don't want you to even think of doing that. In fact, I forbid it. I don't want him to know our private business."

"It will come out eventually, Rick," Lara said quietly. "How can you hide ... what about your mom and dad? Oh God, what about mine?" *If only they weren't on the other side of the world right now.*

"They'll have to accept it." Rick strode to the front door, opened it, and flicked his cigarette out onto the graveled driveway.

Lara sat immobile for a moment and watched her husband as he stood on the threshold staring out at the darkened afternoon sky. A thunderstorm was building. Lightning flashed over the stone-walled ridge beyond the house, followed by a clap of thunder.

"Omigosh, the baby!" Lara rushed to the rear of the house, thrust open the kitchen door and dragged Candace's carriage inside as raindrops splashed on the concrete patio. As she walked back into the living room, holding her infant close, she was surprised to see Rick still standing in the open doorway.

The baby burped. Rick glanced at his wife and daughter. Quickly, he turned away and stood facing the driving rain. "I just hope I find what I'm looking for," he said, raising his eyes heavenward.

"I hope you do too, Rick," Lara said, because, despite all, she knew she still loved him. Hugging their tiny offspring, she made a slow retreat into the kitchen to warm a bottle of formula.

The following days held a dreamlike quality for Lara as Rick made all the travel arrangements.

"Jack Grossman and I agreed you should spend the next six weeks at the best divorce ranch in Reno. We thought it would be good for Billy, too. Jack checked and they take kids Billy's age. But they don't take infants." Rick placed a packet of plane tickets on the couch next to Lara where she sat feeding the baby.

Divorce ranch? My God, thought Lara. *I never heard of such a thing. And in Reno? Sounds like the end of the world.*

"What's a divorce ranch, Rick? Why go so far away? And I can't leave Candace," she said. "What are you thinking?"

"I just found out about such places myself ... from Jack." Rick lit a cigarette as he stood looking down at Lara. "Divorce ranches are dude ranches where people go to establish residence in Nevada for six weeks and get a divorce quicker than they can here in Connecticut, which could take up to a year." He blew out a stream of smoke and shrugged his shoulders. "Plenty of people go there. Been the place to go since the 1920s and even more popular now in the '50s, according to Jack," Rick said, adding, "But you can't travel there with an infant."

"I can't leave her, Rick." Lara hugged the tiny child close, feeling sudden tears well up. *Why is Rick in such a hurry,* she wondered? *This is a nightmare, like being stuck on the tracks when a train is coming and you can't save yourself.* "I can't, Rick, don't you see? I just gave birth to her. Only two weeks ago. I love her. She's part of me. How can you ask me to do such a thing?"

"You'll have to. How in hell can you care for her at a ranch in the middle of the desert? No. The sensible thing is to ask Gladys to care for her. I'm sure she'd love to."

"This is unfair, Rick. I feel as if you're making all the decisions and I have no say in things, just because I'm at a disadvantage and can't get out yet." *God, I'm exhausted,* thought Lara. *Doesn't he see that? I wish I felt stronger so I could stand up to him. But he's holding all the cards and calling all the shots, as usual.*

Lara rose, facing her husband, clutching their baby to her breast. "What you're asking me to do, Rick, goes against my grain. It's wrong. I just can't do it. What's more, I won't." She retreated with Candace to the bedroom.

Three days went by, the tension between her and Rick mounting to the point that Billy noticed. "Mommy, what's the matter?" the boy asked one morning after Rick had left and Lara was folding clothes in the laundry room. "You're always crying and Daddy's mad." Billy's upper lip began to tremble.

Oh, my God, thought Lara. *This is too much. This can't go on. I keep trying to reach Rick but nothing works.* She leaned down and hugged her son. "I'm so sorry, Billy. Sometimes mommies and daddies have problems. But it's not your fault. Not at all. Not ever. We'll work things out." She kissed him on one flushed cheek, knowing she needed to make a decision, for his sake especially. *How,* she asked herself, *can I continue to live like this when Rick seems to hate the sight of me? I can't talk to him. He won't get counseling with me. I'm not allowed to go out yet, even to the market. Doctor's orders. What a mess.* She forced a smile for Billy's sake. "Go get your CANDY LAND game and we'll play for awhile. Okay, sweetheart?"

As her son ran to his room, Lara checked on Candace, dozing peacefully in her carriage in the warm morning sunshine outside on the patio. *Such a lovely, calm little thing,* thought Lara. *Maybe she would do fine with Gladys for awhile. Gladys is so kind, and responsible. But ... oh, God, how can I ... ?* Tears slid unbidden down Lara's cheeks as Billy called to her and she stepped back into the kitchen.

Wiping away her tears with the hurried sweep of one hand, Lara sat with Billy at the kitchen table, the CANDY LAND board between them. Surprised at how peaceful and decisive she suddenly felt, she said, "How would you like to take a trip, Billy? Away out west and see some cowboys? Would you like that?"

The boy's eyes widened, bright with excitement. "Will Daddy come too?"

"No, Daddy has to work. And he says Aunt Gladys will take good care of Candace. Just you and Mommy are going. Would that be okay?" She was glad to see her small son grin at her, nodding his blonde head in evident agreement. She decided to talk about it in more detail with him later as she helped him set up the board to play.

But how can I explain to a four-year-old such a deplorable situation as this, thought Lara? *It's so unreal.*

She felt she'd fought as hard as she could. It seemed to her that Rick was like granite. Immovable. And, day by day, it was becoming painfully apparent to Lara that he wanted her to vanish from his life. Gone. Out of sight. Forever, and as soon as possible.

Maybe, she thought, *Rick wants Eve. How do I know? She's only a kid. Oh, hell. My pride is so shot I feel like killing myself. But I won't, ... can't. Billy and Candace need me.*

Lara pledged to herself that she would never, ever let her children down. Next day she called Gladys and thanked her sister-in-law profusely when Gladys readily agreed to her request. Newly pregnant herself, Gladys told Lara she considered it a privilege and a helpful, learning experience to care for Candace. Lara felt relieved. She trusted Gladys. But six weeks? To Lara, it sounded like an eternity. *But at least I'll know,* she thought, *that my precious baby will be loved and cared for properly.*

On the morning of her and Billy's departure, Lara dressed carefully. *Gosh,* she mused, *since giving birth to Candace, I've not been to the market, or anywhere, and here I am about to embark on a journey to end my marriage. How bizarre. Talk about losing control over one's life. God knows I tried hard to argue against it this past week but it's impossible, like butting my head over and over against solid rock. And I'm exhausted.*

Billy bounded into the bedroom as Lara studied her reflection in the dresser mirror. "Will my Hopalong Cassidy cowboy hat fit in your suitcase, Mommy?" The boy's face was flushed with excitement. "I can't get it in mine."

"Of course, sweetheart." Lara smiled at him as he ran back to his room. *What a blessing he is,* she told herself.

Gazing at her image, she decided the green shantung silk with cap sleeves and matching belt looked good enough on her. In fact, her figure filled the dress out in all the right places. She'd worn it before she was pregnant with Candace when she and Rick attended a tribute to Ed Sullivan in New York. She posed with the great television host, who playfully tweaked her nose as cameras clicked and Rick looked on admiringly. A lucky dress. Perfect for a trip to the divorce capital of the world.

Sighing as she brushed her hair, Lara applied lipstick and buckled the thin ankle straps of her high-heeled black suede pumps. Then she carried her and Billy's luggage into the living room.

Earlier, after feeding, bathing, and dressing Candace, Lara had put her outside to sun in her carriage. Now, through the open front door of the house she saw her in-laws and her husband standing over the carriage admiring its contents. Holding back tears, she wondered, *How can I manage this whole good-bye thing with my dignity intact? How in the name of God did everything come to this? And in such a damnably short time?*

Mom and Pop Treadwell moved slowly into the living room. "We're so sorry to see you go, Lara," Mrs. Treadwell said as her husband nodded then looked away, apparently too embarrassed to respond on his own.

Gladys and Reg arrived. Like his father, Reg seemed uncomfortable with the situation while his wife was more effusive. Gladys hugged Lara and told her not to worry, that she would love Candace as her own.

Everyone tried to be cheerful for Billy's sake. After all, the youngster was going on a vacation with his mom. But Lara suspected that even a boy as young as Billy could recognize an atmosphere as charged with unreality as this one. She hastened to say their good-byes.

Rick and Reg piled the traveler's luggage in the back of the station wagon as Lara walked unsteadily to the car with Billy. *I have to steel myself to pass by Candace's carriage without stopping*, she thought, *or I might not be able to leave*. Somehow she made it to the car and got in the front seat with her young son. As they waited for Rick to get in the driver's seat, Lara saw him turn toward a man coming up the driveway.

Lara recognized Jed Morris, Rick's Air Force buddy. "Hey, guy!" Rick greeted his friend. "Glad you made it. Hop in."

As Jed settled himself in the back seat, Lara flashed Rick a look of astonishment. "What's he doing here?" she whispered.

"Moral support," Rick said under his breath as he backed the car down the driveway.

Shocked, but remembering her manners, Lara said hello to Jed, a pleasant, retiring sort of fellow who lived with his wife and family in Carleton. Lara wondered, *Why didn't Rick tell me of his invitation to Jed to share the trip to the airport? How like him to keep me in the dark—about Jack Grossman, about Reno, about who knows what else?*

The drive down the Merritt Parkway was strained.

Billy, wedged between his parents, looked up at them, first at Lara, then at his father. "Isn't Mommy beautiful, Daddy?" he said.

Lara's pulse quickened. Poor little boy. He's obviously trying to put together the pieces of this sad adult puzzle.

"Yes, Billy. Mommy's beautiful," Rick said flatly.

The boy squeezed his mother's hand and smiled at her. Jaw clenched, Rick drove the car at a steady pace.

As they neared the airport, Rick negotiating heavier traffic, Lara became aware of a strange excitement building in her. *I didn't want to go*, she thought. *Not at all. But we're here, soon to fly away. After all the hurt, all the pain, I feel strangely released ... and slightly guilty because of it.*

Later, settled in their seats in the aircraft, Lara watched as Billy waved at his dad from the plane's window. Rick and Jed could be seen standing outside on a balcony of the terminal, Rick waving a large white handkerchief back and forth. Lara felt sure her husband had thought this out ahead of time. It was a clever way to be seen from a distance in a crowd, and the cloth was probably one Rick used in his act to produce rabbits and doves.

"I'm going to miss Daddy, aren't you, Mommy?" Billy continued to wave his small arms, button nose pressed against the plane's window.

"Yes, Billy, and I'm sure Daddy will miss you."

The plane taxied then lifted off the ground with Billy still waving, though the white cloth could no longer be seen.

Lara sat back in her seat. The ascent of the aircraft lifted her spirits, giving rise to a new purpose within her. *My job,* she told herself, *is to protect my children at all costs.*

She relaxed for the first time in weeks, ready for what lay ahead, whatever that might be.

CHAPTER 3

Ride a cockhorse to Banbury Cross,
To see a fine lady upon a white horse.
—— "Ride a Cockhorse," *anonymous*

Roy Bracken wheeled the ranch's new 1951 Woodie station wagon alongside the tarmac of Reno's Municipal Airport, cut the engine, and looked at his watch. *Plenty of time*, he told himself.

Pulling a pack of Camels from the breast pocket of his shirt, Roy popped a cigarette in mouth, lit it, and inhaled deeply. He sat for a while, sweating in the hot sun and squinting at the sky through the Woodie's windshield.

Shit. A man could fry out here. Might as well go inside to wait for the plane. Besides, he reminded himself, *I'll soon need another pack of weeds and it'll be cooler in the terminal.* The July heat showed no signs of letting up.

Inside the terminal, Roy spotted a fellow rancher leaning against an unattended row of slot machines.

"Goddammit, Les! Where th' hell ya been? Haven't seen ya since the Sutcliffe Rodeo." Roy grinned hugely, knowing without caring how such an expression deepened the wrinkles in his weather-beaten face. He shoved his old-fashioned spectacles up the bridge of his nose.

Les, a tall, rangy fellow in faded denims and a sweat-stained cowboy hat, grinned back. "Hey, Roy. Dudes got to ya yet?"

"Nah. I'm waitin' for a new one. Got a kid with her. Comin' in from LaGuardia. How're things out at the Wheeler place?" Roy lit another Camel with the one he was finishing.

Like Roy, Les managed a ranch northeast of Reno, but unlike Roy and his wife June, Les worked for A.K. Wheeler, whose spread was strictly for breeding race horses, not at all like Roy and June's guest ranch for folks waiting out the six weeks necessary for getting a divorce.

"Things are great now that we have the new foreman," said Les. "Been at Wheeler's about a year. Ex-Marine. Guadalcanal. Knows his horseflesh. You might know him. Chance Darwin's the name. Says he likes to hang out at *your* place and check out the fillies." Les winked at Roy. "The two-legged ones."

"Oh, yeah. Chance. Seems like a good kid." Anyone younger than Roy's fifty-odd years was a mere kid in his eyes. A former seasoned rodeo rider, Roy took pride in knowing he was once a dashing figure in Reno's Wild West era when the town was rife with bootleggers and characters of every persuasion.

"What the hell ya doin' at the airport this time of day?" Roy asked his tall friend, who, like himself, had survived the "good old days."

"Aw, ol' Wheeler wants me to meet some high-rollers and their dames flyin' in commercial from the East. Gonna put 'em up at the ranch for a few days. Lord, give me horses over them types any day. They'll wanna sashay around town and gamble. I hate bein' a god-damn tour guide."

An announcement sounded harshly over the terminal's loud-speaker.

"Aw, hell. That's their friggin' flight." As Les loped off toward the far end of the terminal, he shouted over his shoulder, "See ya around, old fart. Don't be a stranger, y'hear?"

Roy stood and watched the rancher disappear. Turning, he nod-ded at two young Paiute Indian cowhands he recognized who were popping nickels into a jingle-bell-and-whistle slot machine. *Damn kids, feeding their hard-earned wages into those dumb one-armed bandits. But maybe that's better than spending it on booze and driving drunk out to the reservation.*

Roy sauntered, bandy-legged and saddle sore in his worn-out jeans and scuffed-up boots, to the terminal's newsstand where he bought a pack of Camels and a newspaper. Still time to kill. He slumped down in a waiting room seat, lit a cigarette, and stared at the paper's front page. But he couldn't concentrate.

Damn. Why couldn't June do the chore of picking up the new boarders today? She's better at it than I am, he thought. *And she's great with people. Totally unflappable. Can deal with anything that comes up. You name it. Rude, drunken guests, the sad ones, the shy ones, the fakes, the rich, the not-so-rich, June can handle them all. I like that about her.*

Roy leaned back, his legs stretched out in front of him, his cowboy hat tipped forward on his face. *Yep. June is a damn handsome woman, slim, sophisticated, a bottle-blonde that makes you look at her twice. But sometimes,* he mused, *she's too goddamn managing. Makes me want to run off and be a bad boy away from "Mom" always watching me. Face it. I like the ladies. Wish I could play around. Just a little. But I know there'd be hell to pay if I did like in the old days when Reno's hooch-drinkin' divorcees were good for a romp in the hay. How in hell did I survive all that? Not to mention two short-lived marriages before this one, plus a .22 slug still in my liver from that fight in Vern's Virginia Street Saloon. Amazing.*

Thinking of all this made Roy need to pee, and he headed for the men's room.

Coming back he could see a plane touching down on the runway. *Must be the one I've been waiting for,* he told himself. He wished he was more certain about who he was meeting. No pictures to go by except the one June painted in his mind of a young woman and her little boy from Connecticut, or somewhere on the East Coast. *How in hell anybody in their right mind could live in that part of the country is beyond me,* he thought. He'd lived in New York once and hated the place. Felt like a caged coon the whole friggin' time.

Roy's throat felt dry. He regretted not taking Jake, the saddle-maker, up on his offer to buy him a few drinks this noon at the Golden Nugget. *On the other hand,* he reasoned, *I don't dare have liquor on my breath when I'm representing the ranch to a goddamn greenhorn. Wouldn't be right. It's June's and my livelihood and I have an obligation to defend it.*

Then he spotted them. A girl in high heels and a green dress holding the hand of a small, blonde boy in a white shirt, bow tie, and short pants. A greenhorn and a tiny dude. Perfect.

He watched as the rest of the passengers slowly dispersed throughout the terminal. The girl in green stood expectantly in one place. She seemed anxious—*like the mare who wandered off from Desert Lake Ranch with her colt last summe*r, thought Roy. A search party finally extricated the poor animal from a pit by the railroad tracks. Fortunately, the mare proved salvageable, as did the colt. But that horse, forever after, wore the same lost look as the girl in green.

Okay. Time to introduce himself. As he approached the two, he could see what a pretty little thing the young woman was, slim but "well-stacked," about five-foot-two with reddish-blonde hair and long-lashed, soulful eyes. Roy's old heart did a flip-flop and he felt immediately protective of her.

"Howdy. I'm Roy Bracken. I'm here to drive you to our Desert Lake Ranch. And, you are... ?" He fumbled for a piece of paper in his jeans pocket, inwardly cursing himself for not having it at the ready. *I always feel awkward greeting dudes*, he told himself.

"Lara Treadwell. And this is my son, Billy." She smiled, then leaned over the boy and whispered in his ear some sort of direction. Billy responded by extending a small, moist hand.

"Put 'er there, partner," said Roy. "We have horses at the ranch. You can be a cowboy like me." He pumped the tot's hand, patted him on the head, and asked Lara if she had a claim check for her luggage.

The baggage attendant glanced at the check stub Lara produced from her purse, waved it aside, and gestured for her and Roy to pick up the two bags left in the pile by the door. Roy carried the suitcases, motioning for mother and son to follow him through the terminal doors out to the hot, dry air of the Nevada afternoon.

The Woodie stood parked and shining in the sun, all by its lonesome in the lot by the tarmac. Roy lifted up the wood-paneled rear door of the wagon on which was printed in black lettering "Bracken's Desert Lake Ranch." He tucked in the greenhorn's luggage next to the new saddle he purchased in town earlier, along with some dry staples June asked him to buy for the ranch's kitchen.

"Pile in, gang." Roy signaled to Lara to join him up front and said to Billy, "Cowboys have to sit in back and be on the lookout for Indians. Okay, partner?"

As well as he knew little dudes, Roy reckoned the kid would react accordingly, his imagination fired up by a real cowboy. Billy jumped into the back seat with enthusiasm, oblivious to the fact that what the big old cowboy really wanted to do was to get to know his mommy better.

Roy drove them into town through Reno's gaudy main drag, flashy signs beckoning every passing sucker to try his or her luck at a thirsty slot machine, felt-covered gaming table, or dice-enticing wheel of fortune. They drove under the famous archway proclaiming Reno as "The Biggest Little City In The World," then crossed over

the Truckee River Bridge. On their right, next to the Riverside Hotel, stood the county courthouse.

"That's where you'll be getting your final decree, miss," Roy said,
pointing to the courthouse, an impressive-looking building whose
wide marble steps led up from the street's sidewalk to an imposing
entrance graced by huge, Corinthian columns supporting its roof.
"Do you have an appointment with your lawyer yet?" Roy asked.

"I think I'm supposed to see him tomorrow."

The girl answered in such a quiet, pensive voice Roy could barely
hear her. *Probably due to all the hunting and the damn guns I've been
around all my life*, he reasoned.

He hesitated to ask the young filly in the classy green dress to repeat her statement. She still seemed lost, and he felt sorry for her. *She
sure is a looker. I sure as hell appreciate good-looking women, being married
to one, and because of June's good taste, I know to admire a woman's clothes
sense, too. Easy. Like pickin' a thoroughbred out of a pack of mustangs.*

*And this girl is quality. What the hell is she doing out here, anyway?
Of course, to get unhitched, but from who? And why? Her husband must
be a world-class chump*, he decided. *And she's different from the ranch's
usual clientele, a few of them bringing their problems with them. Like the gal
who'd just left, New York society type. Rich-bitch-highfalutin'-pain-in-the-
butt. Always complaining. Never enough salt in the stew, sure of bugs in her
bed, too much chlorine in the pool, the maid stole her diamond ring and so
forth.*

Hell, he thought with a smile, *no bugs in her bed, just up her ass.
Seems like some guests need reining in at times. And I've always been good at
breaking broncos.*

He recalled his days on the rodeo circuit, then quitting that to
work wrangling horses at the old Reno Lodge where he'd met June
and they'd teamed up. *I handle the horses,* mused Roy, *June handles the
people. Perfect. Good combination to run a dude ranch. What a business!
Thank God they only stay for six weeks at a time.* Right now the guests at
the ranch seemed okay, especially now with the addition of this one.
He tried not to get involved with any of them, but this girl riding
next to him made him wish he were twenty years younger. Sneaking
another peek at her, Roy was struck with how quiet she was, lost in
her own thoughts.

As the Woodie traveled further out of the city, it passed row upon row of motels, some with signs like "Truckers and Divorcees Welcome," then picked up speed as Roy drove it out onto a long, flat stretch of desert highway. He decided to break the silence. "Would ya like a Camel? S'all I've got unless ya like chewin' tobacco."

He was pleased to see that got to her. She shot him a smile, wan but warm.

"Thanks. Camel's fine. I don't smoke much 'cause I just had a baby." The girl delicately selected a cigarette from Roy's proffered pack, put it to her lips, and struck a match from the book he gave her. She shielded the flame with pale hands, lit the weed, and puffed away slowly, thoughtfully, making Roy think as he peeked at her, *She doesn't want to inhale, or doesn't know how.*

Then her statement sunk in. A baby? He hesitated a second, then plunged in. "How old... I mean, how long ago did you have it?" He hoped that didn't sound crude. He knew nothing about babies. Well, not the human kind, only horses.

"She's just three weeks old." The girl appeared on the brink of tears.

Oh, crap. Anything but crying. *I can't, no, won't, cope with any goddamn blubbering, no matter who it is,* thought Roy.

The small dude piped up from the back seat, inadvertently lessening the tension. "I didn't see any Indians yet."

Roy noticed the kid had a slight lisp. *Must be that space between his front teeth,* he decided, looking at the boy in the rear view mirror. It was then he thought of engaging the kid in conversation. Might help the mother talk more.

"Maybe the Indians knew you were coming and they're hiding," he said. "But when we get to the ranch, partner, there's a real Indian about your age just waiting for a cowboy like you to play with."

"Really?" Billy's voice sounded a decibel higher. "What's his name? Does he have feathers on his head, and bows and arrows?"

Roy laughed. "Nah. He's a real kid like you. His name is Jimmy. His mom does all the cooking for everybody at the ranch."

As Billy pondered what Roy told him, the mother asked, "How long a drive is it to the ranch from Reno?"

"About thirty minutes, Miss. Oh, sorry... Mrs.... uh, Treadwell. Right?" He thought he remembered, but he wanted to be sure. He couldn't let the baby thing go, either. They didn't get many brand-new mothers sitting out six weeks in the middle of nowhere to get a divorce. And where was the infant? Strange she up and left it. Or maybe she didn't have a choice.

"You say you had a little girl?" Roy hoped she didn't get all teary-eyed on him again.

"Yes. And she's beautiful." The girl looked out the window at the landscape whizzing by, probably, Roy thought, not wanting him to see her chin tremble. But he saw it anyway.

"She must be beautiful to come out of you." He meant it as a compliment, spoken in true horseman's lingo.

He could see she took it as such by the warm smile she gave him.

"I miss her so much," said the girl. "The only reason I left her back in Connecticut was because I knew she'd be in good hands with my sister-in-law. I don't know how I'm going to get through the next six weeks without her, but... " The young mother turned toward the back seat and reached for her son's small hand. "At least Billy and I will be doing it together. Right, Billy?"

In the rearview mirror Roy could see the bond between the two from the quick grin the kid gave his mom. Roy thought of his own mother who had died when he was seven on a ranch in Montana in the dead of winter, a painful memory he kept buried, a damnable thing, but one he couldn't change. So he took pride in the crusty exterior he'd developed to keep himself sane.

Enough of this shit, he thought, banging his foot hard to the floor. The Woodie zipped along the desert highway at ninety miles an hour, lopping off jackrabbits right and left, providing instant roadkill for the vultures circling overhead in the clear blue sky.

Roy again peeked surreptitiously at his front seat rider, admiring her classic profile. She seemed lost in her thoughts. What the hell was her story? All the guests had stories, of course, each one tinged with high drama, which is why they were there in the first place.

He could lay bets his classy passenger was thinking about what went wrong up to this point in her young life. *Good thing we have old Pidge at the ranch to draw her out*, he told himself. *And June is great at that stuff, too.*

He stole another look at her, sure he could see the wheels turning in her pretty head, wheels of reflection on why the hell she was here, racing through the desert like a goddamn rocket.

CHAPTER 4

The horses of hope gallop,
but the asses of experience go slowly.
—— Russian proverb

Lara winced each time an unfortunate jackrabbit plopped under the Woodie. She glanced at the old rancher, his squinty eyes impervious to the carnage created by the speeding vehicle. *Par for the course in these parts,* she guessed, wondering if she dare ask for another cigarette.

The old cowboy must have read her thoughts. He offered her another Camel and turned on the car radio. "How about a little music?" he said.

Lara nodded and smiled. She leaned back, smoking and listening to the dulcet tones of Nat King Cole crooning one of his latest hits, about being too young to really be in love. *Maybe that's it,* she thought. *Rick and I were certainly young when we married. But what went wrong? Is it only about sex? Not enough to suit Rick? No, there are other things, of course. Should I have reacted differently to his demand for a divorce? Been tougher and not so damn emotional? Maybe I should've dug in my heels and not given in to Rick so easily.*

An excited shout from Billy brought Lara back to the moment.

"Look, Mommy, I see water!"

A curve in the road showed the starkness of the desert terrain was changing. A large rock formation now loomed to the right, revealing a startling view of aquamarine water stretching for miles against a backdrop of mauve and indigo mountains.

"That's the Desert Lake, partner," Roy said as he turned the volume down on the car's radio. "We're almost to the ranch."

Lara surveyed several more rock formations, fantastic geological configurations poking up like prehistoric sentinels from the glassy turquoise of the lake water.

"How amazing!" she exclaimed. "It looks like it's been here for centuries. Like a crater on the moon."

"Yeah. Those rock forms are called tufa."

"Tufa? What's that?"

Roy lit a cigarette and slowed the Woodie's engine to a more reasonable speed. "Calcium carbonate deposits that build up over time. This place has quite a history with the Paiute Indians, too."

Lara was beginning to feel glad the lawyer from Carleton, Jack Grossman, had recommended that Rick send his wife and son to stay at a ranch outside the city. *I much prefer the dry air to the humidity of the East Coast*, she mused. *Perhaps this period of forced captivity will help me get my head together. If only I didn't have to leave my sweet Candace behind for six weeks.* It really was so unnatural and she was sure Dr. Collins wouldn't have approved, but he hadn't been consulted. On the other hand, he might have thought it better for Candace to stay where she was, with good care, instead of being dragged halfway across the country. *Oh God, it hurts too much to think about it, like having a knife stuck in my heart.*

The Woodie turned up a dirt driveway to a rambling, rustic, lodge-type structure. A wrap-around porch showed steps leading down to a stretch of well-tended lawn. Across the road was a white sandy beach where a stand of willows shaded the shore of the desert lake.

"Here we are." Roy brought the wagon to a stop alongside the lodge. "Just in time for supper, gang. Hope you brought your appetites. We're havin' a barbecue."

Lara climbed out of the car with Billy as Roy retrieved their suitcases from the trunk. A slim, tanned woman in white halter top and shorts—her blonde hair swept back from her face with a red bandana—came to greet them,

"Hello, Mrs. Treadwell," she said in a low voice as she extended a hand to Lara, appraising her with keen, sapphire-blue eyes. "I'm Mrs. June Bracken. Welcome to our ranch. Roy's taking your luggage to your cabin. Please follow me and we'll have you registered in no time."

Holding tight to Billy's hand, Lara led him up the wide plank steps to the wooden porch of the lodge. There they paused for a moment to take in the view toward the lake where several distant figures appeared to be enjoying a swim.

"The water in our desert lake has a high salt content," said Mrs. Bracken, smiling at Lara. "Swimming in it is especially fun because of the buoyancy. Right this way, Mrs. Treadwell."

Lara breathed deeply, delighting in the dry air tinged with a heady scent of sage. She and Billy entered the lodge and followed the trim, competent Mrs. Bracken to a reception desk in the lodge's main room, a vast, two-storied space with log poles in the ceiling and a giant stone fireplace. The room had Craftsman-style furniture and was decorated with many Indian rugs and artifacts.

I wonder what kind of new experiences lie ahead, thought Lara as she signed the register for the required six-week stay. Tired as she was from her recent journey and the disheartening events that had led her to this place, she felt a surprising sense of release. If this setting, she told herself, with its clean air, pleasant hosts, and engaging surroundings was to be her "prison" for awhile... so be it.

Lara and Billy followed Mrs. Bracken on a gravel path to their designated cabin. It stood fourth at the end of a row of small, board-and-batten structures painted white with shingled roofs shining blue-green in the late afternoon sunshine. Lara noticed the white picket fences in front of each dwelling, with gates opening to patches of grassy yard. Wooden stoops were in front of each cabin's door, and each door was painted blue-green to match each roof.

After opening the screen door and then the door to the end cabin, Mrs. Bracken brought Lara's attention to the window on the cabin's right side.

"This place is more private than the others, Mrs. Treadwell. They all have side windows, but none with a view like this one, which we thought would be nice for you and your son. He can see the horses grazing, and sometimes we get deer down here that eat the apples in the orchard nearby," said Mrs. Bracken. "If there's anything you need, there is someone on duty at the lodge to help you." She checked her watch and directed her attention to Billy. "In half an hour we'll be serving supper on the lawn at the lodge. Do you like hamburgers, Mr. Treadwell?"

Billy, taken aback by this grown-up addressing him so formally, looked at his mother, then back at Mrs. Bracken. "I'm not Mr.
Treadwell. My daddy is. But he couldn't come. My name is Billy."

"Well, I'm glad to meet you, Billy. And there are two boys about
your age who would like to meet you at the barbecue." Mrs. Bracken
gave Lara another welcoming handshake. "Please call me June and
I'll call you Lara. We're not at all formal around here. More like family. Now, if you'll excuse me, I have to go supervise the kitchen. Make
yourselves comfortable and we'll see you in a half hour or so."

Thanking June, Lara watched as the tall, slim figure of her hostess bounded down the steps of the cabin and hurried away towards
the lodge, leaving in her wake a faint whiff of Chanel No 5., a fra-
grance Lara would always associate with this attractive, self-possessed
woman of the West.

Closing the door, Lara stood and surveyed the room in which
she and her son were to live for six weeks. It was sparsely furnished.
Two single beds covered with blue-green bedspreads of sturdy-look-
ing material stood against the cabin's windowless, rough-hewn far
wall, separated by a tiny pine table on which perched a log-based
lamp with a parchment shade. An oval, dark-green, braided rug lay
on the yellow linoleum floor, and a wood-framed Remington cowboy
print hung between the beds. Completing the decor was a wooden,
straight-backed chair and a battered oak chest of drawers. Two side
windows, screened and hung with pull-down, tan shades, provided cross ventilation. The small john had a transomed window high
above the toilet and a sink with a wall-mirrored medicine chest. Lara
guessed showers or baths were to be taken elsewhere, much like the
summer camp she'd attended as a child.

"Can I wear my cowboy holster and blue jeans, Mommy?"

Lara knew Billy looked forward to making friends with the boys
the Brackens mentioned. She hugged him. "Of course. But first,
young man, you have to use the bathroom and wash your hands. You
can wear your Hopalong Cassidy shirt, too. This is going to be fun."

Maybe saying it will make it so, she mused. A creeping feeling of
foreboding began wrapping itself around her bruised and pummeled
psyche. *What the hell am I doing out here in the middle of nowhere? I*

should have stuck it out and stayed where I was. Besides, I miss my baby girl so much I can't stand it.

Lara swallowed hard to hold back tears as she removed Billy's cowboy gear from his suitcase and laid it on his bed. From her own luggage, she selected a pair of white shorts and a blue-and-white-striped, sleeveless cotton top.

Slipping off her green silk travel dress, she hung it in the curtained closet opposite the john and donned the shorts, top, and a pair of last summer's white canvas espadrille sandals.

As she emptied the suitcases and put things away in the dresser, Lara felt an overwhelming urge to flop onto one of the beds, drag the bedspread over her head, and stay there for the whole damned, interminable six weeks. If she had been alone, she might have just done it. But of course she couldn't. She owed it to Billy to be as strong as possible.

When Billy finished dressing, Lara freshened her lipstick and, with her miniature cowboy companion, headed for the lodge. In his excitement Billy ran ahead of his mother.

"Slow down, Billy. I'm too tired to rush."

The boy waited for her to catch up. "I can smell the hamburgers, Mommy. I'm hungry."

Forcing a smile, Lara hurried along. *Somehow*, she told herself, *I'll get through this, but I'm not betting on it.*

CHAPTER 5

A little sunburnt by the glare of life.

—— "Aurora Leigh," *Elizabeth Barrett Browning*

"How d'ya like your hamburgers, pal?" Roy Bracken brandished a long-handled spatula at his foreman, Duke Fenway, anticipating with relish the old wrangler's standard reply every time they held a barbecue.

"Hot 'n juicy, jes like my women!" Duke thrust his plate toward Roy with a flourish.

Both men laughed heartily as they stood in front of the ranch's bricked-in grill enjoying their camaraderie born of long association and mutual adventures.

Duke, a tall, raw-boned, red-haired cowboy, a bit over the hill but strong and spry as any of the mustangs he used to chase when he was younger, watched as Roy expertly flipped burgers. His squinty-eyed concentration soon became diverted by the sight of Lara being shepherded by June to a serving table nearby.

"Hot damn." Duke's flinty, steel blue eyes widened. "Hey, Roy, ya been holdin' out on me? Is that the new filly ya picked up in Reno today? Goddamn, she's a looker. Kinda pale, though. Needs to get out in the sun."

Roy noticed his wife introducing Lara to some guests loading their plates with food. Without warning, he smacked his spatula down hard on top of a half-done burger, causing meat juice to spatter, squirt, and sizzle onto the grill's red-hot coals. "Listen up, pal. Keep your big paws off that little filly. She's special. Needs protection."

"Geezus, Roy. I was only ..."

"So she's pale. Good. Not your type. You only like 'em when they turn the color of cow shit."

"Well, piss on you, Roy. What's got your dander up? I ain't gonna make a move. Hell. I could be her grandpappy. But it's sure nice to see sump'n' nice," said Duke. "Oops, here she comes."

The girl seemed to float towards them, her dark-blonde hair catching the sun's rays with reddish-gold highlights, her long-lashed, olive green eyes shining in recognition of Roy. Even the sad smile she gave them only added to her allure.

"Mr. Bracken. Hello!" Lara held out her plate, which contained coleslaw and baked beans, with space left for a burger. "It's good to see you again."

Roy straightened up and grinned at the enticing newcomer. His grin took in June as she, also with plate in hand, joined the new young guest. He cleared his throat. "Chef Roy at your service, ladies. Rare, medium, or well-done?"

As he took their orders, Roy saw Duke shuffling with anticipation from one foot to another. "Oh, sorry, Mrs. Treadwell. Like ya to meet our foreman, Duke Fenway. Duke, Lara Treadwell."

Duke grabbed hold of Lara's small hand with one huge, sunburned paw, clicked together the heels of his pointy-toed cowboy boots, whipped off his beat-up, straw Stetson, and bowed low to her like a royal page to a princess. "Pleased to meetcha, purty lady. You kin jump on my saddle anytime." His lopsided grin revealed a mouthful of tobacco-stained dentures as he reluctantly released her hand.

"Why, thank you, Mr. Fenway. June's been telling me you're an expert at teaching kids to ride the horses here. My son Billy is four. Is that too young?"

"Uh... oh no, purty lady. Four's jes fine. Bring the kid, I mean, the boy by any time."

"For god sakes, Duke." Roy flipped a spare burger onto a plate and shoved it at his dazed foreman. "Have a burger. You're boring this nice young lady."

"Oh no!" Lara protested. "I've enjoyed meeting you, Mr. Fenway... Duke. I'll tell my son about you."

Roy could swear his long-time friend was blushing, but given Duke's ruddy complexion, it was hard to tell. "Don't mind ol' Duke, Mrs. Treadwell. He thinks he's our resident lady killer, but he's gettin' sorta long in the tooth for that job, so we try to humor him."

"Thank you, Mr. Bracken. And you, too, Duke." The young woman beamed at the two men as Roy served her a well-done burger on a toasted bun. She turned to June. "And thanks, June, for getting

Billy together with Jimmy. If you'll excuse me, I'm going to check on them now. See you all later."

Roy and Duke stared unabashedly at Lara as she strolled out onto the lawn carrying her plate of food, her petite figure casting an elongated shadow on the grass as the desert sun sank lower in the sky.

"You guys are pathetic." June snatched the spatula from Roy's hand and served herself a burger. "Put your eyeballs back in your heads. You look like a damn cartoon." She shook her blonde, smoothly-coiffed head in good-humored disgust. "It's a good thing Tex Otis isn't here today. You guys would be setting a *fine* example for him, and God knows he needs no encouragement when it comes to our female guests." She waved the spatula at Roy. "Remember a year ago? That nasty business with Tex and the oil heiress? We don't need a repeat of that. It's bad enough Kat Kavanaugh, the new gal from Grosse Pointe, is already showing signs of falling for him."

"How d'ya know that?" Roy asked.

"Because she makes goo-goo eyes at Tex every time I see them together, and he gives her plenty of reason to. Speaking of which... " June lowered her voice and directed both men's attention to a deeply-tanned woman with a short, well-endowed figure and curly brown hair, walking unsteadily toward them. "Here she comes now. Be nice to her. You both know how unstable she is, and nipping at that bottle of Jim Beam she keeps in her room doesn't help. I'm going to catch up with Lara and find out what time I have to drive her into town tomorrow."

Leaving the two chastened cowboys to deal with the troubled guest from Michigan, June hastened across the lawn towards Lara. *Amazing*, she told herself, *how Roy and I manage to stay in this nutty business. I'm often tempted to write a book about all the stuff that goes on. But, hell, nobody'd believe it, and besides, I'm honor-bound to protect the privacy of our guests.*

June caught up with the pretty new arrival as both reached Billy and the Indian boy, Jimmy Big Horn. "Wait up, Lara. I have to ask you something."

Lara turned, smiling at June. "Look at those two little guys. One so fair, the other so dark."

Both women stood and gazed at the youngsters who sat cross-legged on the grass, happily chomping on their hamburgers as Billy shared his Hopalong Cassidy gun and holster with the wide-eyed Jimmy. They did, indeed, present a striking contrast, the blonde, crew-cut, rosy-cheeked boy and the brown-skinned Indian child with shiny, blue-black hair, and bright, coal-black eyes.

"Hi, Mommy." Billy's eyes radiated excitement. "Jimmy and I are having fun. Can we play for a while?"

"Of course, sweetheart." Turning to June, Lara said, "Jimmy seems so friendly and polite. His mom must be doing a good job with him."

"Yes," June answered, sotto voce. "And she's doing it by herself. Her husband died in a hunting accident about a year ago leaving Wanda to raise not only Jimmy, but Jimmy's teen-age sister, Nita. Wanda does all the cooking here at the ranch. Would you like to meet her? She's over there by the dessert table."

"Thanks, June, but I'm really tired. It's been a long day." Lara gestured toward a white, wood-slatted lawn chair with armrests. "I think I'll sit over there for a while. As soon as the sun sets, Billy and I will be on our way to dreamland. I hope you don't mind. I can meet everyone tomorrow."

"Which reminds me," June said. "Roy tells me you have an appointment with your lawyer tomorrow. I need to know what time so I can drive you into Reno and back."

"I think it's around 1:00 in the afternoon. But I don't want Billy to be there with me at the lawyer's and I don't know anyone here who can watch him while I'm gone."

June assured the young mother that Nita Big Horn, Jimmy's sister, was an excellent babysitter, and arrangements would be made to employ her services, which were free. Lara seemed near tears as she thanked June for her kindness.

June bid the newcomer goodbye and left her collapsed like a small rag doll in the big Adirondack lawn chair. *Damn good thing Tex Otis isn't at the ranch for tonight's barbecue*, thought June. *There's no doubt he'd single Lara out for his next conquest.* She wished Roy would fire Otis, but Roy kept giving the guy one more chance since Tex was a good wrangler, despite his massive ego. Even so, the whole sorry business a year ago with the oil heiress was a wake-up call. The heiress, sultry and spoiled and older than Tex, had fallen hard for his macho charms. When the cowboy two-timed her with a young waitress from town, the heiress found a gun and threatened to blow his brains out. *Lucky for him he got to keep his brains, much less his balls, intact,* thought June.

As June strode across the lawn to help in the lodge's kitchen, she looked forward to getting to know the young Mrs. Treadwell better. *What is the young woman's story that she leaves a three-week-old infant behind just to split with its father? But I'm sure*, thought June, *there is much more to it than that. There always is.*

She climbed the steps of the lodge, carrying a large empty wooden salad bowl, when the approaching sound of a motor caused her to pause. They weren't expecting visitors. Then she noticed a swirl of dust raised by a car speeding along the dirt road by the lake. Would it stop, or race on to Reno?

But I have work to do, she told herself, and hurried towards the kitchen.

CHAPTER 6

So did this horse excel a common one
In shape, in courage, color, pace, and bone...
—— *William Shakespeare*, Venus and Adonis

Lara sat slumped against the vertical wooden slats of the lawn chair. She felt numb, weary. She peered at the plate of food on her lap and, taking a bite of the burger, chewed slowly. *I'm far too tired to eat*, she thought. She lifted a forkful of coleslaw, then dropped it back on the plate as she observed the pallor of her bare legs and arms. How disgusting. Same color as the coleslaw. A pasty, creamy white. Yuk. And all she saw around her were healthy-looking, tanned bodies grouped on the lawn, eating, drinking, and laughing. It was damn depressing.

She felt like crying but curbed the impulse as she noticed Billy, several feet away, enjoying himself. *I'm happy for him*, she mused. *What a nice little pal he's found in Jimmy Big Horn. It isn't every day a kid from a staid Connecticut town gets to meet a real Indian boy way out in the Old West.*

Thinking of Connecticut made Lara feel even more fatigued. *Did we actually start out from there so early this morning? It doesn't seem possible. But*, she told herself, *if I continue to dwell on Carleton and Rick and all the stress, misery, and hurt involved, I'll go nuts.*

As she fought with her thoughts, she fiddled absently with the wedding band still encircling the third finger of her left hand. She hadn't removed the ring since Rick had put it on her finger in front of God and everyone in Carleton's All Saint's Episcopal Church. What a beautiful day that had been, so full of hope and happy dreams. Now the ring was just a piece of jewelry. End of an era. Death of a marriage. Her eyes misted over. She dabbed at them with a napkin and took another bite of burger.

Munching disconsolately on her food, trying somehow to will the past away, Lara stared out at the vast expanse of aquamarine lakewater. She removed her sandals and wiggled her bare toes in the soft, tickly blades of grass, recalling summer childhoods spent in the backyard of a house her family rented on Long Island. There she had become acquainted with the world of storybooks, reading to herself on a wooden bench under an old maple tree. Her favorite was *Alice In Wonderland. That's what this desert ranch reminds me of,* she thought, *a wonderland into which I, Lara, like Alice, landed after falling down a jack-rabbit hole.* Like Alice's wonderland, the ranch was an oasis removed from reality and inhabited by a cast of characters she imagined she'd find "curiouser and curiouser" as she got to know them all. Of course, they might find her "curious," too.

And, she thought, *that could be the "White Knight" himself coming from the direction of the driveway!* Shielding her eyes from the slanting rays of the sun, she watched as a tall, muscular figure approached her from across the lawn. As he drew closer, Lara noticed how good-looking he was, handsome, really, with his blonde hair cut in a crew style. He was wearing faded jeans, brown cowboy boots, and a white, open-collared shirt with rolled-up sleeves that set off his deep tan.

A tall, reed-thin fellow apparently accompanied the blonde stranger, but stayed a distance behind, as if waiting respect-fully. He stood like a sentinel, smoking a cigarette and facing the lake.

At first Lara wasn't sure what to do, freeze or flee. She certainly wasn't in the mood for conversation, especially not with a stranger. But she felt too tired to move so continued to sit there, feeling some-what stupid while fidgeting with her wedding ring. She noticed a black convertible with its top down, parked in the driveway. *That's probably it. They're lost.* She looked down at her plate and considered taking another forkful of food.

No use. Not hungry. She stared straight ahead at the lake.

The blonde stranger came closer and stood directly in front of her chair. As Lara peered up at him, he seemed to block out the sun like a Paul Bunyan figure stretching interminably to the sky.

"Hi," he said. "You're new. I've never seen you here before."

"I just got here today," she said, feeling a bit overwhelmed and slightly apologetic for reasons unknown. She shifted uneasily in the lawn chair.

The stranger squatted on his haunches alongside her and extended a strong-looking hand in greeting. "Well, I'm glad. Welcome. This place just got better because you're here. I'm Chance. Chance Darwin. And my friend over there is Frank Jensen. You'll have to forgive his manners. He's a bit shy." Chance gifted her with a dazzling, white-toothed smile enhanced by two deeply set dimples. "And who are you, beautiful lady?"

When his hand touched hers, Lara felt a hot, visceral rush. Her heart pumped faster. She felt her face flush as she quickly withdrew her hand from his. "Lara. Lara Treadwell," she said, trying to ignore the effect this man was having on her, particularly when his blonde-lashed, golden-green eyes met hers. "You must know the Brackens then," she added. "They're great people. I like June a lot." For some reason Lara felt like a conversational klutz.

"Yeah, the Brackens are the best." Chance reached in his shirt pocket for a pack of cigarettes as he flashed his dimpled smile. "I've known them for about a year now." He offered her a Chesterfield, a brand with which she was not familiar. She accepted anyway. Maybe smoking would help keep her focused and better able to quell the nervousness she was experiencing in this intriguing young man's presence. What was it about him? He certainly exuded an alarmingly rugged sexiness. *I better be true to my married name and "tread well,"* she told herself.

"I only get over here about once a week," Chance said as he lit her cigarette and then his own. "Frank and I work at a ranch about forty miles from here. The A.K. Wheeler spread. A.K. breeds race horses to run and win. I'm his foreman, and Frank doubles as the old man's secretary and pilot. Wheeler is pretty famous. You've probably heard of him?"

"No." Lara drew on her cigarette. She tried to avoid looking into the fascinating green eyes. Instead, she concentrated on the golden hairs growing on Chance's tanned, smoothly muscled arm. "What's he famous for?"

"Mainly as a Western singing star, like some of his bud-dies, Gene Autry, Roy Rogers, and the rest. He's politically well known, too... U.S. Senate and all. But enough about him." Chance's voice took on a deeper quality, soft, mellifluous. "What about you? Where do you hail from, Lara? Wherever it is, they lost a winner."

She was about to tell him when Frank joined them, changing the interplay developing between Chance and herself. Frank seemed older and more serious than his blonde buddy. He had a narrow, tanned face, squinty brown eyes, and a thin, sinewy build. His brown hair was cropped short and he was attired in black jeans, a matching jacket, and black cowboy boots. His manner was stiff and diffident as Chance introduced him.

"Nice to meet you." He looked at the ground, then shifting his gaze directly, almost sternly at Chance, he said, "We have to go, Chance. They're waiting for us. We were only going to stay for a few minutes, remember? You wanted to speak to Roy." Frank dropped his cigarette butt in the grass and ground it out with the sole of his boot.

"Oh, that's right. Go over and talk to Roy, Frank. I'll be there in a sec." Chance stood up and grinned down at Lara. "We're on a booze run. A.K. has company and they're drinking up all his liquor, so he sent us to see if Roy can sell us some of his. Otherwise, we have to drive all the way into Reno." He took her hand once more and Lara let him hold it longer this time. He seemed reluctant to let go. "I hope we meet again soon, Lara Treadwell."

For one piercing, electrically charged second, their eyes met, made soulful contact, and then disconnected. Chance turned slowly from her and walked quickly across the lawn to where Roy and Frank were conversing near the barbecue area.

The sun was setting over the azure desert lake, infusing everything with a warm, tangerine glow. Lara slipped on her sandals and rose from the lawn chair as if awakening from a long, blissful sleep, when, abruptly, she realized Billy was no longer where she'd last seen him. Heart thumping, she stubbed out her cigarette in the half-eaten food on her plate. It was a messy thing to do, but she didn't care as she stood, trembling, a rivulet of fear washing over her and rendering her temporarily immobile. Terrified, she didn't dare look in the direction of the lake. Billy had only taken a few swimming lessons at the community pool in Carleton. What if...?

A slender young girl with long, glossy, blue-black hair and huge, liquid brown eyes approached Lara. "Are you all right, ma'am? Here. I'll take your plate. Is something the matter?"

"Yes... no, I mean, thanks." Lara felt faint. "I'm looking for my little boy. A little four-year-old blonde boy." She grabbed the girl's thin brown arm. "Have you seen him?"

"Oh, you mean Billy? He and my little brother are playing tag over there." The girl pointed to a large clump of lavender and pink hydrangea bushes near the lodge's front porch.

Lara was so relieved she felt like hugging the girl, who couldn't have been more than fourteen. "Whew! I got really worried there for a minute. You must be Nita... Nita Big Horn?"

"Yes, ma'am. And Mrs. Bracken already asked me if I would watch your boy tomorrow. I'll be glad to. The Brackens have a bunch of board games in the rec room, and Jimmy and I can teach Billy how to play." Nita's smile lit up her dark, olive-skinned face. "I have to go help my mom now. See you tomorrow!"

"Hi, Mommy!" A breathless Billy ran up and tagged his mother. "Look out! You're it!" He laughed happily as Jimmy and another small boy came running from behind the bushes. "Jimmy and Bip and I are having fun."

"I'm glad, Billy. But it'll be dark soon and we have to get to our cabin." To the other boys she said, "We'll see you tomorrow, guys, okay?"

It was obvious to Lara she was being unnecessarily blunt by the crestfallen expressions on the young faces staring up at her. *So what if I'm exhausted? Not fair to take it out on Billy and his newfound playmates.*

She quickly relented, softening the moment by extending her hand to the diminutive Indian boy. "I don't think I've had the pleasure of meeting you. Are you the famous Jimmy Big Horn?" She shook his small brown hand and was instantly rewarded by a brightening of his dark eyes and a sunny, gap-toothed smile.

"And this is Bip, Mommy. Bip's daddy is here but his mommy couldn't come." Billy beamed as Lara shook the grubby hand of a dark-haired, wiry little boy whose yellow-green eyes held a hint of mischief and whose tanned face broke into an animated grin. Like Jimmy, Bip was missing his two front teeth.

Waving farewell to the two boys, Lara and Billy trotted down the gravel path leading to their cabin. As they passed the first cabin, a voice called out to them from the gathering gloom. "Stop! Who goes there? What's the password?"

Alarmed, Lara grabbed Billy to her side and held him tight as she squinted in the direction of the voice, which seemed to come from a woman sitting on the steps of the cabin.

"Don't be scared. All ya gotta do is say, 'Winnemucca.' That's the password. Then the gods won't be mad at ya and ya can go in peace." The woman was slurring her words. Lara, suspecting they had encountered a drunk, took Billy's hand and quickened their pace along the path.

"Hey! Slow down, you two. I don't bite, y'know." The woman, surprisingly agile, caught up with them. "Hi. I saw you at the barbecue. I'm Pidge McCauley. I'm the resident gatekeeper. That's why ya hafta know the password. I report to Roy and June on a regular basis, y'know. They depend on me."

Lara found herself face-to-face with a woman as short in physical stature as she, but a lot older, at least as was apparent in the diminishing light. Dressed in what looked like a long dirndl skirt, white blouse, and an inordinate amount of turquoise and silver jewelry, Pidge's small, twinkling eyes, set close together in her tanned, wrinkled face, wore an expression of delight. Even her hair, a brownish, over-permanented halo of frizz seemed to stand up and cheer. She radiated joy as she waved a long cigarette holder like a lighted torch in one hand and thrust out her other hand to Lara in a jubilant gesture of friendship.

Despite the woman's alcoholic breath, emitting fumes strong enough to knock a passing mosquito into a tailspin, Lara felt there was something vulnerable and innately charming in this "Pidge" person. She returned the handshake. Certainly Pidge was worth knowing, especially in a more sober state. This impression was confirmed when Lara saw how taken Pidge was with Billy.

"Well, you're a fine young fella." Pidge leaned down and took Billy's hand. "I can tell. Pidge sees lots of Lilliputians come and go at this ranch, and you're top of the line. Say... I like to read. I can read you a story sometime, Mister... what did ya say your name was?"

Lara introduced herself and Billy, but the boy appeared relieved when Pidge let go of his hand, and he tugged at his mother's arm, asking to go to their cabin.

"I'm sorry, Pidge. We're really tired. It was lovely to meet you. See you tomorrow, I hope," said Lara. She gave Pidge a little wave and, with Billy, continued on the path.

When they reached their cabin, Billy ran inside as Lara paused on the steps, thinking she heard footsteps behind her. Sure enough, there was the tipsy lady, leaning on the gate to the cabin's tiny yard.

"Jes' wanna remind ya, Larie-love." Pidge lowered her voice to a raspy whisper. "Don't forget th' password. 'S very important."

"I won't. Goodnight, Pidge."

Lara watched as Pidge toddled down the path, the lighted tip of her cigarette holder bobbing up and down in the dimness like a firefly dizzy on dope. *Hopefully the woman will sleep it off and be more with it next day,* thought Lara. But Pidge did seem intelligent, warm-hearted, even well bred. *Wonder why she's here. Sounds like she's been at the ranch longer than the usual six weeks. Is it true the Brackens "depend" on her?*

Later, as Lara tucked him into bed, Billy said, "That was a funny lady, huh, Mommy? What's the matter with her? Do we have to say the password every time? And... what's a Lillapooshun?"

Lara kissed him on his forehead. "Oh, sweetheart, there's so much to talk about. Can we save it for tomorrow? I am so tired, and you must be, too."

She listened to him say the prayer she'd taught him, said goodnight, and fell into her bed, feeling completely wrung out.

This is only the first day of what seems like an endless six weeks, she mused wearily. *Everything feels so unreal. And what is it about the blonde Mr. Darwin? He's attractive in a clean-cut, All-American-Guy kind of way. But he possesses a strong sexuality that bothers me. I better steer clear of him,* she decided. *After all, I just had a baby, for heaven's sake. Besides, I still have a husband. Rick will change his mind.* For a moment she allowed herself to hope. *Surely, after a few weeks, he'll miss me, fly out, and whisk us back to Carleton. Then I won't need to go to court, or even to Denver with the children as planned, and our marriage will be saved. Yeah. Right. I wish.*

Soon she slipped into a dream in which she was a Lilliputian being crushed beneath the heavy boot of a giant, Gulliver-like man, dressed in a black magician's cloak. He kept smashing her down, down, down... until she awoke, gasping for air and soaked with perspiration.

For a long time, lying in the strange bed, she was unable to sleep. It was quiet now, with only the comforting sound of Billy's soft, sweet, rhythmic intake and release of breath. *Maybe this place is really a dream*, she thought, *and I'll wake up in our bed in Carleton with Rick by my side, Billy in his room, and the baby, oh, dear... my baby. Darling little Candace Ann.*

Lara buried her face in her pillow to stifle the sobs rising in her throat. *No*, she told herself, *I might as well face it. I'm here to get a divorce, compliant, as usual, to Rick's wishes. I need to make the best of it. But it all happened too damn fast. I should have fought harder. Why didn't I? Damn! I had no one to talk to, to advise me. Maybe this is all a terrible mistake. Oh, dear God... please help me.*

She rose from the bed, slipped on a pink nylon robe, and sat in the chair by the cabin's view window. Gently, so as not to wake Billy, she raised the shade, revealing a sliver of moon and a myriad of stars twinkling in the indigo sky. Pale moonlight gave a glow to the wedding ring on her left hand resting on the windowsill. Inside the plain gold band were inscribed her and Rick's initials, the date of their wedding, and one word, *Always. Our love song*, she thought. *Now the sentiment seems empty.*

She pulled down the shade, cast off her robe, and crawled back into bed. She was to meet another stranger tomorrow, the "dean" of Reno's lawyers, according to Rick, and she needed a clear head and a good night's sleep.

CHAPTER 7

The law, which is perfection of reason.
— Sir Edward Coke

The man behind the massive, oak-paneled desk rose to greet Lara, motioning for her to take a seat opposite him. "Welcome to Reno, Mrs. Treadwell," he said as he sat down, rifled through some papers, then peered at her with watery, probing blue eyes over a pair of tortoiseshell, half-rimmed glasses.

"Thank you." Lara tried to appear more confident than she felt as she returned the quizzical gaze of Sylvester T. McDermott, the lawyer assigned to her by Carleton's Jack Grossman.

I feel so damn self-conscious, she told herself. *Why is that?* She settled herself in the appointed chair and smiled at McDermott, noting his slicked-back silver hair, florid complexion, and weighty build encased in an expensive-looking, Western-style navy-blue jacket. Her eye stopped, fascinated by the bolo tie he sported, an impressive hunk of turquoise embellished with a border of hammered silver. *Power personified,* she thought as she waited expectantly for him to speak next.

"Six weeks from today you will stand before a judge in the courtroom down the street." McDermott's voice was deep, strong, and low-pitched. "If you answer all the questions the judge puts to you truthfully and satisfactorily, and your witness attests to the truthfulness thereof, you will get a decree of divorce. How does that sound to you?" He smiled benignly.

"Well... uh, fine, thank you, but ..."

"Mr. Grossman assures this office both you and your husband are amenable to these proceedings. Is that the case, Mrs. Treadwell,... from your point of view, that is?"

His tone sparked something in Lara. He seemed so understanding, almost grandfatherly. She blinked back unexpected tears. "Actually... uh, I can't believe I'm here. I didn't want... you see, I brought my four-year-old son out here to the ranch with me, but I had to leave my newborn daughter behind, and ..."

"I see." McDermott sat back against his high, black leather chair, rubbed his chin for a second, then pulled open a drawer in his desk and produced a pack of Pall Malls. He offered one to Lara, who declined politely. Lighting his cigarette, he spoke through a swirl of exhaled smoke. "The fact you are here, however, means you are not contesting Grossman and your husband's demands. Correct?"

"I... uh ..." Lara felt like dissolving into a puddle on the polished wooden floor of this older man's office, three floors up in a granite building on Virginia Street in the heart of Reno's business district. Earlier, June had dropped her off, promising to pick her up in an hour. Lara, dressed in her green traveling costume and high-heeled, black suede pumps, opted to climb the stairs instead of taking the elevator to McDermott's office. Doing so, she felt, should help summon the sheer physical courage necessary to face the inevitable. *Hasn't helped much so far,* she thought. *Oh, hell, I might as well go for broke. Here this man is, like the therapist I never managed to see and wanted to... so badly, for so damn long. I've got to explain how hard I tried to make things work and to get Rick to change his mind in the short time we had. I've got to get across the fact that I was pushed into this, that I didn't really want to, that it was all too crazy, too damn fast...*

"Look, Mr. McDermott," she said, chin held high, "I argued against this 'til I was half-dead. Nothing helped. I was exhausted. I still am. My obstetrician ordered me not to go anywhere for at least three weeks after I gave birth to my daughter. I followed his orders because I respected him. Besides, I don't drive and I didn't know where to turn for advice, even over the 'phone. My husband is well known in Carleton, Connecticut, and all around there. We were a team onstage, dancing together on some New York television shows. I also assisted him with his magic act. But Carleton is *his* town. He grew up there. I didn't. His reputation is sheer gold to him and he doesn't want it tarnished at any cost, so he engaged Mr. Grossman. I never met the man. Never talked to him on the phone, ever. Finally I could fight Rick no longer. He said you were the 'dean' of Reno's lawyers. So here I am."

"Well, well." McDermott stubbed his cigarette out in a black ceramic ashtray shaped like a steer's head. "I may not be the 'dean' of barristers around here, in one sense of the word, but I've certainly been here the longest." He looked at Lara appraisingly. "And you've been in show business. That's all you'll need for your day in court. That, and the honest replies I mentioned before. My job is to see you get a fair deal in division of property, child custody and support, and alimony for you. I'm also here to coach you toward a successful performance. You should be good at that. Let's get to work."

Lara was instructed by McDermott to stand before him. "Now, Mrs. Treadwell. Think of me as the judge, which I have been, many times. After you take the oath, the judge asks why you came to Reno. You are to say, 'to establish a residence here, Your Honor.' The judge will then ask how long you've lived at Desert Lake Ranch, how long you've been married, how many children, and why you want a divorce."

"But what do I say to that last question, Mr. McDermott?"

"Mental cruelty, my dear, incompatibility, irreconcilable differences, all of the above. But 'mental cruelty' will do the job. Just say you were forced to dissolve the marriage against your will, fought to save it for the sake of your children, the youngest a newborn, and suffered mental and emotional distress. Words to that effect. But keep it short and to the point. June or Roy Bracken will accompany you and testify under oath that they know you and have seen you every single day of your six weeks' residence at their ranch."

"Every day?"

"Yes. This is important: swearing falsely to this is a crime in the state of Nevada, punishable by fourteen year's imprisonment. If this law was not strictly upheld the 'dude' business could collapse. So it behooves both ranch operators as well as their guests to cooperate fully in this regard. Any questions?"

By this time Lara felt somewhat intimidated. The former image she conjured up of McDermott as a comforting, grandfatherly type had vanished. But it did serve its purpose. She was glad she'd expressed herself to this forthright gentleman of the law. "No. Thank you, Mr. McDermott. I appreciate your help. If I think of anything further, may I call you?"

"Of course." McDermott pulled himself upright with effort and reached for something from behind his desk chair. Lara saw it was a silver-handled cane and hoped her expression of surprise didn't cause the attorney embarrassment as he hobbled around the desk leaning heavily on the cane for support. He stood looking down from his considerable height and smiled at her, his manner less formal than before.

"Old injury," he explained. "Ancient history. Rode one too many broncos. Tried to keep up with your Desert Lake Ranch owner, Roy Bracken, on the rodeo circuit. We were competing in 1924 at Madison Square Garden when I took the fall that changed my life. Bracken went on to win Cowboy of the Year and I wrangled a law degree from Columbia. No regrets. And, to me, there's a distinct correlation between the practice of law and trying to break a wild horse to the saddle. In a way, I'm still in the business of busting broncos. Esoterically speaking, of course."

"Of course," she said, thinking how interesting it was to meet someone both physically challenged and intellectually gifted. Lara thanked McDermott again, gave him a warm handshake, and left, taking the elevator down to the building's ground floor lobby. She hurried out to the sidewalk and paused to collect her thoughts. Pedestrians passed by her in the bright sunshine. She could hear the jingle-jangle of several slot machines in full orchestration emanating from a nearby drugstore. Ah, Reno. A gambler's heaven, or hell, depending on luck. For once Lara felt Lady Luck had smiled on her. Or maybe it was God who'd dealt her a winning hand in McDermott. She was tempted to dance a jig right there on the concrete. Instead, she glided gracefully across the street when the traffic light turned green and headed toward the ranch's Woodie, parked in front of a bank.

As Lara drew nearer the car, she noticed the driver's seat was empty. Two passengers who bore no resemblance to the other guests that had ridden into Reno with her and June earlier in the day now occupied the back seat.

Lara opened the door of the Woodie and slid into the middle seat, turning to speak to the young woman and small boy in the rear of the vehicle. "Hi. I'm Lara Treadwell. Are you by any chance the new guests June said she was picking up at the airport?"

"Ah, yah." The young woman seemed ill at ease and spoke with an accent Lara surmised was German. "My name is Uta Crouse. Und dis is my son. Please to say hello, Axel."

The boy, stick-thin like his mother, shrank closer against her while staring at Lara, his cornflower-blue eyes enormous in his pinched face, his blonde hair cropped in what looked like a home-executed haircut. "Hello," he said in a tiny voice, holding tight to a tattered teddy bear.

"Ve got up so urly dis morning." Uta mustered a weary smile and brushed her wavy, ash-blonde hair back from her high, pale forehead with long, thin fingers. Her eyes were a deeper blue than her son's, almost violet. "Ve vait here for Mrs. Bracken. She had to go to bank."

"I brought my little boy with me, too. Billy is four." Lara thought the young woman attractive in a nondescript way. "And there are other boys, too, at the ranch. Axel will have lots of playmates. Oh, excuse me. You *are* going to the ranch, aren't you?"

"Yah. Ve flew in from Visconsin. I am going to vait tables und do kitchen vork to pay my vay. My grandmother in Munich pay for plane and lawyer. Is the ranch nice place?"

Lara started to answer when June appeared and got behind the wheel of the Woodie. "Good to see you two have already met," she said, smiling as she maneuvered the vehicle into traffic. "Sorry I took so long in the bank. How did your time with McDermott go, Lara?"

"Great, thanks. I feel good about him. He told me he competed in rodeos with Mr. Bracken years ago. I didn't know your husband was a champion bronco buster."

"Yes. Long before I met him, thank the Lord," said June, driving the short span across the Truckee River and pulling up in front of the Hotel Riverside. "I'm going to pick up the other guests. I'll only be a minute."

As June dashed into the hotel's entrance, Lara turned in her seat to look at Uta and answer her previous question. "The ranch is really pretty. It's by a big lake surrounded by desert and mountains. Billy and I arrived just yesterday so I can't tell you much, except that the Brackens are especially nice. Oh... and the ranch has a swimming pool, cowboys, and you can ride horses there." She was pleased to see the shy young Axel's blue eyes light up at the mention of cowboys.

June returned with the two women guests she'd chauffeured into Reno with Lara earlier. Vida Zembrowski, the older of the two women, was a bubbly, bountifully-built blonde in her fifties. At breakfast that morning, Lara overheard Vida say she owned a Polish restaurant in New York City with her husband, a "son-of-a-bitch" who she caught "screwing" one of their hostesses. As Vida settled her copious self in the front seat, June introduced Uta and Axel to all, then headed the Woodie out of town.

The other female, Kat Kavanaugh, shared the middle seat with Lara. Kat had obviously indulged in a few cocktails since the trip in from the ranch. She smiled tipsily at Lara and set several fancy-looking bags on the seat between them. "What did ya say your name was? I'm so bad at names. S'wonder I remember my own." She laughed throatily and leaned toward Lara as if to share a confidence, her golden-brown eyes uncomfortably close to Lara's face. "Lissen. I found the cutest shop jes' down th' street from th' Riverside. I gotta hot date with an honest-to-god cowboy an' I bought th' sexiest outfit. Very *Harper's Bazaar*. Wanna see?"

"Why,... sure," Lara said, not wanting to be impolite to Kat, an attractive socialite-type with a deep tan, short brown hair, and a buxom figure.

Vida shifted in her seat to shout at Kat over the roar of the car's engine. The Woodie's two front windows were open to let a warm breeze circulate. "Hey, Kat! Why don't you give us all a fashion show back at the ranch? Can you hear me? God, it's so damn noisy in here." She rolled up her window an inch or two and lit a cigarette.

Grinning at Lara, Kat said, "What d'ya say, gorgeous? Should I do it? I used ta model, y'know." To Vida she yelled, banging her hand against the back of Vida's seat, "Damn good idea, Veesi. Cocktail time. My cabin. Okay?" She turned around to get a shaky bead on the German girl in the back seat. "Y'all come, too, honey. It'll be a gas. Oh, an' bring the kid there with ya." At that, Kat sank back in her seat and dozed with her mouth open.

All talk ceased for the rest of the ride, each woman wrapped in her own web of consciousness. Only the occasional pop-plop of an unlucky jackrabbit being transported to "bunny heaven" under the Woodie's speeding wheels jolted Lara from her thoughts and impressions of the day.

She turned to check on Uta Crouse and her son. Both were asleep, Uta with her arm around her small son who was clutching his teddy bear. *I wonder what happened to bring them away out here? Must be painful,* mused Lara. Her heart went out to mother and child as she considered her own situation.

She could hardly wait to get to the ranch to hug Billy.

CHAPTER 8

Our greatest glory is not in never falling,
but in rising every time we fall.
— *Confucius*

"I told Nita 'n Jimmy my daddy makes magic. Do you know any magic tricks, Mommy?" Billy lay on his stomach on the cabin floor, crayoning in his Donald Duck coloring book while his mother rested before dinner.

Lara, now wearing shorts and a halter, stretched out on her bed, happy to have this time with Billy after the trip into Reno. "Not really, sweetheart," she said. "I only learned a few tricks and I can't do them nearly as well as Daddy does." *Yeah, like the slight-of-hand Rick conjured up to do a hatchet job on our marriage*, she thought. "But maybe somebody at the ranch does magic. We can ask. Okay?" She looked at her watch. "Oops, almost time to wash up for dinner."

Though still tired from the lack of a full night's sleep, Lara rose and grabbed a towel, washcloth, and her bottle of Breck shampoo. "Mommy's going to take a shower in that building over there." She directed Billy's attention to a white board-and-batten structure located at the back of the lodge a few yards from their cabin. "I'll only be a few minutes. I want you to stay right here and guard our cabin. Promise?" She raised his chin with one hand and peered into his trusting little face.

"I promise, Mommy."

"And don't let anybody in. Okay?" She kissed his forehead, closed the cabin door, and hurried over to the women's bathhouse, hoping she didn't bump into anyone on the way.

Lara enjoyed her shower. The last time she'd taken one had been the morning before she left Carleton; sponge baths in the cabin's tiny washbasin had served temporarily. She toweled off, dressed again in the white halter and shorts, and was drying her hair, rubbing and shaking her fingers through it vigorously, when someone entered the bathhouse. It was a tipsy Kat Kavanaugh.

"Goddammit, I'm mad at ya, gorgeous. Where th' hell *were* ya? Veesi and I waited to start th' fashion show... an' shit, ya never showed." Kat wobbled to a toilet stall, lifted her skirt, pulled down her panties, and sat, leaving the door open. "What *are* ya, anyhow? Goddamn Miss Goody-Two-Shoes, or what? I knocked an' knocked at your door an' your kid wouldn't let me in. Said ya went ta get cleaned up, goddammit." Kat finished tinkling and was having trouble unrolling the toilet paper. "Oh, shit." She ripped the spool from its holder and threw it across the tiled space, narrowly missing Lara. "Oh, hell. Did I hurt ya?"

Good God, the woman's a nutcase, thought Lara. But she somehow felt sorry for Kat when she saw how contrite the poor thing appeared to be. Kat kept sitting on the john, pink panties at half-mast, tears welling up in her golden brown eyes.

"Nothing ever turns out for me, goddammit. I'm jes' a damn loser with too many big bucks and, I might add, big tits, too. D'ya think I'm pretty? Not like you, but pretty enough?" She stood, swaying for a moment, then attempted to pull up her panties, without success. "I *got to* be pretty for Tex. We're goin' dancin' at th' Riverside tomorra night."

"You'll be the prettiest one there," Lara said, helping Kat pull up her pink silk underwear. She walked the woman out of the stall.

"There you are!" A breathless Vida Zembrowski came bustling into the bathhouse. "God, Kat! I thought you were down at The Trading Post but they said you'd left already. You really had me going for a while." She smiled at Lara. "Thanks. I hope Kat didn't give you a hard time. She was drinking up a storm after we all got back from Reno today. Guess she was nervous about showing off her new outfit,... and when you and that new girl didn't show, she got pissed and hit the bottle with a vengeance. Don't worry. I'll get her back to her cabin. I deal with this stuff all the time at my New York restaurant. When the bouncer doesn't show, I take over."

Considering Vida's bulk, Lara believed her. "I'm really sorry, Vida," she said. "I didn't think Kat's invitation was serious...."

"I know, I know. It was very last minute. And Kat already had three gin and tonics and a Manhattan, sitting at the Riverside bar while we were waiting for June. They'd have to carry *me* out on a stretcher if I did that. I told her to slow down, but she's been so worked up ever since that damn cowboy asked her out." With some difficulty, Vida led Kat to one of the bathhouse sinks and ran the cold water. "Can I borrow a corner of your towel, Lara?"

Lara complied and watched Vida dab Kat's face and eyes, marveling at how quiet Kat now seemed.

"Atta girl. Let's go back to your cabin, Kat," Vida said, handing Lara's towel back to her. "Thanks, Lara. See you later."

Off the two went, leaving Lara wondering why, with the arrival of Vida, Kat had changed into a docile child, as though the older woman was a mother figure to her.

When Lara got back to her cabin she hugged Billy warmly. "A lady kept knocking, Mommy, but I yelled no, no, no... *really* loud and she went away." Billy beamed at his mother.

"I'm proud of you. You kept your promise, Billy." Lara kissed her son on his cheek. "Okay, cowboy. Wash your hands. We have to head out to the old corral and put on the feed bag."

"You're funny, Mommy." Billy laughed and went to get ready, standing on tiptoe to reach the washbasin.

Changing into a white sleeveless blouse, candy-striped capri pants, and sandals, Lara brushed her dark-blonde hair 'til it shone, fluffed up her bangs, and applied bright red lipstick. "Let's go, sweetheart," she said to her son, taking his hand and setting off down the gravel path toward the lodge, their faces caressed by a warm breeze wafting off the lake.

They entered the ranch's main, log-ceilinged room and stepped one step down into the adjacent dining hall, a rectangular, screened-in space with a view of the lake. June Bracken welcomed them graciously, seating them at one of four long, banquet-style tables covered in white oilcloth. A basket containing freshly baked bread, muffins, and biscuits was placed on each table, along with cobalt-blue country crocks of butter. For the first time since her pregnancy, Lara felt the stirrings of a healthy appetite. Something in the dry air? She smiled at the couple sitting across from her and Billy.

June, always the sensitive hostess, immediately circumvented any possible feelings of social timidity and offered introductions all around. "I've been wanting Lara to meet both of you," she said to the couple. "She just arrived yesterday. Lara Treadwell, meet Claire and Nick Janus. Oh, yes, and this handsome young man is Mr. Billy

Treadwell." June patted Billy's head and excused herself to greet and seat other incoming diners.

"Where are you from, Lara?" Claire Janus took a sip from her water glass. She was auburn-haired, with a creamy, lightly freckled complexion, her green eyes sparkling as she smiled warmly. Seated, she appeared to be taller than her husband.

"We're from Connecticut. Are you here for the proverbial six weeks?" Lara asked, then instantly regretted the question. If the couple were already married, seemingly happily so, they wouldn't be here for the reason she was, would they? Lara felt herself blush.

Nick answered. "We thought we'd try roughing it at a real dude ranch for a change,... if, of course, you can call this 'roughing it.'" He smiled.

Nick Janus looked professorial to Lara. She didn't know why, but he appeared to have the distinct air of academia about him, or at least some position of influence. It was a characteristic Lara recognized because several of her father's brothers were professors at colleges and universities. Nick also had a slight accent she couldn't place, a fair complexion, dark brown hair, a receding hairline, prominent nose, and the blackest, most piercing eyes she'd ever seen in a human. An unusual person. Something mysterious about him, too.

Before Lara and the Januses could talk further, Pidge McCauley arrived, plunking herself down to sit next to Billy. "Howdy, young sir," she said with a grin. "What's the password?"

Startled, Billy stared at Pidge, who, to Lara's relief, appeared sober this time. The boy turned to his mother, a worried expression on his rosy-cheeked face. "What's the password, Mommy?" he whispered.

She cupped her hand to whisper in his ear, "Winnemucca, Billy."

While Pidge pretended to wait patiently, Billy tapped her arm and motioned for her to bend down to his level so he could whisper in her ear. "Winnemucca," he said triumphantly.

"Correct, Sir Billy!" said Pidge. "A step in the right direction! In fact, in Indian-land, Winnemucca means to walk on one moccasin. I think this calls for an extra helping of ice cream tonight. Whatta ya say to that?" Pidge winked at Lara and the Januses, put an arm around Billy's small shoulders, and hugged him close, much to his obvious embarrassment, which quickly evaporated when Nita Big Horn came into view with a tray of food.

The pretty young Indian girl served Billy a large plate of meat-loaf, mashed potatoes, corn on the cob, and green beans. Lara noticed Uta Crouse helping to serve the other tables but failed to catch her eye. Hopefully she would soon find out how things were going for the nice young German girl and her son.

As dinner progressed, Lara found out more about the Januses. She had been right about Nick. He was on sabbatical from teaching economics at the University of California at Berkeley. Claire was a teaching assistant in the university's English Department and managed some time off so she and Nick could tour the West and Nick could write. Lara found them both erudite, witty, and charming. Also something else she couldn't quite put her finger on. There was that mystery again, as if the couple were on a second honeymoon and took immense pleasure in it but didn't want everyone to know. *How appealing*, thought Lara. *I feel I could be friends with this couple forever, even though they don't ask in-depth questions about my situation, which is fine with me. Why would such a happy pair want to dwell on anything as depressing as divorce, despite Desert Lake's catering to such things?*

As they all enjoyed the simple, down-home meal, Lara offhandedly mentioned her show business background. It was then the Januses, especially Claire, registered the greatest amount of enthusiasm.

"How fascinating!" she trilled, her emerald green eyes shimmering. "We'd love to see you perform sometime, Lara. We're crazy about anything theatrical. We go to all the visiting celebrity shows and musical events at the university and lots in San Francisco, too. Don't we, Nicky?" She reached for his hand on the table and squeezed it, beaming at him.

"Wouldn't miss a one," he said, returning Claire's gesture warmly. "Because of my faculty position, we meet quite a few important stars from the cinema."

There it is again. Why does he say cinema? *Why not plain old* movies? Lara thought his accent not really British but more European, with a certain measured pomposity filtering through it, so practiced and high-toned.

Pidge joined the conversation, recounting some particularly hilarious, sometimes embarrassing accounts of celebrities who'd visited the ranch. Lara hoped some of Pidge's more risqué tales went over Billy's innocent head and was glad when Nita served the evening's dessert, an enticing apple pie a la mode. Pidge sent back to the kitchen for an extra dollop of ice cream for Billy's portion. "Gotta keep our cowboys well fed around hyar," she drawled, and was instantly rewarded with a huge grin from Billy.

Over coffee, Nick said, "We're going along to The Trading Post for an after-dinner drink." He looked at his wife.

"Yes." Claire smiled invitingly at Lara. "It's a ritual with us. Ever since we got here. We'd love it if you would join us later."

"Oh, thank you. But I need to put this young man to bed." Lara watched fondly as Billy devoured the last of his pie and ice cream. "It's a ritual with us, too," she said, wondering how to explain that particular ritual to someone not familiar with raising kids. At least, the Januses hadn't mentioned having any children. "I'm sorry. I have nobody to watch him and it's too late to find someone." *I hope they understand*, she thought, then added, "I'd love to, though. Maybe another time."

"'Ta-da!" Pidge rose and gave Lara a mock salute. "Your fairy godmother to the rescue, Miss Cinderella. I hereby insist you go enjoy yourself." Concurrently, guests at the next table stopped their chitchat for a moment to stare bemusedly. "As everyone knows, I am also the official gatekeeper. After you tuck this young feller in bed and go to the ball, I will personally keep watch on the stoop outside your lowly dwelling. I will stay there 'til your return and I promise I will not turn into a pumpkin, 'cause guess what?" Pidge cupped her tanned, gnarled hands alongside her mouth and spoke in a loud, hoarse whisper, "I know the password!" She sat down, apparently pleased with her spontaneous performance.

"Me, too! I know the password," Billy piped up gleefully.

Pidge leaned her elbow on the table, chin in hand, and peered intently at Billy. "Yes. And good for you, sir. But do your mommy and you know 'Winnemucca' is also the word for 'go' around here? See, it's like the green light for a car. Everything's on red 'til you say the password. Then you can go! Don't you think Mommy should go and have fun?"

Great, thought Lara, *get the kid involved*. She really didn't want someone persuading her child to make decisions regarding her, nice as that person might be. "C'mon, Billy." Lara wiped her small son's face and fingers with a napkin, then, turning to Pidge, said, "Bless you, Pidge. I know you mean well. Thank you for your offer, but we have to get back to the cabin."

The two were about to leave the dining hall when Pidge came running after them. "I'm sorry, dear one. I get carried away sometimes. I've no kiddies of my own, but I love 'em. I wouldn't hurt Billy for all the world. Honest."

Because Pidge looked so earnest and pathetic standing there, Lara felt her heart soften. "I'm sorry, too, Pidge. It's just... well, I don't want Billy involved in decisions as to what his mother should or should not do. He's an innocent in all this, and he deserves to stay that way. Can we keep things on that level?"

"Of course. You're right. I just thought since you're going to be here for a while you need to give yourself a little fun, too. Am I wrong?"

"Well, no. It isn't a matter of who's right or wrong. I feel guilty about being here in the first place." Lara noticed Nick and Claire observing her and Pidge with interest from their seats at the table. "Oh, okay. Maybe it'll be good for me. But only for one drink, if you absolutely watch over him for me, Pidge, and stay there while he sleeps." She excused herself from Pidge, who waited while Lara walked back, hand in hand with Billy, to speak to the Januses.

"I'll meet you at The Trading Post in an hour, if the invite still stands?" she said, feeling a bit foolish. "Just one drink. Thanks." She smiled. "Billy and I need our beauty sleep."

"You're both beautiful enough," said Claire as Nick nodded smilingly in agreement. "See you later, Lara. Good night, Billy."

Billy waved at the couple. Lara left with Billy in tow and Pidge trotting alongside. The sun was setting and already a slim crescent of moon hung high in the pink and lavender sky.

"Pidge, thank you for helping me out, but I have to be sure you won't, you know, start drinking or anything like that. I don't mean that as a criticism, but I did notice last night you were somewhat … uh … under the weather." Lara hated to bring it up but it had to be said.

Pidge stopped suddenly. "You hit a sore spot, Larie-love. Got ol' Pidge pegged for sure." She looked towards the lake, a pensive expression on her apple-doll visage. "There's lots of us ol' 'alkies' around here. My best bud, Marge Stanley, is one. You'll meet her. Roy looks out for her, keeps her busy serving drinks at The Trading Post every night, testing her. But me, I have to look out for myself. I slip up now 'n then, but never, never when I make a promise. You can count on that."

Lara patted the older woman's arm affectionately. "I believe you, Pidge, and I'm sorry I doubted you even for a minute. Thanks. See you later at my place."

A brisk bout of teeth brushing and sponge bathing in the cabin's small sink, and a pajama-clad Billy was eager for a reading from a special storybook. Lara was in the middle of "Jack and the Beanstalk" when Pidge appeared at the cabin's screen door.

"Cap'n McCauley reporting for duty, sirs." She waved two small flashlights in the air. "I brought one for you, Larie-love, and one to keep me company. It gets pitch-black here at night." She plopped down on the stoop and lit a cigarette, calling out to Billy, "Nighty-night, handsome. I'll be right here if you need me."

Billy didn't answer, having slipped off to sleep. Lara covered him with a light cotton blanket, checked her reflection in the washbasin mirror, and joined Pidge, closing the screen door carefully. "Thank you," she whispered as Pidge handed her a flashlight. "I won't be long."

"Watch out for wolves wearing sheepskins," Pidge whispered back, her pixie eyes glowing like new pennies. "My pal Marge is tending bar tonight. Get her to make you one of her famous Moscow Mules. It's on me, Larie-love. Have fun!"

Lara followed the path in the gathering dusk and rounded the corner of the lodge when she heard a low, contralto voice behind her. "Lara, wait up." It was Claire Janus. "Nick's coming. He's gone back to our place for something. That's The Trading Post over there."

Claire pointed to a log building set close to the road beside the lake. The syncopated beat of Les Paul and Mary Ford's "How High The Moon" grew louder as Lara and Claire approached the brightly lit nightspot. They stepped from the grassy path onto a wooden porch and entered through saloon-style swinging doors. The musky odor of wood soaked with hops and malt reminded Lara of off-campus hangouts at Syracuse as she noted June and a stocky, pale-faced woman with frizzy, orange-colored hair keeping busy behind the bar. A glassed-in cabinet featuring Indian-made jewelry and other artifacts, plus a few sundries, occupied the corner nearest the entrance. *Can this be a real trading post?* Lara wondered. A jukebox, multicolored lights flashing, stood in the rear of the room, and many large posters advertising past rodeo events in and around Reno lined the walls. Several small tables with chairs were set around a mini-sized dance floor.

"This looks okay, don't you think?" said Claire as Lara and she sat down and smiled at several occupants of the other tables. "Oh, good. Here's Nicky." Claire's green eyes sparkled at the sight of her husband, leaving Lara longing for that old feeling she remembered feeling with Rick. If she saw him again, would she still feel it? *Despite everything, I still love him,* she told herself. And the music pulsating from the Wurlitzer was stirring all the old memories, all the beautiful dancing, the magical moments, the good times canceling out the recent sadness.

Joining Claire and Lara at their table, Nick opened a handsome, silver-and-black cigarette case and offered filter-tipped smokes to each. *An elegant gesture indeed,* thought Lara.

The stocky lady with orange-colored hair came shuffling over from behind the bar, pad in hand, pencil poised. "Hi. I'm Marge. I make the best damn Moscow Mule this side of the 'Vulgar' River. Ha, ha." She had a pug nose, pie-face, and an attitude. "So. What'll it be, folks?"

"Moscow Mule for me, please," Lara said, feeling adventurous.

"Hey. You must be the new girl. Pidge told me you'd be here tonight. Mule it is," Marge drawled in her dry, deadpan manner.

As Nick and Claire ordered their drinks from Marge, Lara's attention shifted to The Trading Post's swinging doors. Two men entered the smoke-filled room. One wandered to the bar. As if on cue, like something in a B movie, the jukebox gave sway to the Andrews Sisters singing "I Want To Be Loved", and Lara saw Chance Darwin striding in—in all his tanned, blonde glory—straight toward her.

CHAPTER 9

Rings on her fingers and bells on her toes,
She shall have music wherever she goes.

—— "Ride a Cockhorse," *anonymous*

The Moscow Mule, served in an iced copper mug with a pewter handle, was beautiful, thought Lara. Unusual taste, too... so sensuous, and the smell of it delightfully ginger-peachy. Though she usually stayed away from alcoholic drinks, this creation seemed to hit the spot. She couldn't stop sipping. "What is *in* this?" she asked.

"Vodka, ginger beer, and a dash of lime." Chance grinned at her enthusiasm. "It's well named for a drink. So, watch out. Comes with a kick." He took a swig from his bottle of beer. "It's good to see you again, Lar," he said.

His shoulder brushed hers as he sat close to her at the table they shared with the Januses. Lara gazed into his gold-flecked green eyes. *Never*, she thought, *have I felt such an animalistic attraction towards a man. Scary, but fascinating.*

"Because of You," the next platter on the jukebox, sung by Tony Bennett, caused Lara to smile at Chance, wondering to herself why she felt so comfortable in his presence. *He's so easy to be with,* she thought. *But I hardly know him. I miss Rick, my baby, and ... oh, dear...*

As if responding to her thoughts, Chance rose and extended his hand to her. "May I have this dance, Lar? I'll try not to step on your toes," he said, a wide grin crinkling his dimples.

Chance's cowboy-style two-step was simplistic at best. *Oh, so what? So he doesn't dance like Rick. No earthly man can,* she told herself. *Well, Astaire, Kelly, and the like, but no ordinary guy. I'll probably always miss that part of my life with Rick. No more brilliantly choreographed moves to all kinds of music, all kinds of audiences. Rick was a master at leading me into moves I could never do with anyone else. It was so beautiful. I'll never have that again.*

She sighed inwardly, swaying to and fro in the arms of a stranger whose strong embrace enfolded her as they moved slowly to the music. It felt different to Lara of course, from Rick's holding her. With

Rick, there was always the element of exhibitionism, of "let's put on a show" and he reveled in his crowd-pleasing techniques, having taught her to respond as he did and follow his fantastic lead in dance-floor and stage performances alike. *I did enjoy the spotlight, too,* mused Lara, *so not only have I lost Rick, I've lost...*

"You're so easy to dance with, Lar," said Chance, smiling down at her. "Guess you can see I'm not." His warm, green-eyed gaze somehow put her at ease for the moment.

"Oh, no, Chance," she said, smiling back, "You're fine. It's just that it was my husband's and my profession, and I practiced a lot." She decided to change the subject. "Where's your friend Frank? I thought I saw him come in with you."

"Had to stay at the ranch and draw up some racing contracts for A.K. Why?"

"Well, if it isn't Frank,... who is that guy sitting at the bar? Do you know him? He keeps staring at us. It's creepy."

"Want me to go over there and knock his block off?" Chance pulled her closer, his eyes twinkling. "I'd do that for you, Lar."

She laughed, slightly embarrassed. *What's my problem? It's so difficult to think straight when I'm this close to Chance,* she thought. *But I do like him calling me "Lar."*

The music ended. "Let's sit down," Lara whispered. "Nick and Claire look lonely and I can't stay much longer. Maybe they know who the guy is. Oh no. Too late. He's coming over here!"

Before she and Chance could join the Januses at the table, Lara found herself face to face with the man from the bar. "Can I have this dance with you, miss?" he drawled. "I can't help noticin' how smooth you move on the floor."

"Well ..." The jukebox was now booming out with a jump number. Lara felt tuned up, tempted. On closer inspection, she noted the guy didn't appear threatening, except for what looked like a well-healed scar running the length of one side of his face. He was short, lean, tan and sandy-haired, brown-eyed, and dressed neatly in jeans and a Western-style shirt. *Clean-cut enough,* she thought, amused at the way he shifted his weight from one leg to the other as if he was wired for a fast take-off.

She looked at Chance. "Okay?"

"Go ahead." Chance grinned, adding as he sat down next to Nick, "But, remember. The clock's ticking, Cinderella."

Her answer got lost as she felt herself speedily swirled out and back and out and back like a revved up yo-yo. The guy led her well, given the restricted space, so she let go completely. When the number ended she could barely breathe. People in the smoky room applauded. How invigorating! It was like old times with Rick.

She plopped down next to Chance. Out of breath, she looked up at her whirlwind of a dance partner, standing by the table, also breathless and wiping his face with a blue bandana. "Thank you," she said. "That was fun. Where did you learn to dance like that?"

"Took lessons in Reno. You're great. I'm Tex. What's your name?"

"Lara." For a moment she sensed a tenseness in Chance. *My imagination?* she wondered.

"Let's do it again sometime, Lara. Well, see ya." For some reason "Tex" didn't introduce himself to Chance or the Januses, and, without another word, ambled back to sit at the bar. Lara noticed Marge serving him a drink as he turned his back to the rest of the room.

"If I'd known you could move like that, Lar, I wouldn't have had the nerve to dance with you. You're amazing." Chance lit a cigarette for her, his blonde-lashed green eyes caressing her with approval.

"I guess Lara didn't tell you she's a stage and television performer, Chance," Claire said in her throaty voice. She brightened and smiled at Nick, who nodded back at her as if they shared some secret form of communication. "I know! Let's go over to our place. We have some terrific jazz recordings you might like to hear—you know, Jack Teagarden, Ellington, Armstrong, Billie Holiday. Do you like jazz, Chance?"

"Yeah. Just can't dance to it." He turned to Lara. "You have time, Lar? You said you have to get back. Your boy is okay?"

She didn't recall telling Chance she was a mother. Maybe he found out from the Brackens. "Well... I do like jazz." She felt sure Billy was asleep and Pidge was watching. "Okay." She linked her arm in Chance's and as they headed for the door she glanced back at the bar. Tex had disappeared. Who was he? And why had he picked her as a dance partner?

Next morning Lara awoke with a headache. *Must have been the mixture of Moscow Mule with the bourbon and soda I had at Nick and Claire's*, she thought, vowing to stick to one Mule an outing from now on and no other alcohol.

"Mommy, Mommy!" Billy jumped on her bed. "Can we go see the horses today? Bip said his daddy's taking him riding."

"Sure. But after breakfast, Billy." She groaned quietly as she swung her feet out onto the green braided rug between their beds.

At breakfast in the dining hall, about all she could manage was Lipton tea and unbuttered toast.

"You not feel so good, Lara?" Uta Crouse inquired in her fractured English as she placed a plate of butter patties and a jar of strawberry jam on the table.

"Serves me right. I can't drink."

"Yah. Me not neither. But my husband, Karl, he can. Too much. It make him mean after he come home from war. That's why Axel und me here. He beat us too many," Uta said, her blue-violet eyes glistening. "But now we here we feel better, tanks be to Gott."

Lara smiled, noting the German girl's healthier appearance. "I'm glad, Uta. Where's Axel?"

"In kitchen. June let him play there if he not get in vay."

Lara watched her own son happily wolfing down his Rice Krispies and milk. "Uta, we're going to the stables. Would you let Axel join Billy and me while you finish your shift? I promise to have Axel back in an hour or so."

Uta seemed so grateful, it was almost embarrassing. Poor gal. A battered war bride. *What she's endured,* thought Lara, feeling fortunate by comparison. *I didn't experience physical abuse, thank God, only that of a psychological nature, which can still be brutal.* But the German girl had suffered both. Lara's heart went out to the young working mother and she promised herself to help Uta by including Axel in Billy's playtimes as often as possible.

Trudging down the path to the horse barn, Lara watched her son and the thin, blonde German child skip joyfully ahead of her.

I know nothing about horses, she thought. *They seem like such mysterious creatures. I never got close to one 'til that night last October on the country road with Rick. And that animal didn't seem real. More like a ghost horse.*

She paused by the side of the reddish barn and a weathered sign on which was printed "Tack Room," whatever that was. She and the boys peered into the cavernous opening. "Hello?" she called. No answer. As her eyes adjusted to the stark contrast of sunlight and shadowy dark, she discerned stalls, piles of straw, coils of rope, and a dirt floor. Flies were plentiful and the place smelled of manure.

"Mommy! Look. Everybody's over there." Billy pointed to a fenced-in area some distance from where they were. Several guests were leaning or sitting on the fence. When Lara and the boys drew closer, she recognized Duke Fenway leading a docile-looking horse around in a circle as a small boy in a cowboy hat sat atop the animal, clinging to a raised part of the saddle in front of him.

"It's Bip, Mommy!" Billy and Axel scrambled over to the fence for a better view.

"That's my kid," a slim man said to Lara. His brown hair was slicked-back and his dark eyes were set deep in a pale, pockmarked face. Half-smoked cigarette in hand, he pointed to the little kid on the horse. "He's a regular Lone Ranger, don't ya think?"

An attractive, olive-skinned brunette next to him laughed. "Yeah, but that horse is no Silver. More like the Old Gray Mare with its head in a truss." Like the man, her accent was unmistakably New York. "Hi," she said, turning to Lara while shading from the sun's glare her dark-amber eyes heavily lined with makeup. "I'm Maria. Maria Wexler. And this is Bip's dad, as if you can't tell,... Stan Gorman. Say hello, Stanley."

Apparently ignoring her, Gorman jumped the fence to lift Bip off the horse and carry the excited boy around on his shoulders.

"Oh, well. Stan doesn't like it when I pull that Laurel and Hardy stuff," Maria said. "I hooked up with him the minute I got here. He's divorcing Bip's mom 'cause she's a total alcoholic and won't care for the kid. Stan's a good dad. Good in the sack, too, which is why I stick to him like flypaper."

Something about Maria made it easy to talk to her. After introducing herself, Lara discovered Maria owned a liquor store in Manhattan with her husband Irving, whom she was divorcing. And, according to Maria, she had five more weeks to go before she got her decree and "graduated" from the "Desert Dormitory for Desperate Dudes" as she called it.

"Who's next?" Old Duke led the phlegmatic mare over to the fence near Lara, Billy, and Axel. "Well, purty lady. Which one is th' young 'un you told me about?" He winked at her and leaned down to peer at the two youngsters, his crinkly blue eyes shaded by a dusty Stetson, his yellow-toothed grin gleaming in the sun.

Billy went first, looking ecstatic as he clung tight to the saddle horn and rode the horse slowly round and round the ring. Lara decided Duke was cautious enough with kids so she let Axel have a turn or two also. As the sun beat down unmercifully, Maria offered to share a cooler of soft drinks she'd brought with her when Lara heard her draw in her breath sharply.

"Uh, oh. Here comes trouble," Maria mumbled, pointing with her bottle opener to something in back of Lara.

Lara turned to see Tex, her inscrutable dance partner from the night before, sauntering towards them. His frayed cowboy hat was worn at a rakish angle, his jeans, boots, and shirt were dusty, and his dark, nut-brown eyes seemed more piercing and insinuating than she remembered. A small shiver ran down her spine despite the heat of the day. *I wouldn't dance with him out here in the daylight*, she thought. Why, then, had she been willing in the smoky dark? *I better watch those drinks from now on.*

"Hey, Lara. How's it goin'?" Tex glanced at Billy. "This your kid? Your mom's a beaut, bud." He patted Billy on the head and the boy recoiled slightly, a puzzled look on his face.

Tex sidled up to Maria. "Hey, baby. When're we gonna meet in town again an' shoot some dirty pool?" Lara saw him about to give a scowling Maria a quick pat on the behind but apparently think better of it when he saw Stan approaching. "'Scuse me, ladies an' gents. Gotta get to work." Tex tipped his hat, grabbed a saddle off the fence, and headed for the barn.

Maria handed a bottle of orange soda pop to Billy and a Coke to Lara. "That Tex Otis is a snake, believe me. He flirts with every skirt he sees. He helps Roy and Duke with the horses and I guess he does okay at that, but... basically, he's slime. How come he knew you?"

"Tell you later," Lara said, ashamed for dancing with such a sub-standard person. *Am I really such a poor judge of character? Rick is right*, she decided. *What is there to love about me when I make such stupid moves?*

Duke lifted a glowing Axel over the fence to join Lara and Billy. "Come again, purty lady," the wrangler said, his craggy features erupting in a wide grin. "And bring th' troops with ya."

After thanking the old foreman, Lara gave a promise to Maria to join her on a short trip into Reno the next afternoon to buy a few necessities. Roy was driving and would drop them off. "I'll go," added Lara. "But only if Billy is well looked after."

Later in their cabin Lara told her son about the next day's plan Maria had arranged with Stan. "Is that okay with you?"

"Will Bip's daddy watch us swim in the pool? Bip said he has new swim fins and I could try them out, too."

With Billy's lisp, "swim fins" came out "thwim finth," but Lara hardly noticed, so glad was she to see her son adjusting to the life here. "I'm sure that'll be fine, Billy," she said.

What fun, she thought, *to share some talk time in Reno with another female, something missing from my life for far too long.*

CHAPTER 10

Tranquility! thou better name,
Than all the family of Fame.
—— Samuel Taylor Coleridge

Lara leaned against the railing of Reno's Truckee River Bridge and focused on the rippling waters below. Bright sunlight sparkled and shimmered across the surface of the water, highlighting the tops of river rocks in diamond-like patterns. Such a pretty sight. But, she wondered, how many souls, disillusioned over losses in love or cards, had jumped from this same bridge? What a morbid thought. She knew in her heart she would never make such a decision. *I've been hurt, yes*, she told herself, *but my children need me, and...*

A tap on her shoulder brought her back to the cacophony of Virginia Street traffic. "Whoa there!" she heard Maria say. "C'mon, kiddo. I don't think you're ready to toss your wedding ring to the Truckee River fishes like a lotta babes do."

"You mean it's a tradition? I would never do that."

"I know," Maria laughed. "I would. But not until the judge gives me my walking papers. I'd keep my engagement ring 'cause real diamonds are as good as sex in my book." She grabbed Lara's arm. "Let's pop over to the Riverside and tie one on. My treat," she said, guiding Lara across the street to the hotel on the corner.

The dark, cave-like coolness of the Hotel Riverside's cocktail lounge provided a respite from the heat of the day. A red Dubonnet over ice with a twist of lemon encouraged Lara to talk, as did her friend's uncanny knack for probing.

"So, kiddo. For a looker like you, you can write your own ticket," Maria said in her distinctive New York accent, producing a pack of Kools from her purse and offering one of the filter tips to Lara. "From what little you've told me so far, you let that guy you were married to walk all over you. I can't believe it. Why didn't you tell *him* to hop the next plane to Reno?" She lit her own cigarette and shoved a book of matches to Lara across the polished surface of the cocktail table. "Why didn't you take a stand? You weren't the one hot to trot. He was. And you just had his baby, for pete's sake."

Lighting the cigarette, Lara said, "Believe me, Maria, every day, after he shocked me by insisting we get a divorce... I kept at him trying to get him to change his mind, give it some time, find a counselor, get help... but he would have none of it. I was desperate. And because I'd just had a baby, I didn't feel like my normal self. I cried buckets. I couldn't think. I felt like a robot."

"Wasn't there someone you could at least talk to on the phone?" asked Maria.

"No." Lara sighed. "Honestly, Maria, it was like trying to swim upstream when the current is pushing so hard against you you just stay in place flailing your arms and getting nowhere. It was exhausting. And Rick was like a stone. Once he makes up his mind, forget changing it. It was his way or nothing." Lara took a drag on her cigarette, blowing the smoke out slowly. "So... here I am. I feel like I've been through a hurricane and lucky to have survived... if you call getting a divorce against your will surviving. And it really hurts that I had to leave my baby at home. I... I miss her so much." Lara swallowed hard, trying to keep from crying. She bowed her head, staring down at the table. "Even someone as strong as you, Maria," she said, "Even you, in the same circumstances, would be challenged."

"Well, I never had a kid, so I don't know. My natural inclination would be to tell the guy to go to hell."

"I was angry, yes, mad as hell... besides being hurt. But I had two kids to consider. I don't know." Lara stared into space, "I've thought about it alot, Maria. It's devastating to be hated the way Rick seems to hate me. And for what reason, really? Unless he ..."

"Yeah." Maria laughed. "Wake up and smell the coffee, toots. It's obvious there's someone else on the horizon and you're in the way," she said, reaching across the table to touch Lara affectionately on the arm. "Oldest story in the world. Frankly, I think he's nuts to give you up. I've noticed the guys at the ranch staring at you,... aside from that devil Tex, of course."

"Yes, and it makes me uncomfortable." Lara blew a smoke ring and gazed out beyond the lounge to the hotel's lobby where two men in Western garb were playing the slot machines. She thought of Chance. *Best I don't talk about him with Maria 'til I know him better,* she thought. *Besides, I shouldn't be thinking about* any *man when my life is in such disarray.*

"Why should guys staring at you make you uncomfortable? I don't get it. You told me you were in show business. People stare at you all the time when you're performing. Why should it be any different when you're not?" Maria's large, dark amber eyes begged the question.

"I don't know, Maria. Onstage is fantasy. Real life changes things. I know I should've told Rick he's the one who should go. When we're dancing together, I feel strong. I love moving to the music, expressing myself that way. I love performing. All my inhibitions melt away when I'm in the spotlight and I feel totally free, as if nothing matters but that moment. It's so creative. Like my art, like painting, too. I get lost in it and troubles seem to melt away. It's like another world, Maria, so beautiful," Lara shrugged her shoulders. "Then, offstage, somehow I seem to lose it, like I have no will of my own. Of course, that may be because of Rick. He's extremely critical and I bent over backwards trying to be perfect for him in our act." Lara took a sip of her Dubonnet. "I wish I were more sure of myself, like you, Maria."

Maria grinned. "Well, I'm Sicilian. In my New York neighborhood when I was a kid, if you didn't stand up for yourself, you got creamed. End of story. Maybe life didn't kick you in the butt enough when you were growing up."

"Could be." Lara laughed, then turned pensive. "My parents were so protective of me. My dad is a minister... well, an army chaplain now. They were strict with me. Maybe because I was the oldest and they expected more from me than from my sister. Or maybe it was my long recovery from an accident I had when I was little made them overly protective. I don't know."

"Oh? What happened?"

"I fell off a high four-poster bed and landed on my head." Lara made a comic face, crossing her eyes and sticking out her tongue. "And I've been like this ever since."

"Not funny, toots."

"Okay. Seriously,... I had a cerebral hemorrhage from the fall, was paralyzed for ten days, and almost died at the tender age of three and a half. Had to learn to walk all over again. Even now I limp a little when I'm tired."

"So? I should feel sorry for you? Look at you! You survived, turned beautiful, and ended up dancing with your husband on TV."

"Yeah, and now I'm *here*!" Lara sighed, sipped her drink, and changed the subject. "What happened with you and Irving, Maria?"

"Oh, don't ask!" Maria rolled her eyes. "Irving had some bad business deals and got in hock with the Mafia. He messed up our books and all our plans for the liquor store. I thought when we got hitched six years ago I was joining up with a smart Jewish business man, but he got too greedy for his—and my—good. He owes the damn mob, for pete's sake. Being Italian, I know how bad *that* can be, so I ran for the fastest plane to Reno."

"How scary, Maria. Won't you be afraid to go back to New York?"

"Why? I didn't do anything. Irving made his bed. He can lie in it." Maria stubbed her cigarette out in an ashtray and signaled for the check.

"You're amazing, Maria. I could never be that tough. Did you ever love Irving?" asked Lara.

"At first I did, or I never would've married the guy, but towards the end I got fed up. Thank God we didn't have kids." Maria peered at her watch. "Roy might be back from his errands by now. Maybe we should wait outside," she said, finishing her martini and getting up from her seat at the table.

Lara gathered up the bags of purchases she made in town that afternoon, among them lipstick, toothpaste, aspirin, and a new color-ing book for Billy. "Thanks for the treat," she said as Maria paid the bar tab.

Outside, waiting for the Woodie in the hot afternoon sun, Lara smiled at her new friend. "I really appreciate talking with you, Maria. I haven't shared anything about Rick and me since I got here. Well, except with my lawyer, but only 'cause I had to."

Maria squinted in the sunshine, and lit another Kool. "Ever think how lucky you are, kiddo? You've got two cute kids, talent, looks. So your ball 'n' chain dumped you, maybe for that teenage girl you told me about. Big friggin' deal. Could be Rick did you a favor. Ever look at it that way?"

Maria is right, thought Lara, *at least on some level*. But it was hard to change when there was no road map to follow.

As the Woodie pulled up in front of the lodge after the ride back from Reno, Lara saw June standing in the driveway. Alighting from the car, Lara felt startled when June drew her aside, saying, "Lucky I caught you in time. A call just came in for you. You can take it in my office, Lara. Long distance. From Connecticut. Your husband asked for Billy, too, so I got Stan to bring him over from the pool."

Lara's thoughts went immediately to her baby. Heart in her throat, she hurried inside past Pidge and Marge sunning themselves on the lodge steps. Billy, a white towel draped over his small shoulders, grinned widely at Lara as he spoke into the phone. "Here's Mommy, Daddy. She wants to say hello, then I'll say good-bye. Okay?"

Lara's hand shook as she took the receiver from her son and lifted it to her ear. *Please God,* she prayed, *please let Candace be all right.*

Moments later, Lara found herself limping out onto the lodge's porch. *I need air*, she thought. *Lots of it.*

"Larie-love. What happened?" said Pidge, who was sitting on the steps smoking with Marge. "Here, dear one. Rest awhile." She patted a space next to herself and Marge and held out a tanned, wrinkled, silver-ringed hand to Lara.

"Billy's inside talking to his dad on the phone." Lara felt hot tears slide down her cheeks, tears over which she seemed to have no control. "I'm so... confused." She sat down, leaning her elbows on her knees and burying her face in her hands. "We shouldn't be here.

I still love my husband," she sobbed. "When I heard his voice again I knew I missed him. I miss my baby, too, terribly. " She cried for a few moments more, then straightened up, making a vain effort to wipe her eyes. "I'm sorry. I seem to be always teetering on the edge of tears these days."

"We're all teetering on the edge of something, m'dear: life, death, guilt, fear, indecision, you name it." Pidge patted her gently on the shoulder.

"Goddamn quickie divorces," Marge muttered. "Makes my blood boil." She took a deep drag from her cigarette and flicked it out onto the dirt. "C'mon down to the Post, girl, and ol' Marge'll fix you a drink."

"Good Lord, Marge. She doesn't need a drink. She needs a good ear," Pidge said, shaking her head at her friend. She turned to Lara. "Pick your 'teeter,' m'dear. I mean, what edge are you trying to balance yourself on?"

Wiping her eyes with the back of one hand, Lara sighed. "Oh, Pidge. I don't know. All I know is I feel shaky, sorry, and sad. I wish I felt solid and peaceful inside like you."

"Ha!" Marge hooted with a shake of her orangey, frizzy-haired head. "That's a laugh. Pidge an' me both are teetering' on the edge of 'where's our next drink comin' from.' If it weren't for this here ranch and Roy makin' me tend bar every night, I know where I'd be, and her with me." She pointed a crooked thumb in Pidge's direction.

Pidge pursed her wrinkled lips in defiance. "Speak for yourself, Marge. As long as I stay tranquil inside I'm not teetering on the edge of temptation. It's tranquility keeps me going. Perhaps that'd help you, too, Larie-love." She laughed and stuck a Viceroy in her cigarette holder. "My, my. Aren't we waxing philosophical?"

Billy appeared at the top of the steps in his royal blue Superman swim trunks, holding a corner of the white towel and dragging it behind him. "I said good-bye to Daddy, Mommy. Daddy said he'd call again." The boy's young face appeared flushed with excitement. "I told Daddy it's fun here. But I miss him, Mommy, don't you?"

Lara rushed up the steps to hug her son, hoping he wouldn't notice her tear-stained cheeks. "Yes, yes, Billy." She took his small, warm hand in hers. "Let's go back to the cabin, sweetheart. I bought a new cowboy coloring book for you. Then maybe we'll go play on the beach before supper. Would you like that?" Pleased to see him nod enthusiastically, Lara smiled and waved at Pidge and Marge. "Thanks, you two. See you later."

Walking back to their cabin, Lara decided she would have a long talk with Billy soon. If only there was a way to turn time backwards, to change the course of events, to make everything better, different, happier. *I should have duked it out back there in Carleton, should have stood up for my rights, shown more guts, used my head to see the bigger picture, especially for the children*, she chastised herself. *But, no, as usual, I gave in to a stronger power. I feel guilty, and the old limp is still here. I can disguise it physically, but not emotionally.*

Hearing Rick's voice on the phone again had made her heart soar initially then, like a kite, crash in a tailspin. Relieved to hear from her spouse of Candace's doing beautifully under Gladys's diligent care, Lara asked him how things were going otherwise.

"Oh, okay," he said. "Went into New York yesterday for a spot on Fred Waring's show."

"How'd it go?"

"They loved us."

Us? "Oh,... you must have done The Shadow Number with the Double-Dove Trick?"

"No. The Apache. With Eve. Mom and Pop drove down and back with us, of course. Would you put Billy on again, please?"

At least he'd said please.

After supper and an early bedtime story, Lara tucked a sleepy Billy into bed. She sat out on the cabin's stoop in the soft, plum-colored twilight and wondered if she dared go over to The Trading Post. One Mule, one "kick" a night. Too much to ask? Besides, there were other souls there she could mix with, talk to. And there was music. A beat to jump to. An intoxicating rhythm to undulate to, slow, fast, who cared? *I'll dance solo if necessary. Who gives a damn? But I can't, no, won't,* she told herself, *leave Billy alone.*

She sighed, pulled herself up from the stoop, and had her hand on the cabin's doorknob when she heard the gate click behind her. She turned and gasped audibly. It was Chance Darwin.

CHAPTER 11

My purpose is, indeed, a horse of that color.
—— *William Shakespeare,* Twelfth Night

"I found you, Lar. Last little cabin in the sky." Chance came close, so close Lara could smell him, a clean, musky male scent mixed with tobacco and a faint float of some kind of aromatic aftershave. The effect was devastating. She stood one step above him on the stoop and, without thinking, let him lift her down by the waist to clasp her body tightly to his.

"Oh my God. Chance, don't,... I can't." Lara broke away. "Someone might see us."

"I'm sorry, Lar." Chance backed away a few steps. "I get so damn carried away. You do something to me and I don't know what it is. Well, that's not true. I do. You're so... oh, hell." He drew a pack of Chesterfields from his shirt pocket with his free hand. "Smoke?"

As he lit their cigarettes, Chance said, "I came over to The Trading Post looking for you and bumped into Nick and Claire."

Lara puffed away, trying to calm herself. "Oh? I was thinking of going there tonight."

"The Januses are going for a swim in the lake, probably around midnight. They invited us to join them. Are you game?"

"I can't leave Billy alone, but maybe Pidge can watch ..."

"Pidge? Oh, yeah. Marge's friend. Funny old gal. Once at the bar, Marge told me how Pidge is loaded with dough, worth over a million, and how she keeps hanging out here from getting divorced years ago because she doesn't want to go back to Philly's Main Line, or whatever. Too snooty a life for her, according to Marge."

"Where are you from, Chance? I mean, where did you grow up?"

"Chicago. Suburbs mostly. 'Til I joined the Marines and saw the world. That's when I really grew up. War does that to you."

"Do you still have family in Chicago? Omigosh. You're not married, are you?" The thought hadn't occurred to Lara until now. She stubbed out her cigarette. "Chance, I, uh, I think I'd better go in now."

"Whoa. Take it easy. You're like a colt spooked by its shadow." He stood up, facing her, looking deep into her eyes. "Dammit, Lar. I wouldn't hurt you for anything. No. I'm not married. Not now. I was, but we were dumb kids and it didn't pan out. As for family, my dad died when I was in high school, my mom's in Chicago still, my younger brother Bruce is on a football scholarship at Northwestern, and Frank is all the 'family' I need right now."

Lara relaxed, feeling like a first-class dunce. But after the warning from Maria regarding Tex Otis, and the brief touch by telephone with Rick, she felt confused and skittery about almost everything.

For an hour or so she sat with Chance, huddled together on the steps of her cabin. She told him as much as she felt safe to share with him about her life, including the recent split with Rick, when two shadowy figures, aided by the pinpoint of a flashlight, approached the gate to Lara's tiny yard.

"Just us!" Claire Janus's mellifluous voice called out.

"We thought you were coming back to The Trading Post sometime tonight, Chance. But you didn't. So we went looking," Nick said.

Claire laughed melodiously. "Guess you were otherwise occupied."

"Yeah. Sorry 'bout that," Chance said, strolling the few feet to the gate and grinning at the two. "We got to talking." He motioned for Lara to join him.

"Chance tells me you're going for a swim," Lara said to the couple, smiling as she stood close to Chance at the gate. "If I can get Pidge to check on my son, I might go, too."

How brave of me, she thought. *Chance seems to impart a certain strength directly to me. How safe I feel in his presence! What is it? Magic? Osmosis. What?* She didn't know and she realized she didn't care. It was enough to be affected by it. For now.

Around midnight, Lara and Chance—wearing their swimsuits—walked down along the shore of Desert Lake, past a shadowy stand of willow trees whose branches swayed in the soft, warm breeze like dancers moving erotically to some tribal beat.

"Oh, look," said Lara, stepping onto the sandy beach and removing her sandals, "They're already here!" She waved at Nick and Claire who were splashing happily a few yards out in the moonlit lake where sooty silhouettes of tufa-rock formations loomed like murky sentinels, and the protective rim of mountains stood silent guard.

Before she could think to resist, Lara found herself swooped up in Chance's strong arms. "Hey!" she laughed. "Put me down!"

"We're taking the plunge, Lar! Together!" He ran, carrying her into the lake, and set her down gently in the waist-deep water. "We could've walked in, but it's more fun this way... and we get wet faster." He grinned at her as he held her tightly to his hard-muscled body. "I'll let you go if you kiss me, Lar. I promise."

"Right here? In front of God and... " She peeked over his shoulder at the Januses, several feet away. "... everybody?" Her heart was beating so fast she felt it might jump out of her chest and swim away without her. She lifted her face up to his and touched his cheek, caressing slowly, methodically, the smooth warmth of his skin, tracing with her finger the fullness of his lips. "What if I don't want you to let me go, Chance?" Her boldness surprised her. Where did *that* come from?

"Then we'll just be the Siamese Twins of Desert Lake." He laughed. "The Brackens can set us up as a side show and make a ton of money, renting us out to circuses, maybe to Ringling Brothers. We'll be stuck, but hell, we'll be rich!" He let go of her and pecked her on the nose. "I need to move, Lar. Gonna swim to the raft and back."

She stood watching him slice expertly through the water, wishing she hadn't reacted the way she did. She still didn't have a handle on how to interact with him, and how to deal with the emotions he so easily aroused in her. *I was attracted to Rick, yes*, she thought, *in the beginning. But this is different, much more organic. It feels like it's rooting itself in the deepest parts of me. A new sensation, and it scares me.*

She waved again at the Januses, who waved back, then she sank into the water and puppy-paddled around in a small circle. Desert Lake's water was air-temperature and delightfully buoyant; the moon,

Marilu Norden

a thin slice of silver in the vast, inky, starlit sky, shone brightly, its reflection dancing on the water's surface. She was relieved when Chance
swam back to her, grinning as he rose like the Loch Ness Monster
from the lake. "Ah, ha!" he exclaimed, beads of moisture dripping
down his smooth, blonde-haired chest. "You look familiar. Have we
met somewhere?"

Lara laughed. "I've never seen you before in my life." She splashed
him playfully, then, as she started to swim away, was pleased when he
grabbed her and pulled her to him. She didn't struggle as he kissed
her full on her lips, sweetly, tenderly. She fell away from him into the
water to float on her back. "I take it back. We *have* met before." She
laughed.

"There's a helluva lot more where that came from," Chance shot
at her. Belly-flopping, he disappeared underwater for so many seconds Lara felt anxious. When he jumped up beside her like a playful
dolphin, her relief was palpable. *This man is truly getting to me,* she told
herself, *and I hardly know him.*

Minutes later, as she and Chance floated along together, Lara
thought how wonderful it was of Pidge to agree to look in on Billy for
the next hour or so. This was so much fun, and so relaxing. She glanced
over at Nick and Claire who were gleefully splashing each other.

"Nick wants us to go skinny-dipping!" Claire called out and
swam over to Lara and Chance. "He says when he was a kid in Greece
they did it all the time. Especially in the dark. Nobody sees you and
the water feels so-o-o great all over you without a suit. Hope you
don't mind, but we're doing it!" She swam back to Nick who, Lara
could see, was flinging his swim trunks away with wild abandon-
ment out onto the sandy, moonlit beach. Claire joyfully did the same
with her bathing suit.

Lara wondered if she was up to such shenanigans. *I'm not a prude,
or am I?* She stood still and shivered, filled with indecision, her feet
touching the lake's bottom, the water just up to her shoulder blades.
The question was how much she really wanted to be a part of this.
And, what in hell did I get myself into?

Chance's arms encircled her as he stood behind her and pressed
his firm body against hers. "Lar ... Lar," he whispered. "I'll help you
if you help me." He started pulling down a strap of her suit, a two-

piece black Jantzen she'd purchased in Carleton last summer before getting pregnant with Candace.

"No. Chance, don't... I don't think ..."

"That's it, Lar. Don't think. Just feel. Let go. Feel how warm,... how right." His breath was hot on the back of her neck. "Oh God, Lar. You're so damn beautiful."

Before she could protest more, she felt Chance cradle her bare breasts in his two hands, felt his hardness grow against her back. Somehow her suit was off. Where? "I, uh, I don't ..." But the water felt so soft, so silky on her naked skin that before she knew it she felt herself losing her inhibitions with Chance's strong arms holding her so deliciously close. All her emotions so carefully contained, the fear, the hurt, the sadness, drifted away in a moonlit, watery dream of passion awakened. It felt as though she were drowning, but happily, gloriously... for a moment.

And then it stopped.

"Wait," Chance's voice sounded soft but urgent in her ear. "God-dammit. Somebody's watching. From the beach. I saw them. Look. Behind that big willow tree."

Lara opened her eyes and saw Chance turn his head in the direction of the shoreline. "What did you see?" she asked, a cold claw of fear clutching at her heart. She looked around for Nick and Claire and spotted them floating a yard or so away, the nude parts of them slightly, fuzzily discernible on the rippling surface of the water like nighttime lilies in a Monet painting.

"Shit. I threw our suits out to shore. Hope the bastard doesn't pick them up, whoever it is," Chance said.

For one crazy moment, Lara felt like laughing. The whole scene tickled her funny bone, like watching a silly Milton Berle comedy routine on the tube. "I hope they didn't take my suit. It's the first time I got to wear it since I gave birth and I looked pretty good in it. Think I did, anyway," she said.

"You did, Lar, but you'd look good in anything. And nothing." Chance kissed her softly, holding her close, shoulder-deep in the silvery, ink-blue water. "I can't get enough of you, know that? Question is, how in hell are we going to get you back to your cabin if some maniac took all our cover-ups?"

"Fig leaves?" laughed Lara, amazed at how relaxed she'd become. "Oh, Chance! Look." She pointed to the Januses who were rising up from the lake, two fair-skinned alabaster figurines brought to life and splashing towards shore.

"Hope all our damn suits are still there. At least the towels we brought," Chance chuckled. "Or we'll be dashing from bush to bush like a bunch of naked jailbirds on the run."

Funny image, thought Lara, as she swam alongside Chance, then waded the rest of the way through the gentle waves lapping against the white sandy beach. She tried not to stare at the Januses as she ran to retrieve the dark green towel she'd brought from her cabin, mercifully still where she'd left it. Wrapping her nakedness in the towel, she searched around in the sand for her suit.

"Sorry, Lar." Chance already had his towel knotted around his waist and was holding her suit toward her. "It's full of sand." He waved it at her, teasing, "But I'll give it to you for a kiss."

She grabbed for it and he whipped it out of reach. Again she lunged for it, giggling, and fell against him. He caught her just as Nick and Claire approached. Lara quickly pulled her towel around her, hoping parts of her she didn't want revealed, weren't. She noticed the Januses were both wearing robes. *So*, she thought. *They'd come prepared for skinny-dipping. Had Chance?*

"Would you two like to come up to our place for a drink? I could loan you a robe to wear to your cabin later, Lara," Claire said sweetly, as though nude bathing and mixed drinks were *de rigueur* in this desert hostel of broken dreams.

Oh, hell, why not? I've come this far, thought Lara. Besides, her swimsuit was too wet and sandy, and, facing Pidge later, she'd look better in a robe than wrapped in a skimpy towel with nothing underneath.

Lara was glad she was wearing sandals as she and Chance followed the Januses up the beach, across the dirt road, and up the rocky rise to where their cabin stood. Nick and Claire's place was luxurious compared to the tiny cabins on each side and in back of the lodge. It boasted a screened-in veranda and a lovely view of the lake. Nice spot for a vacation. Undoubtedly more expensive, but without the taint of divorce.

Lowering her voice, Lara said, "You said you saw someone watching us, Chance. What do you think they could see? I mean, it was pretty dark, and, whoever it was, was kind of far away." She felt a pebble in her sandal. "Wait a minute."

"Here, let me help you," Chance said as she leaned against him, standing on one leg like a crane, shaking the other leg to loosen the tiny stone. "I've got you."

"Yes, you have, darn it." She laughed quietly and snuggled close to him, making sure the towel was still wrapped decorously around her. "And I don't know what to do about it."

"Don't have to do anything. Just enjoy. See where it leads us." He kissed her upturned nose and ruffled her hair, still damp from the lake.

His reference to the future caught her up short. "I'm not in a position to do that, Chance. Can't you see that?"

What more could she say? How could she help him understand the conflict raging within her? She didn't want to hurt his feelings. She was beginning to care for him. And not just that. She wanted him, too. Wanted him as a woman wants a man. Basic desire of the flesh. But she was still bound to Rick, a man who said in no uncertain terms he didn't want her anymore. A man for whom she still had feelings, had love, as her earlier conversation had revealed. *How can I let go, feel free, under these circumstances? Then there's the danger of being discovered. Oh God, I can't risk losing my children for a dalliance at a divorce ranch.*

"I, uh... Chance, I think I'll skip the drink and the robe. Would you tell Claire and Nick I don't feel well, or whatever?"

"Sure," Chance said, "But I think it'd be better if you tell them yourself, Lar. Then I'll walk you back to your place. It's too damn dark out here for you to go alone."

They walked further. "Did you really see someone out there watching us?" she whispered, turning to face him.

"Yeah. It looked like a figure skulking in the shadows by the trees. Then I definitely saw whoever it was run up behind the lodge."

"Do you think they're still out there? I hate the idea we're being spied on."

"Look, Lar. I may have been seeing things. God knows you have that effect on me. I promise I'll check around before I get in my car to drive back tonight." He drew her close to him again. "I was going to tell you later,... but don't expect me for a few days. I have to oversee some breeding business for A.K. So I'll ask you now. How about a date to do the town? Saturday okay?"

"Well, I don't know," Lara sighed. "I have to ..."

"Think about it. I'll check with June Thursday and she can call you to the phone." His voice took on a deeper, throbbing quality. "Meanwhile, Lar, I'll miss you like crazy."

"Hey, you two!" It was Claire, calling down from the cabin. "We're waiting for you. C'mon up."

"What about it, Lar?" Chance asked softly. "Shall I walk you home now, or after we have that drink?"

He seems so sure of himself, thought Lara, searching the dark for the nameless spy. She grabbed Chance's hand. "No hard liquor this time," she said. "I need to think straight for a change."

CHAPTER 12

The malicious have a dark happiness.
— *Victor Hugo*

Tex Otis leaned against the bar at Harrah's Club, his nut-brown eyes squinting through the blue haze of smoke waffling up from the cigarette in the corner of his mouth. He scanned the busy room. Bright lights blazed throughout, accompanied by the din of jangling slot machines, the occasional shout from somebody's win, and the brassy, bumping beat from the latest lousy lounge act.

Two a.m. and the joint's jumpin', he thought. *So's my brain.*

Tex pushed his black Stetson to the back of his head, savored a swig from his Whiskey Sour, and smiled at his reflection in the bar's mirrored back wall. *Goddamn. This has to be the sweetest little scam I dreamed up yet. And*, he chuckled to himself, *I've dreamed up plenty.*

"You're lookin' pleased with yourself, cowboy." A tall, curvy redhead in a low-cut black gown slithered up to him and lit a cigarette. She smiled like a cat with heavy-lidded, greenish-shadowed eyes, her pale face and plucked eyebrows giving her a Mona Lisa expression. "Hit it big yet, Tex?"

"What hole did you crawl out of, Bea? How's tricks?" he sneered.

"Slow." The redhead blew a stream of smoke out of one side of her blood red, pouty mouth and stared him down. "No shit, Tex. You look like you got a deal goin'. I know that look."

"You a mind reader? Yeh. I'm lookin' at a big one this time. But don't tell Deb. I want it to be a surprise."

"It's a shitty shame the way you treat that dame, Tex. Who knows how many rich bitches you're ballin' at that goddamn dude ranch, and her workin' her ass off waitin' tables at some two-bit joints and shillin' for the big bosses. Why she ever hitched up with you beats me."

"You should talk, Bea. At least she's not turnin' tricks, far as I know. Deb knows I'll do good by her yet. An' I got a whopper cooked up this time. Best ever. Road to Easy Street, I swear."

"I'm not holdin' my breath, big boy. Gotta go. See ya." Bea sa-shayed off, tottering on her high heels and heading directly for a nearby gaming table where a group of out-of-town conventioneers were noisily winning at roulette.

Tex paid his bar tab and high-tailed it for the nearest exit, know-ing he had to get back to Desert Lake and grab some shut-eye before working with Duke rounding up horses for some early riders at the ranch.

As his '46 Ford truck streaked out of town, Tex's brain was stir-ring up a stewpot of possibilities. *No question that rich but kooky Kat Kavanaugh and that high-steppin, classy little newcomer Lara were gonna be the stars of the setup. Talk about hittin' th' jackpot.*

He slammed his boot hard to the gas pedal, hands gripping the steering wheel, eyes narrowed, mind racing, calculating, as the truck shot down the highway like a rocket from hell.

Only fly in the shit, Tex figured, *might be that damn foreman from Wheeler's spread. Chance. He might get in the way. But I'm every bit as hot, sexy, and smart as that big, blonde stiff any day*, thought Tex. *Babes always fall for ol' Tex-boy.*

He laughed out loud, and, for emphasis, banged the palm of one hand hard on the truck's steering wheel as the speedometer soared into the nineties. In the pale light of a waning moon, smart bunnies ran for cover. Every couple of miles... plop went another jackrabbit. Tex loved it. Easy hunting. Like his scam.

Arriving at the ranch, Tex slipped into the bunkhouse john to pee. He pulled the chain on the one nude lightbulb that hung over the dirty sink and appraised his image in the medicine chest mirror. *Damn good-lookin' bastard.* The scar on his left cheek from a brawl over some long-forgotten chick in Vegas gave him distinction, he thought. Sorta mysterious, too. Chicks dug that. Fact is, the Kavana-ugh dame had said as much on their date Tuesday night: "Oh, Tex, darling, I love that scar."

Have to keep butterin' the bitch up. She's money, man. Old money. Her father is loaded. He's paying her bill here so's she can get free of the jerk she married. Mucho bucks there, jes' for the takin'. And her ol' daddy-o will pay, I know it. She's stacked, too, and if I keep my eyes closed, sex with her is toler-able. Have to get her so damn bonkers fer me she'll do anything. Make her so

*jealous whenever I dance with th' new filly, Lara, ol' Kat'll sign away cash
to me just to keep in my good graces. And, maybe, when Kat gets unhitched,
she'll marry me. Then I kin buy a ranch and have other damn schmucks
lickin' my boots, workin' their balls off. Money is* it, *man. When you're born
a poor friggin' Okie like me, you'll kill fer cash if ya hafta.*

Tex flopped down on his bunk, pleased with himself. "Yeah, Tex-boy, you're worth every penny of Kit-Kat's bankroll," he murmured to himself. "Jes' keep screwin' her, don't take crap from her ol' man, an' th' money'll roll in." Meanwhile he'd get to dance with Lara, who was one hell of a looker.

He was glad he was well-hung, something he was proud of, something he knew what few buddies he had in his past, especially in school, were envious of. He thought back to the day he found out he was 4-F because of a busted eardrum. Probably brought on by beatings his drunken pappy had given him every time he messed up, which was often. He chuckled, recalling cursing the whole U.S. Army and the vow he'd made to get even by "makin' it" with all the chicks guys left behind,... his contribution to the war effort.

Tex could hear Duke snoring in his bunk at the far end of the bunkhouse. Tex pretended to be asleep himself as the Paiute Indian stable boy, Pedro, padded past on his way to early chores in the horse barn. Poor son of a bitch, thought Tex, recalling his own boyhood shoveling shit for rich ranchers. Well, no more. The dame-game was on and old Tex held all the cards.

Full of himself, he extinguished his weed and settled back for a short snooze.

CHAPTER 13

O! for a horse with wings.
— *William Shakespeare,* Cymbeline

Several days later, as they were sunning themselves by the pool, Maria asked Lara, "What's eating you lately? You've been down in the mouth all afternoon. Yesterday, too, for pete's sake."

"Chance said he'd call, and he hasn't. I'm fed up with men, Maria." Lara's eyes held a glassy expression as she watched Billy, Axel, Bip, and Jimmy splash happily together in the shallow end.

"That pasty-white hide of yours'll turn red-hot if you don't oil up. Here." Maria handed Lara a half-bottle of Johnson's Baby Oil. "I added some iodine. You're supposed to turn golden-brown, like toast, in minutes."

Lara stared at the bottle, feeling tears puddle up unexpectedly. "That baby oil reminds me of Candace," she sighed.

"Oh. I'm sorry." Maria retrieved the bottle, unscrewed the top, and spread some oil on her own, already tanned legs. "Let's change the subject. Tell me about this guy, uh, what's his name,... Chance? Whatever. Where'd he get such a name, anyway?"

"He told me his real name is Charles. Charles Darwin. Can you imagine? He's no relation to the famous Darwin, but when he was a kid he got flak from his schoolmates about it so he tried to make up for it by taking chances, in sports, with girls, in everything. So Chance is his nickname, and it stuck."

"I haven't seen him yet. What d'ya like about him?" Maria offered Lara a stick of gum. "Want some? It's Teaberry."

"Thanks." Lara chewed reflectively. "I don't know, Maria. He's ..." She paused, noticing June signaling from the back door of the lodge.

"Telephone for you, Lara!" she heard June calling.

"Oh, Maria, please watch Billy for me. Thanks." Lara took off at a half-run across the green expanse of lawn to June's office, her heart thumping wildly.

Chance. Let it be Chance. Out of breath, she lifted the receiver.

It was Rick, asking to speak to Billy.

That night, Lara tossed and turned in her narrow bed. She wondered, *Did I hear Chance correctly? He did say he wanted to do the town with me on Saturday, didn't he? Maybe I'm just another notch in his silver-buckled belt of near conquests ..."near" because nothing's been consummated.* For that, she was glad. *I probably shouldn't even* think *of such things 'cause I've no idea when my next period will start. A dumb chance to take. The man's very name should be a red flag. Sure, it's flattering, all the attention he's showing me. But I hardly know him. Only been with him... what? Three times?*

She made a valiant attempt to direct her thoughts elsewhere. As she looked at her sweet young son sleeping in the next bed, she was filled with guilt and regret. While Billy had chatted with his father earlier that day, Lara had kept thinking how unnatural this whole situation was. What were she and Rick doing to their children?

Lara sat upright in bed and tried to pray. *Dear God, show me the way.* It was then she thought of her dad, and her mother, so far away on the other side of the globe. How could she relate to them such dire news? And she would have to write to them soon. They didn't know where their eldest daughter was. But it would be so shocking for them. *Divorce. Not a one in all the generations of Dad's family.*

Lying back, conflicted, Lara stared up at the wood-beamed ceiling of the cabin, and decided to give herself a break. *I'm not here because I chose to be. So why not go to The Trading Post tomorrow night and kick up my heels? I'm sure Pidge or Nita can watch Billy for an hour or two. Five more everlasting weeks in this godforsaken place and I'm entitled to a little fun, aren't I? Chance, or no Chance.* She turned on her side, willing her mind empty and open to sleep.

CHAPTER 14

Everything that deceives may be said to enchant.
— *Plato*

Saturday night and The Trading Post was crowded, smoky, dark, and loud. Lara, entering through the swinging doors, saw Marge, June, and even Roy doing triple duty at the bar. She also noticed Kat Kavanaugh deep in conversation with Vida Zembrowski at one table, and Maria and Stan at another. Lara smilingly acknowledged Maria's motion to join them.

"Looking good tonight, kiddo," Maria said with a grin. "Got a sitter, I see."

"Yes. Pidge, bless her. Who's watching Bip?"

"Nita's mom. You know, Wanda? The cook?" Maria jumped from her chair. "Uh-oh. They're playing our song. Stan and I are gonna shake a leg. 'Scuse us." She and Stan broke into a fast Lindy, leaving Lara wondering if she should go to the bar and order a Mule. She decided to stay at the table for now.

"In the mood, Lara?"

She turned to see Tex Otis smiling down at her, holding out a well-scrubbed hand. She was surprised at how different the cowboy appeared from the dishabille he displayed at the corral. Tonight he was clean-shaven and dressed presentably in blue jeans and matching shirt. *Oh, gee*, she thought. *Why not?* There was no one else to dance with, and the music was so great. "Okay," she said, realizing she couldn't sit still for long when one of her favorite jump tunes was booming from the jukebox. "In The Mood," indeed!

As Tex swung Lara out and in, back and forth, fast and furious, she could feel the ruffles of her chartreuse dirndl skirt swirl round and round her bare legs, and she gloried in it. *How I love to dance*, she thought as she let go, rejoicing in the creative freedom of it.

Next, Tex led her in a smooth fox trot. "I never had as good a dance partner as you, Lara," he said as they moved expertly to the strains of Nat King Cole's "Mona Lisa."

"I'm sure you had some terrific partners where you took lessons in town, Tex," said Lara, smiling, gliding, and humming to the music. "Did you learn at Arthur Murray's?"

She could see she'd surprised him. "How did ya know that?"

"Well, they hire good people. Back in New York, my husband met Mr. Murray." *I probably shouldn't share too much with this cowboy,* thought Lara, *but, golly, he* is *being nice. Maybe Maria was wrong about him.*

"No kiddin'?" Tex was saying. "Wow. You're really somethin', Lara, y'know that? I gotta say you're the best lookin' girl I've seen here yet. And that kid of yours. He's quite a boy." He led her in a well-supported dip as the music ended.

For a moment she felt awkward standing alone on the floor with Tex, even though they were surrounded by other couples waiting for the music to start again. *After all, this Otis guy is a complete stranger,* she reminded herself. *And Maria, whom I respect, seems determined to hold him in low regard.*

But Tex had just said something nice about her young son. "Billy's wonderful," she heard herself say. "Of course, being his mom ..." She smiled, suddenly self-conscious.

"How High the Moon" sprang like gangbusters from the Wurlitzer and Lara felt herself vigorously led by Tex, the whirling dervish of a devil-may-care cowboy, in a lilting, tilting, throw-away-your-cares Lindy Hop. She forgot herself, forgot everything but this exuberant display of toe-tapping energy, this flight into a fantasy world where time hung suspended and music and dance melded like magic.

Other couples cleared the floor to watch them. Lara loved the sensation of total freedom, complete release. Playing to a crowd pleased her, too. What a thrill to perform again.

Enthusiastic applause rewarded her and Tex's terpsichorean efforts as they left the floor to catch their breath, both warm and perspiring. Besides, Frankie Laine's "Mule Train" was next up on the turntable... *good to listen to but less conducive for dancing,* thought Lara.

"Can I get you a drink?" Tex asked as he seated her at Maria and Stan's table.

"Thanks, Tex. A Mule would be great." Lara watched him go to the bar. She turned to smile at Maria and was taken aback by the expression in her friend's dark amber eyes. "What?" Even unflappable Stan seemed to stare at her disapprovingly. "Why are you guys looking at me like that? Was I that bad?" she said.

Maria shook her head. "Didn't I warn you about that jerk? I'm surprised at you, Lara."

"Gee, Maria. You sound like my mother, for heaven's sake."

"Well, I warned you. That guy thinks he's Casanova and Errol Flynn rolled up into one. And it's no joke. He's been known to turn women on like faucets."

"I don't see what ..."

"No. You don't see. That's the trouble. And get a gander at poor, kooky Kat Kavanaugh over there. She's got 'Tex-fever,' too. Right now she's so hot under the collar she's about to burst."

"Why? I knew she dated him once, but ..."

"You don't know she's got the hots for that piece of cowboy crap? It's all over the ranch." Maria propped an elbow on the table, cigarette in hand, took a drag, and squinted through the smoke. "Oh, boy. Look out," she said. "Steamboat comin' 'round the bend."

Lara whirled around in her chair to see a highly agitated Kat Kavanaugh stabbing her with a stare of pure hate.

Supporting herself with both hands on the table, Kat leaned alarmingly close to Lara's face and snarled at her through clenched teeth. "He's *mine*, goddamn you. Think you're so fuckin' la-de-da gorgeous."

Shocked, Lara shrank back from the alcoholic breath of her accuser, aimed straight at her like a dart to a dartboard.

"Think cuz ya dance better'n everybody you're goddamn Queen of th' May around here," Kat raved. "Think ya kin grab all th' men ya want." She leaned even closer, spittle spraying. "Well, lay off, sister. He's mine. Get it?"

Despite the loud music, Kat's behavior was attracting the crowd's attention. Vida arrived, and placing a copious arm around her inebriated friend's shoulder, murmured to Kat, "C'mon, honey. Let's go back to your cabin."

"No! Goddammit." Kat wrenched clear and pushed Vida rudely aside. "I don't wanna go to my fuckin' cabin. I want Tex!" she yowled.

Tex approached with drinks in hand. Lara was amazed to see him smile, as if nothing unusual was occurring. "Now, now, babe," he said to Kat, who, at the sight of him, seemed to change from a raving tigress into a purring pussycat. The cowboy set a cool, brass mug of Moscow Mule in front of Lara. "Sorry 'bout this, Lara," he whispered. He took a swallow from his bottle of beer, put it down, and, arms outstretched, said to Kat, "C'mon, baby. Ol' Tex is here. How 'bout we get some air, sugar?"

"Oh yeah, han'some." Kat lurched toward him. "But first I wanna dance with ya, ya cute cowboy, you. I'm better'n *her* any day." She threw a dagger of a look Lara's way.

"We'll dance in th' moonlight. Jes' you 'n me, Kit-Kat."

The thoroughly sloshed Kat, a lopsided grin on her face, fell against Tex, who supported her with both tanned, well-muscled arms. "I'll be back, Lara. Save a dance for me, huh?" He winked at her as he and the unsteady Kat stumbled out into the night.

"What in hell was that all about?" asked Stan Gorman. "You're right, Maria. Something about that guy doesn't add up."

"The question is, how does it add up for Lara?" said Maria.

Lara held out her hands. "Ye gads, Maria,... Stan. Don't talk about me as though I'm not here. I feel bad enough."

"Tex is not exactly a straight-arrow kind of person, toots, you have to admit," said Maria. "I'm not saying it's your fault what happened. But that poor excuse for a cowboy is leading Kat Kavanaugh down the garden path and you're just there for fishin' bait."

"Why would he do that?"

"Because he's twisted, kiddo. Can't you see that?"

"Not really. I mean, he can be so nice, and he's such a ..."

"Good dancer? If I recall what you told me, your soon-to-be ex is a whiz on the dance floor, too. Get the connection?"

"Not exactly." Lara glanced over at Vida sitting dejectedly alone. "But I do feel sorry for Kat. She's so darn vulnerable. Even though what she said to me hurt, I can see it's only because she's drunk. She's lucky to have a friend like Vida, don't you think?"

But Maria was off dancing with Stan again, so Lara dropped by Vida's table to say a few words. "I'm so sorry, Vida. I didn't know how much Tex meant to Kat. I feel awful for even dancing with him."

"Kat lives in a dream world, Lara. Don't worry yourself about it," Vida sighed, holding tight to her glass with both plump hands. "She reminds me of my younger sister in Poland, so I guess I care about her. I never know where I stand with her, but I do know when we met here at the ranch we hit it off somehow."

Strange how that happens, mused Lara, observing her own new friend, Maria, now swaying to a slow fox trot with Stan. *This ranch has a certain unreality about it, like purgatory, somewhere between heaven and hell,* she told herself. *It's like a way station on the way out of something not so good to something better, or worse, depending on how the cards are played with the hand we're all dealt. That such a place exists in a town dedicated to gambling makes perfect sense.*

Going back to her table, Lara finished her Moscow Mule and said her goodbyes, eager to return to her cabin and the sweet innocence of her young son. She walked out onto the portico, thinking she might bump into Tex and Kat, and hoping she wouldn't. There was no sign of them.

As she picked her way home in the dark, wishing she'd brought her flashlight, Lara recalled a wry college roommate of hers saying, "Take it from me, Lara. Life's a crap shoot." Here at Desert Lake that particular philosophy applied in spades.

What a crazy night, she thought. *Maybe Kat is correct in her assumptions that I, in my rush to shine as usual on the dance floor, am not sensitive enough to those around me. Of course, I didn't realize how possessive Kat is about Tex. Or, for that matter, how unbalanced she may actually be.*

More and more Lara wished she could fast-forward her sentence at this desert detention center, pleasant as it was. More and more she found herself eager to arrive at "Graduation Day" at the county courthouse so she could fly away to a spot where life might take on some semblance of normalcy for her and her children.

In mid-thought, she stopped. What was that? A twig snapping on a nearby bush? Over there, by the lodge. She called out, "Who... who's there?"

Nobody. She hurried on, rounding the corner of the lodge, thinking, *If Pidge is asleep, I might just let myself in. But...* She reached for the shoulder strap of her handbag to get her key. *...what? Oh no! My purse!*

She must have left it at The Trading Post. Or maybe she'd dropped it along the way. The shoulder strap had been giving her trouble lately, slipping off often due to a faulty snap needing to be replaced. She'd tried to repair it, but didn't have the proper tool at the moment. Darn, thought Lara, I shouldn't have taken it with me tonight. I could've charged my drink. June keeps a tab for everyone.

Trying to keep calm, she retraced her steps. *I have to find the purse.* Not only did it hold the key to her cabin but it also held her wallet, which was especially valuable as it contained a tiny photo of Candace taken in the hospital just after her birth. Irreplaceable.

With eyes now accustomed to the dark, Lara searched the ground as she scurried along the path back to the Post. As far as she could determine, her purse was not outside, so she pushed through the swinging doors and made her way to the table where Maria and Stan sat with Vida and also June, who was taking a break from bar duty.

"Hi, Lara! You missed us so much you had to come back?" Maria started to laugh but stopped when she saw the expression on Lara's face. "What's wrong? Billy okay?"

"I'm missing my purse. Did I leave it here?" Lara bent over to search under the table, to no avail. "I've got to find it," she said, holding back tears.

All at the table moved back their chairs and joined in a quick probe of their immediate vicinity.

"Tell you what, Lara. I'll have Roy turn off the jukebox and make an announcement," said June, patting her sympathetically on the shoulder. "I'm sure it'll turn up. We'll get the guys to look outside with flashlights. What did your purse look like? "

Lara gave June as detailed a picture of the lost purse as she could and then sat down, accepted a cigarette from Maria, and watched as June went to the bar to speak to Roy.

"Okay," said Roy, raising his voice as Teresa Brewer's recording of "Music, Music, Music" came to a grinding halt. "Lissen up, everybody. We got a lady's purse lost here tonight." He paused as June whispered something in his ear. "Okay. Lessee. It's a... what?" He seemed to have trouble hearing what his wife was trying to convey. "Oh, hell. Let June tell ya." Roy ran one hand over the top of his balding pate, shrugged, and grinned self-consciously at the crowd in the Post.

June's alto voice carried well. "Mrs. Treadwell, Lara, has lost her handbag. She had it with her when she came in and sat over there with Mrs. Wexler and Mr. Gorman. She only got up to dance a few numbers, and when she left here she thought she had her bag with her. She's looked outside but can't find it. So we'd appreciate anyone joining in the search. The handbag is small, square-shaped, made of white leather, with a short strap and a brass fastener. Anyone finding it gets two free drinks from the bar. We've got flashlights to help look outside."

Roy plugged in the jukebox again and Brewer's tuneful ditty wound itself up to its former bounce. While some people stayed at their tables, Lara, accompanied by Maria, Stan, and Vida, joined several young Paiute Indian cowboys and other men searching outside The Trading Post. Nothing resembling the lost handbag showed up.

"This it, missus?" asked an old Paiute wearing a beat-up, ten-gallon hat. He held up a small, off-white, fringed leather pouch and grinned at Lara with jagged, yellow teeth. "Found it by the lake."

"No. But thanks. It's so pretty, I'm sure someone's missing it," said a dejected Lara. Then she brightened. "Oh, maybe it belongs to Wanda or Nita Big Horn. Better give it to Mrs. Bracken." She watched as the elderly Indian nodded and triumphantly tramped into the Post with his find.

Moments later, June stepped out on the porch of The Trading Post. "Lara, I think your purse has been found," she said, and beckoned for Lara to join her. "I can't believe it, but, well... you'll see. It certainly looks like what you described. Don't be shocked at who found it. I'll say no more."

Lara followed June over to the bar. There, holding up her lost purse, stood Tex Otis, flashing a wide grin. "Found this outside th' lodge, Lara. You must've dropped it on your way home." He handed the handbag to her.

"Oh! How can I thank you, Tex?" Lara felt overcome with relief, clutching her purse with both hands. "I've got five dollars here. Would you take it as a small reward?"

"Nah," Tex laughed, his piercing, nut-brown eyes actually appearing softer and warmer to her. "How 'bout I give that boy of yours a coupla riding lessons instead? My treat," he said, lighting a cigarette.

"Billy would love it. When?"

"Why not tomorrow morning? At th' corral?"

"We'll be there. Thank you so much, Tex." Lara reached to shake his hand. To her surprise, the cowboy lifted her hand to his lips and kissed the back of it. Flustered, she smiled at him. *Is he trying to romance me? Whatever the reason, it feels extremely weird. But I do owe him for finding my purse*, she reasoned. She turned to go, "Tex, thanks so much again. See you tomorrow."

Outside, Lara bumped into Maria and Stan. She waved her handbag in the air, feeling exulted.

"Oh, great!" Maria exclaimed. "You found it. Thank God."

"Wasn't God," Lara said, laughing. "Though He probably had something to do with it. Tex Otis found it. And he's going to give Billy free riding lessons, too. Gee, Maria, don't be so hard on the guy. He can't be as bad as you say."

Maria exchanged glances with Stan. "Sorry, kiddo. I hate to think you're going to find out the hard way. So he found your purse. So what? He probably stole it when you weren't looking and the whole thing's a stinkin' sham." Maria dropped her cigarette in the grass and stomped on it for emphasis. "Hey, sweets," she said, putting a hand on Lara's shoulder. "Do yourself a favor. Watch your step. You're young for your age. Twenty-five and still way too gullible. Don't forget about Kat Kavanaugh. He's pulling a fast one on her, too," Maria sighed. "'Nuf said. See ya at breakfast tomorrow."

With Maria's words of caution ringing in her ears, Lara hugged her handbag and hurried along the path to her cabin. Not until she got within ten feet of her place did she think to check the purse's contents. How stupid. Maybe something was missing.

Lara saw Pidge, wrapped in what looked like a geometrically-configured red-black-and-gray blanket of Indian design, sitting slumped on the stoop of the cabin. Coming abruptly awake, Pidge murmured, "What's th' password?" Then she laughed. "Oh, it's you, Larie-love. Wasn't sure at first." Pidge's bright, button eyes narrowed. "Hey, you look worried. Can I help?"

"Yeah, thanks. Would you shine your flashlight over here, please? Sorry I woke you. I thought you might be inside stretched out on my bed like you usually do."

"Was at first. Conked out after reading 'The Emperor's New Clothes.' Had a dream I was in the altogether, nude, like the emperor. I was half asleep. Wasn't sure if I was indecent or not, so I wrapped myself in my trusty blanket. Then I got too warm 'n came out here. Where d'ya want me to shine this mighty beacon, dear one?" Pidge clicked on the flashlight.

"Just want to check my purse here."

Pidge obligingly held the light steady as Lara peered in her handbag. Everything was there, including her wallet containing the photo of Candace. "Oh, thank goodness," Lara sighed, grateful again to Tex. "Did I ever show you a picture of my baby girl?"

A sliver of moonbeam shown through the slit in the cabin's drawn window shade, providing enough light for Lara to check the contents of her suitcase. Quietly, so as not to wake Billy, she dragged the brown leather case from the alcove closet, opened it, and stuck one hand in an inner elasticized cloth pocket. Thank God. Two hundred dollars in cash and more in traveler's checks as well as her plane tickets to Denver, all safe and sound.

After what had happened that night, she felt especially wary and self-protective. She removed her wallet from her purse. Another reason to be concerned regarding the loss of her wallet; it held the key to her suitcase. Lara used the key to lock the luggage, both hers and Billy's, shoved the cases back in the closet, and returned the suitcase key to her wallet. *Now the key to my present situation is safe*, she told herself, *at least the one I can hold in my hand.*

Placing the wallet under her pillow, Lara stooped to kiss the sleeping Billy on one warm, rosy cheek, and crawled into her bed across from his, thinking how good it was of Tex to find her purse, wallet, and all. And how kind of him to offer to teach Billy how to ride a horse, to actually teach the boy instead of just being led around the ring by Duke. Of course, it might be scary, she told herself, but she would be there to watch, and Tex knows horses well, that being his job.

Chance knows horses well, too, she mused, *but so far he hasn't expressed much of an interest in Billy.* Of course, he hadn't met the boy yet. Lara tossed fitfully, unable to relax. *Where is Chance, anyway? And why hasn't he called me?*

The night dragged by. A weary Lara rose early, and after breakfast, she and her excited four-year-old son traipsed through tall, dry grass in the torrid morning sunshine, bound for the horse corral.

CHAPTER 15

For slander lives upon succession,
Forever housed where it gets possession.
——*William Shakespeare,* The Comedy of Errors

"There's a new girl on campus," Maria whispered at breakfast several days later.

"You mean... a guest?" Lara asked as she used a napkin to wipe away a mustache of milk from Billy's mouth.

"Nope. Worker. Hired hand." Maria buttered a piece of whole wheat toast. "I happened to be checking out the latest copy of 'True Confessions' in the lodge this morning when I look up and see this dame coming out of June's office. The girl was walking on air like she just won at roulette. I heard June say, 'Go down and talk to Marge. You start work tonight, Deb.' So... " Maria broke off a corner of toast and popped it in her mouth, munching as she talked. "Looks like we have a brand new barmaid at the Post."

"Did you get a good look at her?"

"Sort of," Maria said, munching away. "She's skinny, short, but stacked, if you get the picture."

"You make her sound like a side order of pancakes. Is she old? Young?"

"Younger than you, I'd say. Certainly younger 'n me. She's got jet-black hair with one of those new poodle cuts. Looks okay, I guess, but she's heavy on the makeup. Makes her look older, kinda tough."

"You noticed a lot in a short time."

"Yeah. I'm a regular Dick Tracy." Maria lit a cigarette. "Maybe I should open up a detective agency when I get sprung. Beats the booze business." She brightened. "Hmm. Not a bad idea. Then I could keep tabs on old 'Snake-In-The-Grass' Irving."

"You'd be good at anything. Let's hope the new girl does well, too," Lara said, recalling summers spent waitressing in her teens. "It's not an easy job."

"Changing the subject, kiddo, how'd the riding lesson go?" Maria turned to Billy. "Did you have fun, Billy? Bip wants to take lessons, too."

"Well ..." The boy looked at Lara before answering, a tentative smile flickering on his rosy-cheeked face. "... at first it was fun," he said, his lisp prominent on the "s" sounds.

Lara intervened, her arm around her son's small shoulders. "Tex took him around the ring a few times. He started showing Billy how to work the horse's reins. Then Kat and Vida showed up with two guests I never saw before, and, for some reason, Tex had to turn us over to Duke for the rest of the lesson."

"I like Duke," Billy said, both small hands encircling his glass as he downed the rest of his milk.

Maria shook her head and gave Lara a knowing look. "Yeah, Billy. Duke's a good guy. I hope you can take some more lessons. Bip, too. Then you both can be cowboys." She smiled, tight-lipped, and crushed out her cigarette in the dining table ashtray. "Bip's playing out on the porch, Billy. He and his dad finished eating before me."

Billy glanced expectantly at Lara. "Can I go play with Bip, Mommy?"

Lara smiled her consent at the youngster, adding, "Just for a while, Billy. I'll be out in a few minutes." She turned to her brunette friend. "Thank you, Maria, for not saying anything derogatory about Tex in front of Billy. I appreciate it."

"Credit where credit is due, toots." Maria finished her coffee. "Look. Far be it from me to burst your bubble. So I'll change the subject again. Stan and I heard Frank Sinatra is headlining at the Riverside in Reno. Nick and Claire are driving in to catch his act and they asked all of us to join them. They thought maybe Chance could come, too, but ..."

Sinatra? In Reno? Lara's pulse quickened and she reached for her pack of Viceroy cigarettes. "Oh my gosh," she said. "Rick and I were on Sinatra's television show recently in New York. Well... Rick was. I was eight months pregnant and had to watch from the studio control booth."

"Wow! Did you get to meet Frankie? My cousin Rose in Brooklyn is nuts about him. She keeps his autographed picture over her bed, next to her crucifix." Maria lit a cigarette.

"I did meet him," said Lara. "When Rick introduced me to Sinatra after the show, we watched his screaming fans mob him at the stage door on the way to his car. Those teen-age girls literally crawled over Sinatra's limo with him in it, and the driver couldn't budge."

"So. You wanna go? Tomorrow night. Ol' Blue Eyes'll probably remember Rick and you. Maybe you could talk to him."

"Yeah,... maybe." Certainly the star would remember Rick, whose performance was especially brilliant. Eve O'Brian and her mother had joined her and Rick on the train ride into the city, Lara recalled. It had been Eve's first professional appearance as Rick's magician-assistant. Little to do: no dancing, just bring stuff onstage and off for Rick's tricks. She'd handled it quite capably for fifteen years of age, thought Lara.

Sighing, she looked at her watch, and rose to leave the table. "Billy and I are going back to the cabin, Maria. Can you believe I'm still working on that letter to my parents? I'll be 'graduated' and gone to Denver before they hear from me." She hugged her friend. "And... I don't know about Chance. He didn't call. Not yet. But I'd love to go with all of you, with or without Chance."

"It's a date, then," said Maria. "We meet at Nick and Claire's tomorrow night at eight sharp. Wish your Chance was going. Is he for real, or are you just conjuring him up to keep yourself warm at night?" Maria laughed as she and Lara ambled out of the dining hall together. "Just kidding, of course, but I do want to meet him soon. After all, he's gotta pass muster with 'Mother Maria.'"

Later, in her cabin, Lara endeavored to put pen to paper while Billy played tag outside with Bip, Jimmy Big Horn, and Axel. Using *The Saturday Evening Post* as a lap support, she sat on her bed and tried to concentrate on the letter to Ankara, Turkey. But her thoughts soon wandered. *Why*, she wondered, *didn't Chance call me? I miss him. Miss his tender, sexy touch, his dimpled smile, and his "up" outlook on life.*

If Chance doesn't call before tomorrow night, she told herself, *I'll find a sitter and join the group without him to hear "The Voice."* She sighed, peering hard at the notepaper on her lap.

"Dear Mother and Dad. I'm writing to you from a ranch in Reno, Nevada and I am... ." Hmmm.

She looked up to see Billy standing at the cabin's screen door, sweaty from playing tag in the heat. "Mommy, can I have a orange soda?" Billy lisped, excitedly. "Jimmy knows where to get some."

"Where, Billy?" Lara padded with bare feet to the door, thinking her son was becoming as fond of orange soda as she was of Moscow Mules. Probably not good for either of them.

"Over there. Behind the lodge." Billy pointed, smiling at Jimmy, Bip, and Axel, who had joined him.

"It's a big box, Missus," Jimmy piped up, his black eyes shining.

"You mean, a big cooler, Jimmy?"

The small Indian nodded. "By th' kitchen. My mom lets me. It's fer guests. Lottsa soda pop."

"Okay. But come right back, so I know where you are." Lara watched as the four junior-sized, would-be cowboys ran enthusiastically to the corner of the lodge, then bounded out of sight.

On second thought, maybe I'd better check, Lara warned herself as she slipped on her sandals. She slammed the cabin door and was about to open the yard's pint-sized gate, when she heard a high-pitched scream. A child's scream. Her child's?

The gate latch was stuck. Damn! She jumped the fence, scraping her leg, and ran so fast she almost collided with a tearful Jimmy.

"Missus, Missus! Billy bumped th' rope! Come quick!" the frantic little Indian yelled.

Rope? She followed Jimmy, dashing around the corner of the lodge, and spied the small figure of her son sprawled on the ground. He was crying. Bip and Axel stood by, looking scared, and—who was that, squatting on his haunches, trying to comfort Billy? Lara got closer. Tex Otis!

Tex looked up at her and pointed to a rope someone had stretched from an old hitching post on the kitchen's back stoop, across the dirt to a telephone pole between two cabins. "Guess th' Brackens put that up ta keep cars outta here," he said.

"Oh, Billy, Billy!" Lara cried, kneeling over her small progeny. "Are you okay, sweetheart?"

"He'll be fine, Lara. Jes' got th' wind knocked outta him is all," said Tex.

"Ow," said Billy, trying to sit up without success. "I fell down, Mommy."

Bip offered his version. "I saw him! He went down. Bang! Pow! Fast. Like that!" The boy clapped two small grubby hands together, his yellow-green eyes dancing, reveling in the excitement.

Alarmed, Lara felt a large lump forming at the back of her son's head, a trickle of blood oozing from it. "Isn't there a first-aid kit somewhere, for heaven's sake?"

Tex handed Lara the bandana he'd been wearing tied around his neck. "I think you're supposed ta keep pressure on it." He watched as she tenderly pressed the cloth to the back of Billy's head. "Better?" he asked.

Lara shook her head. "Still bleeding." Her eyes filled.

"Follow me," said Tex, and before Lara could protest, he scooped up Billy and went sprinting down the dirt path through tall grass to the horse barn. Lara and the three boys ran after him. "Hey, Duke!" Tex yelled, depositing a dazed Billy on a flat bale of hay outside the barn. When Lara and the boys caught up with Tex, she put pressure on Billy's lump again with the not-too-clean scrap of cloth, feeling dazed herself.

Duke came loping around the corner of the rustic building. "What th'... ?" Taking in the scene, the old cowboy leaned over and said to Billy, "Hey, podner, what happened here?"

Billy's mouth quivered. "I fell down, Duke. It hurts." He looked at his mother. "Mommy, am I bleeding bad?"

"We're going to fix it so it won't, Billy." Lara tried to be brave for his sake, but... where in the world was there a bonafide doctor when she needed one?

"Ol' Duke's got jes' th' cure." The wrangler patted Billy gently on the arm and said to Tex, "Get th' box. You know. Th' stuff I used on Pedro's elbow th' other day."

In no time, the blood matting in the short hair on the back of Billy's head was cleaned off. Duke painted the lacerated lump with something purple.

"What's that?" Billy asked, staring at the old apothecary bottle Duke held in one huge, gnarled paw.

"Good ol' gentian violet, cowboy. Duke's granny back in Texas used ta paint me an' my brother's sore throats with it." He grinned at the amazed reactions on the faces of all four boys. "Okay, there ya go, Billy-boy. Good as new. Hey, you weren't in no war, was ya?" The old horseman bent down to look Billy in the eye. "Could swear ya was. You was a brave soldier, too."

Billy frowned, still a bit dazed. "I wasn't ..."

"Ya sure been, podner. Cuz ya got a purple heart!" Duke laughed. "Go back to your cabin an' look in th' mirror."

Billy felt the back of his head. "I don't ..."

Duke lifted Billy off the hay bale, set him on the ground, and showed off his handiwork to all. A perfectly-shaped heart, painted in gentian violet, decorated the raised lump on the back of the small, blonde, crew-cut cranium.

The other three boys gaped. "Billy! You *do* got a heart on your head!" shrieked Bip. They crowded around their little pal in wonder.

"I didn't know you were artistic, Duke!" Lara threw her arms around the old cowpoke's sun-browned, wrinkled neck. "Thank you so much."

As Duke grinned, shuffling his boots in the dirt, apparently at a loss for words, Lara noticed Tex staring at her. "Don't I get th' same, Lara? No thanks for what I did?"

She hesitated, not wanting to hug Tex in case he might misconstrue her motives. Still, he was right. He was on the spot helping, carrying Billy down to Duke. *Somehow*, she thought, *I'm always in hock to this guy, first my handbag, now my son.* "Thank you, Tex," she said sweetly. Perhaps a quick kiss on his cheek? Impulsively, she planted a light brush of her lips on the unscarred side of Tex's face, feeling her own cheeks flush as she took a step back from him. "You're so helpful. I don't know how to thank you, really."

Tex's hard eyes seemed to bore straight into hers, making her uncomfortable.

"Jes' keep on dancin' with me, babe. 'S all I need for now."

CHAPTER 16

What a horse should have he did not lack,
Save a proud rider on so proud a back.

—— *William Shakespeare,* Venus and Adonis

Two nights later, Chance called. Lara answered, alerted by June to take the call in the outside phone booth on The Trading Post's portico, away from the noise inside at the bar.

"Hi, Lar. God, I missed you. I kept seeing your pretty face everywhere, in skies, clouds, even the hind ends of horses... and I saw a lot of those." Chance laughed his warm, baritone laugh.

"Gee, thanks a lot." Lara laughed, too, though not quite sure how to take what he said. She suspected he was joking. But she still didn't know him well enough to tell, and wished she did.

"No, no. That didn't come out right. What I mean is, I'm a horse's ass for not calling you sooner, Lar. Just couldn't get the time to phone anyone, except the boss, that is. Frank and I were flying all over hell and gone. A.K. had us recruiting new breeding talent at stud farms from here to the East Coast." His voice softened. "Did you miss me?"

A rush of emotion left her almost breathless. "Of course," she gasped, attempting to keep things light when all she wanted to do was jump through the phone line and kiss him. "Chance, I'm here at the Post having drinks with the Januses and my friend Maria. I don't suppose you could ..."

"I'm practically there, Lar."

For the second time that night, Tex Otis asked Lara to dance. "I'd love to, Tex. Maybe later. I'm waiting for someone," she said, as sweetly as she could. She still wanted Tex to know how grateful she was for the help he gave her with Billy, but she didn't want to be swirling around the dance floor and miss Chance's arrival. She watched as Tex sauntered laconically back to sit at the bar and talk to the new female bartender. Lara thought she recalled the girl's name. Deb? Did Tex know this "Deb" from somewhere? They seemed to be involved in an animated conversation.

Lara felt restless. She wished Claire would stop running on about seeing the Sinatra show in Reno and how terrific it was of Lara to take everyone up on their dare for her to talk to the crooner.

It had taken guts to do it. Lara recalled going first to the Riverside Hotel's ladies room to gather enough courage to approach the great Frank Sinatra. While there, freshening her lipstick, two girls joined her at the long, marbled sink counter. They smiled at her but were involved in their conversation. Both obviously worked in the hotel's casino, one as a cigarette girl, the other dressed in the uniform of a croupier.

"When Frankie sings 'All Or Nothin' At All' I get goosebumps up my you-know-what," said one, loading more black mascara on her upper lashes.

"Yeah. He sings good for havin' trouble with his throat."

"What d'ya mean, trouble?"

"I dunno. But his doctor placed a bet at my table and was talkin' to some Hollywood-type guy about it."

"Well, he's got th' dreamiest blue eyes an' he sings fantastic. Ava Gardner thinks so, too, b'leeve me. I can't b'leeve she's really *here*. All th' guys can't stop gawkin'. God, is she drop-dead gorgeous or what? She bought a carton of Luckies off me an' she was watchin' the show like Frank was singin' just for her."

"Betcha he was. I wonder what color lipstick she wears? I want it. I want Frankie-Boy, too."

The two giggled. They turned on the sink's faucets, ran water over the butts of the cigarettes both had smoked while primping, tossed the wet weeds in the trash, and left. Heart in her throat, Lara waited 'til she heard what she knew from showbiz experience was the finale, then joined her group at their table.

"Now's your chance, Lara," Claire said, Maria, Stan, and Nick nodding their accord. "Sinatra's going over to Ava's table."

Lara pushed herself, like some wind-up toy, around white-clothed, cabaret-style tables, across the red-carpeted room, to find herself facing the famous singer as he stood near his paramour Ava's table. Lara'd forgotten Sinatra was only slightly taller than herself, forgotten how dark his hair was, receding at the hairline like Rick's, forgotten how penetratingly blue were his eyes, as he stood staring at her. Sinatra was pleasant and polite, remembering Rick and asking if he was there. When she said, "Well, no, I'm here alone, because ..."

Her reverie was interrupted by Claire bringing her back to the present. "Tell us again, Lara. When you told Sinatra you were here divorcing Rick... I just can't get over what he said to you. And Ava right there with him. I mean, his reaction was obvious, given his own tangled situation. Please tell us again, Lara." Claire's emerald-green eyes pleaded.

As if by rote, Lara repeated Sinatra's parting words to her, words somehow magical to celebrity-conscious Claire, but "ho-hum" to Maria, Stan, and Nick. "I'll say it for the last time," laughed Lara. "He just shrugged, didn't say he was sorry we were divorcing or anything. Just said, 'Well, that's how the cookie crumbles.' Then he sat down, that was that, and I left."

"Who sat down? Anybody I know?" A familiar, resonant voice sent a thrill through Lara as she turned to see Chance beaming down at her. For a second she couldn't muster enough breath to respond.

Chance pulled up a chair to sit next to her, his gold-flecked, blonde-lashed, green eyes drinking her in. "Got here as fast as I could, Lar." He lit a cigarette and smiled, acknowledging the group at the table. "Hi, folks. Long time, no see."

Lara recovered enough to remember her manners. "Oh, Maria, Stan. This is Chance Darwin." *I can't take my eyes from him*, she thought. *I feel like a sailor lost at sea, finally sighting land.*

Nick Janus clapped Chance on one broad shoulder. "We missed you, guy. How's the racehorse business?"

"Racy," Chance said, laughing. "And profitable. My boss is happy. We picked up a star stallion and two top brood mares this trip." After ordering a beer from the new barmaid, Chance turned to Lara. "Care to shuffle up some dust on the dance floor, Lar?"

As they swayed to the tuneful strains of "Dream" sung by the Modernaires, Chance whispered in Lara's ear, "I'm no whiz as a dancer, Lar, I admit. This is just an excuse to hold you again. I want you so bad I can taste it. Better said, I missed you like crazy. I want to make love to you. When, Lar, when?"

Lara felt her face redden, her heart pump wildly. She was so drawn to him she felt like copulating with him in front of everyone. God, what a shocking thought! Containing herself with effort, she whispered back to him, "Chance, Chance. Please. It's hot in here. Can we go outside for some air?"

Excusing themselves from the group at the table, and carrying their drinks, Chance and Lara made their way out to a bench on the Post's portico, and sat, shoulder to shoulder, hip to hip. Neither said anything as they breathed in the fresh, summery night air and sipped their drinks.

Chance spoke first. "I thought of you so often on this trip, Lar. Frank was after me to keep my mind on business. So, I've come to a decision. Only one solution I can think of, if you agree, of course." He took a long, slow swallow from his bottle of Rheingold beer. "I've been visiting you here, and I was wondering... how about you coming to visit me where I live, at Wheeler's Ranch? I can show you the horses, maybe give you a little supervised ride on one, barbecue a steak, and get you back to Desert Lake way before anyone would know."

"Oh, Chance, I couldn't ..."

"'Course you could. Pidge can watch Billy for supper and after, and bunk in with him. It'd work out fine."

Lara was about to protest again, albeit less vigorously, when she was distracted by the sight of Kat Kavanaugh and Vida Zembrowski approaching the entrance to the Post. Vida smiled at Lara as Kat, nose in the air, sailed past and pushed through the swinging doors.

Vida stopped and spoke softly to Lara. "Kat's in a snit again, I'm sorry to say. I hope she doesn't make another scene."

"I hope so, too, for your sake especially, Vida," said Lara as Vida shrugged sadly and followed Kat into the smoky saloon.

"Scene?" Chance asked.

"Oh nothing, really. Kat just got jealous when I danced with Tex Otis. You know, the guy who helps with the horses for Roy and Duke? Seems she's got a 'thing' for him."

"I saw him when I came in, sitting at the bar. He was talking to the new bar help." Chance paused and lit another Chesterfield. "Y'know, I've seen that bar girl before. In town somewhere. Lots of different places." His green eyes narrowed. "She sure gets around. I wonder if the Brackens checked her out."

"It's late, Chance. I should be getting back. Would you walk home with me? I keep forgetting to bring a flashlight." Lara ran into the Post, left her empty Moscow Mule mug on the table, bid a quick goodbye to her friends, and joined Chance on the path.

"Can I think about your invitation?" she asked him, as hand in hand, they neared her cabin.

"Mull it over in that beautiful head of yours, Lar. I'm a patient man. But only if I get a kiss tonight."

He smiled, pulling her close, so close his golden chest hairs peeking out of his white, open-collared shirt tickled her nose. She turned her face willingly, eagerly up to his. Their lips met, tongues engaging, teasing sensuously as though both were created for this moment only, both born to meld together in one wild explosion of ecstasy, never to part.

Lara managed somehow to break away, to stop before …"Oh my God, Chance. Good thing I have a child in that cabin there," she said, her breath coming in short spurts, "or I'd lose my inhibitions completely." She kissed him lightly. "Call me?"

"This time for sure." Chance let go reluctantly, a smile wavering on his deeply-tanned face. "Oh God, Lar." His smile faded. "If I hang around with you much longer, I'll get so damn horny you'd have to fight me off. I can't do that to you." He ruffled her hair affectionately, turned quickly, and walked away into the soft, sultry night.

She stood by her gate, feeling as though part of her walked away with him. *What's happening? How can I be so attracted to another man,* she wondered, *when I still love my husband? Even after Rick treated me so cruelly, I still feel something for him. But is that love?*

Lara leaned on the gatepost. Stars, twinkling like fairy lights in the evening sky posed the question, stars once glimpsed romantically by her and Rick. *How,* she asked herself, *do I forget him, cast him from my heart of hearts after we shared a life together, brought children into the world, built a career?*

Yet, here I am, she thought, *bursting to make crazy love with a man I barely know. Is it because I'm starved for affection, starved with a hunger I don't understand, a need so strong I'm willing to gobble up whatever crumbs are thrown my way? Sounds pathetic... and downright dangerous. But...*

She leaned heavily on the gatepost, thinking, *The whole five years of my marriage I tried to please. But what did I actually do to be so unceremoniously thrown aside by Rick? In trying to fit in to his life, I lost sight of myself, my own uniqueness, my own spirit. Maybe it's time for a new approach.*

Standing there, she felt a surge of anger in response to Rick's devaluation of her as a woman, a human being.

She opened the gate, a vision of Chance combining with the image of the horse whose spirit had "spoken" to her on that rainy October night. *This*, she told herself, *is my "chance" to find freedom through a new love, to find myself and give of myself. I'll no longer be a doormat to Rick. I'll make my own decisions, wherever they take me.*

It's like learning a new dance routine. At first you're awkward. But with practice you get better, one step at a time.

I can do it. I will *do it.*

CHAPTER 17

Four things greater than all things are,
Women and Horses and Power and War.

— *Rudyard Kipling*, The Ballad of the King's Jest

Next morning at the corral, Tex lifted Billy up on Miz Betsy, a gray-and-white-spotted older horse best suited for novice riders or children. If the cowboy was miffed because of Lara's not dancing with him at the Post the night before, he didn't show it. In fact, it seemed to Lara he was particularly keyed up and in a good mood.

"This'll havta be a short lesson today, Lara. Sorry, but I gotta haul some guests to town, then pick up Deb." Tex adjusted the saddle and stirrups for Billy.

"Deb? Oh, you mean the new girl at the Post. She a friend of yours?" Lara, standing by the horse, looked up and smiled indulgently at her young son, the loop of his Hopalong Cassidy cowboy hat tied under his chin. He'd insisted on wearing the hat earlier, because, he said, "It'll keep the sun off my purple heart, Mommy."

"Friend? Um ... uh, no. She's... Deb's my sister. She's new in town, y'know, jes' in from Oklahoma. Needed a job so I put in a good word fer her with th' Brackens." Tex checked the bit in Miz Betsy's mouth and lit a cigarette.

Lara noticed how "spiffed up" the cowboy appeared, dressed in his black Stetson, clean white shirt, and blue jeans. Even his boots looked recently polished. He smelled good, too, some new brand of men's cologne. "Bet Deb's proud of you, Tex, and happy to be working at the same place where you work. You look nice. Are you showing your sister around Reno?"

"Well... not exactly. Her truck's in th' shop. Broke down last night, so she's stuck in town. I'm jes' pickin' her up so's she don't miss work tonight. Wish I could show *you* the town sometime, Lara."

Tex took a step toward her, his mouth curling in a hard-edged grin, his nut-brown eyes bold, penetrating. Instinctively, Lara backed away. The horse whinnied, flicking its tail nervously.

"Tex!" Billy gripped the saddle horn with both small hands. "Is Miz Betsy okay?" Sudden fear made the boy's lisp more pronounced.

Lara, alarmed for her son's safety, stood stock-still, figuring, since she knew nothing regarding horse psychology that it was the best thing to do.

Calming horse and boy, Tex showed Billy how to hold the reins. "Lissen, Lara," he said. "All I meant was maybe we could go dancin' in town, you 'n' me. I could show you off at Arthur Murray's sometime." He dropped his cigarette in the dirt, mashing it with the sole of one boot. "C'mon, Miz Betsy. Let's make a cowpoke outta Billy-bud here." With a parting wink at Lara, Tex walked horse and young rider into the ring.

Duke Fenway joined Lara at the corral fence. "Your boy'll do fine, purty lady. That mare's as gentle as a breeze off Desert Lake. Sump'n we could use more of on a day like this." The old wrangler removed his battered Stetson and wiped sweat from his ruddy forehead with the back of one work-shirt sleeve.

Watching him, Lara wished she'd packed some form of head protection herself. "Thank you again, Duke, for finishing Billy's lesson the other day... and especially for doctoring my son so artistically. He wishes that heart would stay on his head forever."

Duke clamped the Stetson back on his reddish-gray hair, took a hand-rolled cigarette from behind one ear, stuck it in his mouth, and lit it, inhaling with fervor. "Shucks," he said. "S'long as I got time, I do like workin' with th' lil' shavers. 'Sides, Tex has been kinda in a spin lately. Gets Roy's 'n' my dander up." Duke instantly looked sheepish. "Oops. Shouldn't share such stuff with purty things like you." He took another long drag, holding the weed between thumb and forefinger, and stared at the ground, his craggy face more crimson than usual.

"I guess Tex feels responsible for his sister Deb, her just starting work at the Post a few nights ago," Lara said amiably.

"Sister?" Duke seemed surprised. "Deb? Nah, I mean, well... yeah, I guess. But I don't 'member Tex sayin' she was his sister... if I rightly recall. 'S funny." His brow furrowed, the wrangler crushed the butt of his cigarette out against a metal fencepost and flicked it away with one ham-like, dirt-nailed hand. "Well, purty lady. Looks like I'll be takin' over where Tex left off with your boy. He's got a guest he's gotta drive to town. He *did* tell me that."

Sure enough, as if Tex heard what Duke said, the cowboy walked out of the ring with Miz Betsy and Billy in tow, his eyes lighting up at the sight of someone coming down the path. Lara turned to see Kat Kavanaugh, dressed in a long, Western-style, turquoise fringed skirt, white shirt, and boots. She was further bedecked with a plethora of silver jewelry. Her cropped, russet-brown hair shone and her makeup was more elaborately applied than usual. Lara felt grubby by comparison.

"Tex, am I late?" Kat gushed, barely acknowledging Lara's presence—or Duke's and Billy's, for that matter. "I know we have to get to the rodeo dance by 1:00. All the big people in Reno will be there and we don't want to keep them waiting," she said in a singsongy, girlish voice as she strolled seductively toward the cowboy, her ample hips causing the fringed skirt to sway to and fro. She paused to simper at Lara. "Tex is taking me dancing at a charity affair at somebody's big ol' ranch near Reno."

Lara wasn't sure if she preferred Kat sober or snockered. Either way, the woman was disturbed, more to be pitied than judged. But she did look extra attractive. "You look lovely, Kat," Lara said, smiling at Kat as Tex handed Miz Betsy's reins over to Duke. "I hope you have a great time."

"You bet I will with this sexy cowboy by my side." Kat batted her large, golden-brown eyes at Tex, who, it seemed to Lara, delighted in the attention. "Walk me to your chariot, handsome," Kat said, snuggling up to him.

"It's parked behind the barn, babe." Tex turned and gave a "thumbs-up" to Duke. "Thanks fer fillin' in," he said to the old cowboy, then, grinning at Lara, disappeared around the side of the barn with Kat in tow. Seconds later, Lara heard an engine start up and saw a red truck roar up the dirt road past the railroad tracks, wheels stirring up a trail of dust, headed for Reno.

After another fifteen minutes or so, Billy was tiring of the lesson, and Duke and horse were puffing from the heat. Lara thanked the old wrangler and trudged up the path with her son. Puzzled by Duke's reaction at the mention of Tex's "sister" Deb, Lara wondered if Tex really was a liar, as Maria so insistently contended. If so, why lie as to

Deb's real identity? And if Kat wanted Tex she could have him. Why was Kat so jealous, anyway?

All Lara knew was how tired and disgusted she was with such pettiness. *I'm far more interested in finding out Maria's reaction to Chance*, she thought. *I'm hoping, of course, it's positive. Even if it isn't, I'm definitely taking Chance up on his invitation.*

That night, after reading to Billy, kissing him goodnight, and tucking him in bed, Lara decided to sit outside on the cabin's front stoop. Gazing up at the constellations, she resolved again to conquer her feelings of low self-worth. So often, Rick insinuated she was lacking when it came to sex, calling her "frigid." However, she thought, if they'd relaxed more, cuddled more, were more playful together, if their sex was more *fun*, then maybe... Surely somebody was to blame. *It must be me*, she told herself.

But did she dare "take a chance" with Chance Darwin, in whose arms she might find a stronger, braver "her"? *Or*, she wondered, *will I be rejected again, for being ..."frigid?"*

She stretched, taking a last glimpse at the stars, glittering like jewels in the dark velvet sky. Then she heard something. At first she thought it might be a coyote. High. Shrill. Like a woman shrieking. Then she heard a deeper sound, a masculine voice, shouting. It seemed to be coming from a cabin behind the lodge.

Lara slipped inside her cabin, checked Billy to be sure he was asleep, grabbed her door key, locked up, and followed the sounds.

CHAPTER 18

There is no rampart that will hold out against malice.
— *Jean Baptiste Molière*, Tartuffe

Guided by the pale light of a half-moon, Lara rounded the corner of the lodge and proceeded past the women's bathhouse. The voices seemed to be coming from a cabin at the far end of several white clapboard dwellings standing on the narrow dirt road behind and directly across from the back door of the lodge's kitchen.

Where, she wondered, was the rope that felled her son? Tex told her the Brackens ordered it installed to prevent cars from parking there. Was it but a temporary measure? Perhaps it was stretched across the road only during the day. Strange.

Stranger still was the fact she seemed to be the lone person around at this time of night. *What is it? Nine, nine-thirty?* Lara traced the voices as emanating from the one cabin with lights on. *Everyone else,* she thought, *must be down at The Trading Post. If not, whoever resides in the neighboring cabins have to be sound sleepers indeed.*

As she drew closer, she recognized certain inflections in the voices, punctuated by pop-like, staccato bursts. No question. It was Kat Kavanaugh's cabin and Tex Otis was with her.

Her curiosity satisfied, Lara turned to go back to her cabin, when, surprisingly, she heard her own name shouted by Kat. "That damn *Lara* bitch again! Why th' hell ya hafta keep dancin' with her? And in th' truck tonight ya kept tellin' yer shit-of-a-sister you and Lara were goin' dancin' at Arthur Murray's."

"Now, now, Kit-Kat. Calm down. Ol' Tex-boy'll pour ya another lil' drinky-poo... hey! Watch it, goddammit!"

Lara heard the sound of glass breaking and pictured something hitting the wall, window, or door of the cabin.

"Geezus Kee-ryst, Kat! You coulda clobbered me throwin' that goddamn lamp. C'mon, baby, let Tex-boy put ya to bed an' we'll have a lil'... "

"No! I wanna promise from you, dammit. Don't dance with that goddamn Lara again!" Kat screamed.

Concerned the ruckus would attract others, Lara was about to leave again when she heard Tex's response, spoken so low she found herself straining to catch the words.

"Okay, babe, but it'll cost ya."

"What d'ya mean?"

"I mean, babe, cash, an' lots of it. You don't want me dancin' with Lara or givin' her th' eye? Okay. Or gettin' sweet with any of th' other babes I danced with tonight, who were a helluva lot better-lookin' than you, I might add. Okay. If not, ya gotta pay."

"But, Tex, that's not fair," Kat wailed. "I thought you loved me. You said ya did, and ..."

"Yeah, yeah. I do, babe. But you know nothin' comes free. Love has a price. I can't promise unless you pay me." Tex's tone sounded harsh, cruel. "Get it? Or do I hafta twist yer arm, goddammit?"

"Ouch! Tex, don't. You're hurting me." Kat was sobbing. Lara immediately thought of going in to try to stop things... but of course that would be foolhardy. She certainly was no match for the virulent creature Tex was revealing himself to be.

A minute of silence, then, Kat stammered, "All right... okay, all right. I... I'll pay. Jes' gimme another drink."

"No drink til' I get th' cash, Kit-Kat. I need about five grand up front. The rest we'll haggle over later. I'm gonna contact your rich daddy-o in Grosse Pointe. I know how to ..."

"No! Oh no! Oh God. Please, Tex, not that. He's already bailin' me out from the skunk I married."

"Okay. Okay, then. I'm gonna dance, babe, dance with th' filly. And a whole lot more... or else."

"Or else?" Kat sounded played out, exhausted.

"Game's over, babe. Five grand. I know ya got some stashed here in yer place an' we kin phone yer Michigan bank fer th' rest."

"Oh, Tex. Don't I even get a lil' drink first? Or a kiss an' a lil'... you know... ?"

Lara had heard enough. She ran like a startled deer to the safety of her cabin, feeling guilty for staying so long and hearing more than she wanted to hear. It occurred to her that she'd been far too gullible in trusting Tex and the fact that she now knew his true character made her feel less trusting of herself and her decisions up to now. She vowed to be more careful in her interactions with people, a vow she knew would have to include her involvement with Chance. *Serves me right*, she chided herself. *I know better than to listen in on other people's lives when it's no business of mine. But, in a way, it is my business. I am involved. I was stupid to dance with that despicable, lying cowboy. I trusted him, just as Kat is doing now. I was dumb enough to treat him like a friend because I felt I owed him. How disgusting. Damn. I'll have to learn not to be so gullible. Maria's been right all along.*

She checked Billy, who was sleeping soundly, then lay on her bed in the dark, her stomach in knots. She thought of Kat,... poor, over-emotional rich girl, the innocent victim of a con man, an extortionist. Tex should be reported. *But*, she thought, *I can't be the one to do it. I'm guilty of eavesdropping, to say nothing of befriending that low-down creep of a cowboy to begin with. But somebody should be warned before Tex's shady scheme succeeds. June? Roy?*

Lara's head ached thinking about it all. She took a couple of aspirin, washed her face, undressed, donned her nylon nightie, and slid under the light cotton sheets and blanket. She kept hearing Kat's pitiful pleas, made all the more pitiful due to too much alcohol. Kat was weak, and Tex took full advantage, thought Lara. It felt familiar. *Like my relationship with Rick. Of course!* The realization hit her with the force of a cannon ball. *Dear God! I've been just as weak! How sad.*

Well, no more, she told herself. *Time to grow up, change. Not an easy task, but I'll work on it.*

"So, what did you think of him?" Lara asked Maria. "You know. Chance. Chance Darwin? I know you only met him briefly, but... what was your first impression?"

It was lunchtime in the lodge dining hall. Uta Crouse smiled at Lara, Maria, Stan, Billy, and Bip as she served each of them plates of Chicken à la King, green peas, pear salad, cornbread, and carrot sticks. "You eat goot." Uta winked at Billy and Bip. "Chocolate-chip cookies for dessert. Axel had five already."

"So," said Lara, nodding a smiling thanks to Uta and enjoying watching Billy attack his lunch with gusto. "Back to my question, Maria. I really want to know."

"You want the short version or the long?" Maria teased, taking a bite of raw carrot.

"Short and to the point."

"Handsome, sexy, and *watch out*." Maria grinned as she chewed indelicately with her mouth open.

"Okay. Now the long version."

"Ditto, ditto, and etcetera."

"Ye gads, Maria. That doesn't help," Lara said. "Be a sport. I value your opinion."

"Okay," said Maria, taking a long, thoughtful sip of iced tea. "Here's the deal. He's beautiful, like you. He's been around the block sexually. I'm sure. Often. Unlike you. He seems decent and honorable, but you never really know 'til you spend a lot of time with somebody. He's intelligent and charming. But is he your Prince Charming? I don't know. That's all I see in my crystal ball." She gestured with open palms and faked a gypsy accent. "Ze great Madame Maria can speak no more. That'll be fifty cents, pliz. Zank you, O Divine One."

Lara was about to reply when she noticed June at the entrance to the room, evidently about to announce someone standing behind her. "Everyone, I'd like you all to give a warm welcome to our newest guest who just arrived this morning from Greenwich, Connecticut,... Mrs. Harriet Renquist."

The new guest stepped forward, a smiling, cool, collected-looking brunette, elegantly attired in a navy-blue linen suit set off handsomely by several pieces of expensive gold jewelry.

At the sight of the newcomer, Lara nudged Maria and whispered hoarsely, "Oh my God. Oh no, Maria. I know that lady. I think she's the same one... yes, I'm sure of it."

"Out with it. You're foaming at the mouth."

"Rick and I performed at her Greenwich estate once. At a huge party she had there. Oh God. What a coincidence. I can't believe she's ..."

"So? You have something in common. You can make friends with her while she's here."

"No. Don't you see? She knows Rick. What if it gets back, through her, that Rick Treadwell's wife is having a fling with a Reno ranch foreman?" Lara felt her heartbeat speed up. "Oh, dear. I could lose my kids. What if... ? Now I'm going to feel like I'm being watched all the time."

"For pete's sake. Quit borrowing trouble. Shh. Here she comes."

June led the new guest over to the table where Lara sat with the others. "I thought since you're all from the East Coast you'd help Mrs. Renquist feel at home," June said as she seated Harriet next to Stan and Bip and across from Lara, Billy, and Maria. Before she left, June introduced everyone to Harriet, including Billy and Bip, who both smiled shyly at the new lady.

Harriet was tall, attractive, with high cheekbones and angular features, her dark hair parted in the middle and gathered in a bun at the nape of her neck. Lara remembered how striking the woman had appeared on the night she and Rick had performed, wearing a strapless, red taffeta evening gown as she played hostess. Her home was spectacular, all white marble and mirrors, with a special dance floor built out on the terrace for "The Talented Treadwells." Harriet paid them handsomely, too. Now here sat the same woman, still elegant but looking a little frayed and forlorn. She smiled at Lara, her dark-lashed, gray-green eyes questioning. "You look so familiar. Have we met before?"

Haltingly, Lara brought Harriet up to date. The older woman extended her sympathy to Lara. "I'm so sorry, my dear. But I do understand. I myself had a marriage of longer duration, twenty years, three daughters. But, sadly, my husband was quite ill for part of that time, became dangerously mentally deranged, and had to be institutionalized. He doesn't know me now, and I hardly recognize him. His doctors recommended I come to Reno to dissolve things, for my sake, and especially for the sake of my dear girls."

It was Lara's turn to be sympathetic. Even Stan, a man of few words, offered his condolences to Harriet, mentioning his wife's alcoholism and how difficult it had been to admit his marriage was over because of it.

It was hard not to like Harriet Renquist. *But*, thought Lara, *how can I trust the woman to look the other way whenever I spend time with Chance here at Desert Lake?* Spies, it seemed, were everywhere. Hadn't Chance sworn he'd spotted someone spying on them skinny-dipping? And after discovering the true nature of Tex Otis, who could anyone really trust? She had trusted Rick, and look how that had turned out. Lara felt her faith in human nature at an all-time low. *Can I even trust Chance?* she wondered.

She pondered for a moment as she sat eating and listening to the lively buzz of lunch-table conversation. There was so much to consider, so much hanging on any decision she might make. It was like being on a long, difficult journey following a certain path, then suddenly arriving at a crossroads sign … this way, or that way? Which to take? *Should I follow my heart,* she asked herself. *Or do I know my heart well enough to feel safe following it? Or should I not deviate and just keep on the same, safe path, never giving my heart an opportunity to know itself better, more fully? Somehow, that heart sign seems to lead directly to Chance. I HAVE to trust him. I WILL trust him.*

Sitting there, she smiled to herself, relieved with her decision and thrilled with the thought that she would soon be alone with Chance, even if only for a few hours.

CHAPTER 19

A policeman's lot is not a happy one.
—— *W. S. Gilbert*, Pirates of Penzance

Signing in at the ranch's reception desk, Vince Caparelli told June Bracken he needed a quiet cabin so he could concentrate on the novel he was writing. The typewriter case he set down as he wrote his name on the register provided proof—enough to cover from Mrs. Bracken the fact that he'd been hired as a P. I. by Rick Treadwell to check on a certain Lara Treadwell while she sat out her six weeks at Desert Lake Ranch. The typewriter was a necessity, of course, but not for fiction writing, only for the typing of reports which would be filed for reference back in Vince's New Jersey office.

A cowboy he hitched a ride with from the Reno airport dropped him off here. Turns out the cowboy worked wrangling horses at Desert Lake. That there was something unsavory about the guy was apparent to Vince, whose bloodhound instinct always went for the freshest scent. Now all he had to do, once he'd settled in, would be to keep his nose to the ground and sniff out any improprieties regarding Mrs. Treadwell. The ex-cop-turned-detective often found his job distasteful, but the money was too tempting to turn down.

Later, at lunch in the dining hall, Vince managed to meet several guests. But no Lara Treadwell. He thought he saw a little kid who looked like the snapshot Treadwell gave him. The kid was eating with another kid and an older lady. It was time to move in, get some answers.

"Hi. Mind if I join you for dessert? I'm getting lonely sitting by myself," he asked them.

"Have a seat." The older lady smiled, pointing to an empty place setting directly across from her. "But, first, ..." She winked at the two boys, their faces smeared with chocolate from the pudding they were gobbling with delight, using their spoons like miniature shovels, missing their mouths sometimes but savoring the process. "First, mister... ," the older woman said, her apple-dolly face creasing even more with a Barry Fitzgerald grin aimed directly at Vince, "what's th' password?"

The kids put down their spoons, muddying the white tablecloth, their eyes wide, staring. They clapped their small hands over their sticky mouths, smothering gleeful anticipation.

Vince hesitated, then decided to play along. He raised his arms in the air like so many suspects he'd arrested in the past. "Okay. I give up, guys."

"Shall we let th' gentleman pass, fellas?"

The kids nodded in mock seriousness. But the little blonde, crew-cut one couldn't contain himself, shouting out with a slight lisp, "It's Winnemucca!!" The other boy, skinny, with an unruly mop of dark hair, his yellow-green eyes glinting with enthusiasm, squealed, "Yay, yay! Winnemucca!" He bounced in his chair. "Mucca, mucca, mucca." Both went back to shoveling in their chocolaty treats.

"They love that game, so I couldn't resist," the older lady said as she extended a gnarled, tanned hand loaded with silver and turquoise jewelry. *Geez*, thought Vince, *the dame should open up her own Indian Market like some I've seen in Santa Fe.*

"I'm Pidge," she said. "What's your moniker, mister?"

"Vincent." He smiled.

"Vincent." A twinkle danced in her bright, beady eyes. "Are you a painter?"

"I wish. Can't draw a straight line. Good at crooked ones, though." He chuckled. It was fun sparring with the old broad. Something about her reminded him of his great-aunt, a formidable old gal who raved and ranted at radio newscasters during the war, swearing she alone could boot Mussolini off the map.

A dish of whipped-cream-topped chocolate pudding was placed in front of him by a thin waitress with dullish ash blonde hair. "I vas serving you und you vasn't there." Hmm. German, obviously. She handed him a napkin and a spoon and turned to smile at the attractive brunette who came over to sit next to Pidge and the boys. "Could Axel play mit boys after lunch, Mrs. Vexler?" the waitress asked the newcomer. "I not see Lara so I ask you."

"Of course, Uta. Have him get his swimsuit. We're going to the lake," the brunette answered, smiling back at the German girl who picked up some dirty dishes and went off to the kitchen.

"Maria, meet Vincent," said Pidge. "He can't draw straight, so I guess he's not a painter." Pidge looked him in the eye. "So. What do ya do besides draw crooked, Mister Vincent?"

Great, he thought. *My new name. Sounds swishy. Maybe I'll say I'm in the decorating business. No. Better stick to my cover.* "I'm writing a book." *Mmm. Delicious pudding. And the brunette looks tasty, too.* "I'm just out from the East getting ideas for a story set in Nevada," he lied.

"You'll get plenty from around here, I would think. Where in the East do you hail from, Mister Vincent?" Maria asked, lighting a cigarette, inhaling, then blowing smoke out of one side of her burgundy-lipsticked mouth, her dark eyes probing his.

He found her slightly unnerving. A true toughie. Smart, uncompromising. With her looks she could be Spanish, Portuguese... maybe Italian, he thought. He settled on Italian; didn't know exactly why, but something about her resonated deep within him. Blood ties, possibly? "Newark," he said, finally. "How 'bout you?"

She smiled, white teeth gleaming. "Across the river. Manhattan." She turned to Pidge. "We've got to get these guys cleaned up, in their suits, and ready for sand-castles by the lake." Turning back to Vince, she said with a shrug and a grin, "We're the sitters."

The blonde youngster piped up, "Not *baby*sitters!" He screwed up his chocolate-smeared face at the other boy who responded the same way back to him. "Yeah, we're not babies. We're big!" said the little dark-haired terror. They both ran from the now empty dining hall into the main room of the lodge. "We're big! We're big!" they chanted, happily skipping around the large space.

Finished with his dessert, Vince followed the women as they rounded up the chocolaty cowboys and walked out into the desert sunshine. He spoke to Maria as he lit a cigar. "Nice day for a swim. Mind if I join you at the lake?"

She looked at him quizzically, putting her cigarette out in the sand-filled pot by the lodge's door, then, grabbing the dark-haired kid's hand, said, "It's your call, Mister Vincent. The lake is for everyone."

"I'd feel better if you called me Vince." He hoped that didn't sound like he was making a pass, but he had to get on her good side to find out why the Treadwell woman wasn't tending to her own kid like every mama should. He noticed Pidge greeting a thin little boy who joined her and the Treadwell kid on the gravel path. *Must be the waitress's child,* he reasoned.

"Well, Vince. We're going to our cabins first. Nice meeting you," said Maria. "See you at the lake." With the dark-haired kid scrambling alongside her, she trotted off at a fast clip to catch up with Pidge and the other youngsters. She turned to glance back at him and seemed to say something to Pidge, who looked around, too. Vince waved at them, hoping it came across as a friendly gesture. Pidge waved back. Maria, however, turned away, continuing to walk briskly. *A tough nut to crack,* he thought. But she and Pidge—as sitters for the Treadwell boy—were the only leads he had at the moment. And old Pidge had seemed to like him, which was a plus. The Maria broad would require more effort.

And where the hell was Treadwell's wife? Sick? Couldn't make it to lunch? Off for the day? Or... went to Reno to see her lawyer, maybe? *Well, she'd better show up for roll call come midnight or she'd be in deep doo-doo according to the laws around here,* mused Vince.

He had a black-and-white glossy of Lara, also given to him by Treadwell of both of them dancing, dolled up in evening clothes. She looked petite, pretty and pleasant. Vince wondered why they had split, especially after she'd just had a baby.

Vince remembered catching Rick Treadwell's act on the Sinatra TV show once, just as a fluke. Watched it while having a beer at Clancy's. Impressive. But all that hanky-panky magician stuff left him cold. Too many slippery, tricky bastards out there in the real world to make the stage version appealing... card sharks, pimps, murderers, extortionists, you name it. *Seen 'em all,* he mused.

The day was a hot one. But dry, thank God. Not like summer in the city. *A swim will feel good,* he thought, as he chomped on his cigar, unlocked his cabin door, and proceeded to fish in his suitcase for his one pair of bathing trunks—purple, with a yellow stripe down each side. He hoped they still fit.

As he changed clothes, he pondered his P.I. progress. *Uh-oh,* he thought, as he tried on the trunks. *Gained a little weight. The waistband is too damn tight from all that pizza and beer at Clancy's Bar.*

Donning the blue jeans and a short-sleeved shirt, Vince determined to make a good impression on the Maria dame. *Not bad*, he decided, glancing in the oak-framed mirror on the cabin's wall. The new Panama hat helped. So did the recent growth of a salt-and-pepper goatee. All, he hoped, lent credence to his cover as an author. Hemingway? Fat chance. But he had been mistaken once for the writer. Of course, the guy who'd said so was three sheets to the wind. Oh well.

Vince stuffed a cigar and his special lighter in the pocket of his red-and-white striped shirt, grabbed a small notebook and a pen, and headed for the blue-green Desert Lake, the water and white sandy shore glittering in the afternoon sunlight like the answer to a city kid's dream of heaven.

But my real luck, he mused, *will be getting the goods on Treadwell's wife. First I'll need to find out where she is. And why.*

CHAPTER 20

Life is like a wild horse;
You ride it or it rides you.
— *anonymous*

Lara delighted in the feel of the dry desert wind stinging her eyelids and whipping her bangs as she and Chance zoomed along the two-lane ribbon of road in his black Ford convertible, top down, speed in the eighties, making their early afternoon getaway. They'd long since passed the placid, aquamarine Desert Lake and were now heading towards a ragged range of lavender-pink peaks shimmering in the distance like a majestic, heat-stoked mirage.

The sun blazed high in the cloudless blue sky. Its warm incandescence prompted Lara to push the elasticized neckline of her white cotton, puff-sleeved peasant blouse down off each shoulder. *Might as well work on my tan.* Already her skin glowed satisfactorily golden all over, except for the two-piece bathing suit demarcations. *More sun can't hurt,* she thought.

"You, you gorgeous woman, are way too much for the likes of me," said Chance, shooting a quick dimpled grin at Lara as he drove. "Think you'll like Wheeler's ranch as much as I do. I wanted to show you off to A.K. but he and his wife Zoe are away. Went to visit her brother in Texas to check out some ranch land. So we'll have the place to ourselves, except for the ranch hands, and Frank, of course."

As the car shot down the roadway, Lara glanced at Chance's handsome profile and felt at once ebullient yet apprehensive at the prospect of spending time alone with this new man in her life. But how "alone" would they be with Frank Jensen on the premises? And why was Frank so much in the picture, anyway?

A stand of majestic cottonwoods, leaves swaying in the arid breeze, lined each side of the long dirt road that Chance said led to

A.K. Wheeler's ranch. The Ford had turned off the county road about half a mile before and Lara could now glimpse what she assumed to be the end of their journey. Not far from the base of the stark, lavender-colored mountains seen from afar stood an imposing, two-storied, apricot-hued adobe structure resembling a pueblo. It looked like those Lara had often admired in art books on the Southwest. "My God! Chance! Is that the main house?"

"That's it, Lar." Chance drove toward the house and swung the car to the right onto a circular, graveled driveway. In the middle, on a grassy mound, stood a life-size bronze statue of a sleekly proportioned horse, head held high, its sculptured mane flowing as though blown by the wind. "That's A.K.'s all-time stakes winner, Kane's Able." said Chance. "Wheeler's initials stand for Angus Kane. And the horse certainly was 'able.' Won every race he ran. A.K. got him from Kentucky, where the horse was bred, and raced him at all the major tracks from Belmont to California's Santa Anita and Del Mar. Helluva racehorse." Chance stopped the car so Lara could better observe the work of art.

"Fantastic sculpture! And I love the name," said Lara. "Is Kane's Able in the stables here?"

"No. Unfortunately he had to be put down after an accident at the track. Broke A.K.'s heart. So he had his favorite horse's image cast in bronze by a world-famous sculptor... whose name escapes me at the moment."

Chance started the convertible up again, piloting it past the statue, past the large adobe house and onto a stretch of road bordered on each side by horizontal planks of white fencing. To her right, towards the rugged mountains, Lara saw horses grazing on a wide expanse of green pastureland. "Ahh," she said, sniffing the air, tilting her head back to gaze up at the bright blue sky, "A special perfume. Hay, mixed with 'eau de manure'! I like it. It's honest."

"I'm so used to it, I can't smell it," said Chance. He pointed to a low, rambling building, painted white, with a green-gabled roof and on a slight rise of ground above this, an exact version of the same structure, only smaller. "That's the main barn and stables. In back of it is the bunkhouse. There's even a new landing field. A.K. keeps several small planes. A riding ring is further on, near the pond and corral." Chance slowed the car. "We're almost to my place, Lar. It's rustic, but clean. At least last time I looked."

The Ford came to a halt in front of one of three log cabins, set wide apart from each other, surrounded by well-tended lawns and sheltered by several towering cottonwoods. "Welcome to my humble abode." Chance helped her from the car. "We'll take a tour of the ranch later. I thought you'd like to freshen up first." He led her up several steps to a narrow, roofed porch and opened the cabin door.

"It's cozy, Chance," she exclaimed, surveying the one main room—which obviously served as living and dining areas—and a kitchenette. A door to her left revealed a little room with a single bed. "The bathroom is... ?"

"Next to my king-sized bedroom," Chance laughed and showed her the tiny john. "I know," he apologized. "It's downright cavernous. Let me know if you get stuck trying to turn around."

Emerging from the bathroom, feeling refreshed, her windswept hair brushed and shiny, Lara found Chance removing a tray of ice cubes from his fridge's freezer section. "Thought we'd have a cool drink then walk around the ranch," he suggested. "Lots to show you. Later, we'll check in with Frank at the house. Steaks are marinating as we speak, thanks to the Wheeler's houseboy, Igor. "

"Igor? Sounds like someone from a monster movie. You know, someone who takes orders from Boris Karloff."

"Not this Igor." Chance grinned. "Mind of his own. He's Filipino, believe it or not. Married to Nadia, the housekeeper. She's from the Ukraine. Great couple. Unfortunately, you won't get to meet them, or they you. It's their day off. They went to Reno to stay overnight and gamble."

What an unusual place, thought Lara, storing up impressions to share later with Maria. Thank God Maria and Pidge were looking after Billy. Pidge would stay in the cabin with him tonight. *She and Maria are such good friends to me, and discreet as well.* Both had urged her to go, and even Billy, as she kissed him good-bye, said, "I'm a big boy, Mommy." *What a trooper. Of course, he doesn't know the feelings his mommy has for the man with whom she drove away "to see some horses at a new ranch."*

Oh dear, she thought suddenly, *what am I doing, betraying his trust?*

"You okay, Lar?" Chance asked as he handed her a glass of Coca-Cola over ice. "You seem a million miles away."

"Only a few miles, Chance. She sipped the Coke slowly, thoughtfully. "Thanks for the Coke. Hits the spot." She was almost afraid to look at this tall, attractive man next to her. Why did he seem like a stranger all of a sudden? And what in hell was she doing here? She was crazy to put herself in such a compromising position. "I don't know, Chance. Maybe I..." Lara set her half-empty glass on the linoleum counter next to the kitchenette's white porcelain sink. "Can you take me back to Desert Lake?" She felt hopelessly foolish, on the verge of tears.

Without a word, Chance wrapped two strong, tanned arms around her and drew her so close she could feel the steady beat of his heart. Enfolded thus, she relaxed. "I'm sorry, Chance. I'm such an idiot."

He tipped her face up to his and looked deeply, tenderly into her eyes. "Forget sorry, Lar. You're safe with me. You only have to stay as long as you want to."

A knock sounded on the cabin door, a man's voice shouting, "Hey, Chance. Saw yer car. Ya in there?"

Alarmed, Lara withdrew from Chance. "Is that Frank?"

"No. Sounds like Les,... our senior foreman." Chance kissed the top of Lara's head, walked over to the door, and opened it. "Yeah, Les. What's up?"

A tall, rangy fellow, sixty or so—in dusty cowboy get-up complete with chaps—peered into the cabin, crinkly eyes in a half squint. "Oh, sorry. Didn't know ya had company, Chance."

"Come on in, Les."

As the foreman stood, hesitant, his hat in hand, Chance introduced him to Lara. "Pleased ta meetcha, miss." Les turned his attention to Chance. "Got a problem at th' stables. Vet's in from town. Mare's in trouble. Vet says it might be, uh, diss... diss... oh, hell. You know. When th' foal ain't comin' out right." Les appeared fired up for flight at any moment.

"You mean, dystocia?" Chance clarified.

The older man nodded vigorously in the affirmative.

"Uh-oh." Chance turned to Lara. "Lar,... I have to go help. One of our top mares is foaling. We knew she was due but ..."

"Chance," The wrangler's voice sounded strained. "I'm leavin'. See ya at th' barn. Doc needs ya, man."

"I've got to go. Wait for me here, Lar." Chance squeezed her arm and kissed her on her nose.

"I'm coming with you." She hurried down the porch steps and followed him at a rapid pace toward the stables. She'd never seen the birth of a horse, and she was not about to miss the opportunity, trouble or not.

Inside the barn, Lara saw a couple of Mexican or Indian-type cowboys standing by a horse stall. One was short and roly-poly, holding a gray metal bucket; the other tall and skinny, sporting a black handlebar mustache and holding a coil of metal chain. Chance and Les, the wrangler, were already in the stall. The afternoon sun sent a slanting beam of light through a high window over the small space, making it easy to see clearly. Drawing closer, Lara tried to find a spot for viewing without getting in the way.

"Get her up! Get her up and hold her!" Lara heard a man command in a thickly accented voice. She determined this to be the vet, and, peeking, saw a stocky fellow with a ruddy, balding pate fringed with black hair and dark beady eyes shadowed by bushy black eyebrows. He had a long plastic sleeve on one arm. When Chance and Les managed to get the mare to stand up in the straw-strewn space, the vet reached his sleeved arm and gloved hand up under the horse's tail. "Atta girl. Easy now." He seemed to be feeling around inside the horse. "Got to turn this baby around. Damn. Stuck at the knee joint." A second or two went by. No one spoke. "Ahh. Think it's working," said the vet. "Let's get Mama walking... just a few feet around the stall. Then I'll try again."

But the mare gave a huge sigh, her legs buckled, and she collapsed on her side in the straw, despite the men's efforts to keep her going on all fours. Lara prayed inwardly, prayed for the dear animal having such a vexing time of it, and for the baby horse, too. She felt an immediate kinship with this beautiful creature, obviously a Thoroughbred, a lovely blondish caramel color. The horse had a distinctive white, diamond-shaped marking on her head between her eyes.

"C'mon, Lil. You can do it," said the vet. On his knees at the mare's hind end, he lifted her tail and reached inside again. For a minute he looked worried. "Hmm. Big foal. Now if I can just... ah, that's better. C'mon, Lil-girl. Give us a push, eh?" he said to the horse, who seemed to respond with a strong contraction. "Good... good. Push, *mamalita*, push, dammit." The vet's dark-blue shirt was wet with perspiration. "Hell. Okay, guys," he said to Chance and Les. "She's tired. I'm going to have to pull this baby out. Hold Mama down, hard but gentle, thank you." The vet sat himself at the horse's rear, set his black cowboy boots firmly against each side of her rump, and commenced to pull mightily at something with two hands. Lara peeked over the side of the stall and saw what appeared to be two little horse's feet encased in a white membrane beginning to emerge to meet the world.

All was quiet except for Lil's heavy breathing. The two Mexican cowboys watched, Lara noticed, with a kind of restrained reverence at this miracle before them, though she felt certain they'd seen it many times before. Chance and the older foreman knelt, frozen in concentration, and patted the mare gently, holding her down.

The vet's face was red, his mouth set in a determined expression as he pulled some more, hard on one side, then the other of the mare's rump, huffing and grunting, muttering half in English, half in Spanish, until suddenly, a baby horse shot out from the mare with such force it knocked the vet backwards into the straw. "Well, I'll be goddamned!" He sat up, grinned, and proceeded to wipe the milky-colored membrane off the foal's startled countenance. "It's a good-looking boy, that's for sure."

An exuberant whoop went up from everyone. Lara felt like crying. What a beautiful sight. What sweet, trembling new life! The little foal, a hefty young fellow, strong and healthy-looking, lay still for a second, then struggled to stand up. Mama horse looked over her shoulder, resting and watching as the vet put iodine on the stump of the umbilical cord, which seemed, with the foal's movement, to have broken off naturally.

"Welcome to your new home, little horse," said the vet. "Your mama did *muy bueno*." He uttered more words in Spanish to the two cowboys, who, beaming at him, handed the bucket to him, hung the chain on a nail by the stall, nodded shyly to all assembled, and left the barn.

Outside, Chance came up to Lara. "That was a rare experience, Lar. I'm glad you could see it. It was touch-and-go there for a while, which doesn't happen often, thank God. A.K. will be pleased. This foal looks great—a fine, big, future stallion, maybe a champion." He squeezed her hand, and his dimpled smile filled her with contentment and relief.

"I'm so glad it turned out okay, for mother and baby alike." She peered in the stall at the little foal, a handsome, reddish, chestnut color, with a similar mark like his mother's between his eyes. "What a darling. Can I possibly pet him?" she asked the vet.

"Better stay where you are, young lady. Diamond Lil and her boy need to get acquainted first." The vet stepped out of the stall, wiping sweat from his own face with a small blue terry cloth towel. "Mares are quite protective of their foals the first few hours after birth."

"I can relate to that. Thank you," murmured Lara, smiling at the vet.

"Thanks so much again, Doc," said Chance. "Oh, this is Lara Treadwell. Lar, meet the man of the hour, Doctor Felipe Montano, a savior to all ranchers from here to Tucumcari, New Mexico."

"Which is where I'm from, originally." The vet grinned. "But I have to wash up before I shake the hand of a pretty señorita like yourself. Nice to see Chance has such good taste." Montano turned to Chance and Les, who was filling the bucket with water from a spigot a few feet away. "You fellows were a tremendous help, as usual." Doctor Montano consulted his watch, produced a pad and pencil from his back pants pocket, and wrote on the pad. "Here's the approximate time I've been here." He showed it to the two men. "Just so we're all in agreement once Mr. Wheeler gets the bill. Now if you'll excuse me, I have some post-foaling to do." He took the filled bucket from Les.

Les stepped quickly aside for the vet to enter the stall again. "Thanks, Doc. Hope no more mares give us a hard time like Lil here," said the older foreman. "I thought it was gonna be a breech problem like that poor ol' mama last year. A goddamn Sis-air-ian. Don't cotton to those, no way. No siree-bob." The tall, weathered wrangler lifted a packet of chewing tobacco from his shirt pocket, but, glancing at Lara, shoved the packet back in his shirt. "Well, folks. Gotta see a man about a horse." He winked at Chance. To Montano, he said, "I'll be back, Doc." Then Les took off down the corridor of horse stalls toward the bunkhouse beyond.

"Can I get you something to drink?" Chance asked the vet.

"Thanks, Chance, no. I've got a thermos with me. I'll be on my way, soon as I settle these two and get Junior here to nurse. Then the rest is up to Les and the boys."

Chance and Lara left as Doctor Montano was offering the mama horse a drink of water from the bucket. Stepping out into the sunshine, Chance said, "Are you hungry, Lar?" He put his arm around her and smiled down at her. "Now don't tell me you could eat a horse."

Lara laughed. "Horse, definitely no. But didn't you say something earlier about steaks?" She put an arm around Chance's waist as they strolled toward his cabin. "On second thought, it seems a crime to eat one of God's four-legged creatures. 'Specially after today. I think something vegetarian would be better. Or maybe ..." She glanced sideways at him, feeling her face flush with a devilment surprising to herself. "Or maybe just *you*, Chance." She stood still, surprised at herself. "Oh!" She caught her breath and stared straight up into Chance's gold-green eyes, mesmerized. "I mean... I, uh ..."

"Dammit, Lar!" Laughing, Chance swooped her up, cuddling her protectively in his strong arms, up the steps to his cabin, through the door and into his bedroom where he deposited her carefully, tenderly on his bed. Unprotesting, she gazed wide-eyed up at him as he leaned down to kiss her full on the mouth, at first softly, then hungrily, his hands cupping, fondling her breasts. She kissed him back, responding with pent-up passion, her hands on his back, then moving down his athletic physique, daring to grab his muscular buttocks. "Oh God, Lar," he groaned. "I want you so much. I know you want me, too. Please, let's ..."

"Yes. Oh, yes. I want you, too, Chance. Wanted you the first time I ever saw you," she murmured, feeling a sense of letting go she'd never before experienced, never knew existed.

"A little protection, Lar. For your sake. Be right back."

Lying there in the rustic room, she heard a drawer opening in the john then bang shut. She hadn't considered protection. *Good for him*, she thought. Anticipation rising, she undressed quickly.

Chance returned, naked as she was now. "Oh God, Lar. You are so sweetly, painfully beautiful," he said, smiling down at her.

"You're beautiful, too, Chance. Like a magnificent stallion. A champion." She pulled him down to her to kiss him over and over, on his full lips, sculpted face, his golden-haired chest, his neck, his ears... feeling his tongue caress her nipples, fingers touching everywhere, bodies hot with primitive desire, aflame with passion begging to be satiated.

Together they moved rhythmically to a symphony of rapacious longing unleashed at last. She moaned softly, in tune with her lover, as they hurtled to a crescendo, a climactic explosion, in her brain, her loins... spreading oh-so-sweetly, incredibly, down her legs, to the tips of her toes and back again. She cried out. Lost. Not of this world. She heard him cry out, too, matching her, cry for cry as through a veil, a fog, far away. Why did she feel like crying real tears? *Oh my God, my God.* What a strange reaction to a joy so delicious. And yet tears were streaming down her cheeks. Then she laughed. "Chance. Oh, Chance. What... ?" She lay there, unable to express anything in mere words.

"You're incredible, Lar," he whispered. He kissed her softly on her lips then turned on his side to reach for a pack of cigarettes on the bedside table. They lay together, quietly smoking, snuggling, tranquil, at peace with themselves, with the universe... when the insistent jangling of a telephone sounded in the next room.

"Damn." Chance, cigarette in hand, rose to answer it. Lara watched his Adonis-like form as it disappeared from her view somewhere in the living room. "Yeah. Hi, Frank. Right. Lost track of time. See you soon," she heard him say.

He leaned against the bedroom doorjamb and smiled at her. "You, Lar, are too much. Too much. I want to make love to you all over again." He pulled her up from the bed and held her close, his fingers stroking the skin on her back, up and down, making her long for him to do more, feeling herself like clay in the hands of a master sculptor. "But," he continued, "no such luck. For now, at least. We're expected at the main house. A different kind of feast."

"I don't need another kind of feast, Chance. Not after the one we just had. You gave me a gift I never in this world expected."

He beamed his dimpled smile and led her to the tiny john. "Now that we're one, let's see how we fit in the shower stall, Lar."

So much for seriousness, thought Lara, wondering if Chance had any idea he was the first man to bring her to orgasm. Of course, he was only the second man she'd ever had complete sex with, and that wasn't saying much, given her and Rick's hapless experience in that department. She shared her body with Chance beautifully. Now she wished to know him better as a person, to share each other's innermost thoughts, feelings, and history.

The warm water beating down on her felt exhilarating and it was fun soaping each other. But frolicking together and washing off the soap under the shower's spray failed to wash away the questions building in her mind. What had she and Chance ignited here today? And where would it all lead?

CHAPTER 21

Once a horse is born,
someone will be found to ride it.
— *Hebrew proverb*

Vince Caparelli sat braced against the trunk of a willow tree on the grassy stretch facing the shore of Desert Lake, Panama hat tipped forward on his forehead, squinty eyes scanning the scene on the shoreline a short distance away as he recalled the last half hour or so when he'd rolled up his jeans to wade in the cool lake water. Refreshed, he'd planted himself near Maria and Pidge, who were helping the three little boys build a sand castle. He offered to help, too, saying he thought the castle needed a turret or two; but he might as well have said "a turd or two" from the scathing look Maria sent his way. "Mr. Vincent," she said. "We're into our imaginations here. We want to see what these kids come up with on their own."

Hmm. Tough babe. "Just a suggestion," he said, then, undeterred, added, "Do you and Pidge babysit often? Just wondered. Fine boys."

Pidge answered, standing up with effort from a kneeling position while shaking wet sand from her gnarled fingers. "Guess we missed our manners, Mister Vincent." She pointed out each boy to him. "Bip, Billy, and Axel. A fine lot, 'tis true. Boys, say hello to the nice man. He may write about us someday," she said, smiling her wrinkly grin.

The boys peered briefly in his direction, acknowledging his presence with smiles, then all three returned to their enthusiastic sand-patting and digging. They seemed oblivious to the irritation emanating from their other sitter.

"Mr. Vincent. These children are not supposed to interact with strangers while in our care," Maria stated, rising from her knees on the white sand and reaching for a pack of cigarettes on a nearby beach blanket, "as you will discover when Bip's father arrives, which should be any minute now. Ah... good. Here he comes." She flashed a bright smile at a thin male with a pockmarked complexion and brownish, thinning hair, who seemed glad to see her in a flaccid sort of way. *So the Italian babe was spoken for. Oh, well,* Vince remembered thinking.

At least she'd introduced him to Bip's dad—a Stan Gorman, also from the East, Long Island, he'd said. After the usual pleasantries, Vince had excused himself, thinking, *I need to get out of the sun and find some shade. Actually, I feel a bit dizzy.* It had been a long flight from LaGuardia to Reno and he'd gotten up in the middle of the night to make the plane.

Now, leaning against the tree, Vince puffed on his cigar, closed his eyes, and plotted his next move. *Okay. Stick close to the old broad and the little blonde kid, Billy. Both seem to be friendly and forthright. Through them,* he assured himself, *I'll find out where Lara Treadwell has gone, when she's expected back, and how often she leaves her mothering duties to others.*

He stretched and yawned. Meanwhile, a nap wouldn't hurt. Vince shook the ashes from his cigar, folded his arms across his expansive middle, pushed the Panama forward on his brow, and settled back against the tree trunk.

The setting sun tinted the sky a dazzling peach-vermillion, providing a dramatic backdrop for the once lavender, now deep purple mountains visible from the rear of the adobe ranch house.

Lara, seated in a comfortable white canvas lounge chair on the large flagstone patio, sipped red wine from a crystal goblet and smoked the Chesterfield that Chance had lit for her. She watched him as he stood a few feet away at the brick and wrought iron barbecue apparatus, checking the grill's readiness for the fillets of beef that Frank was now going to the kitchen to retrieve. Just the sight of Chance thrilled her soul.

"The Very Thought Of You," warbled by Doris Day, wafted from a radio inside the house. The music matched Lara's mood. She shivered with pleasure, remembering the passion of her coupling with Chance and how this sexy man's lovemaking, like magic, had turned the tide of her womanhood forever. Some primitive part of her, a part she was only now beginning to recognize, wished she and Chance could run away together, wished they could be like two wild horses, a stallion and his mare, roaming, loving freely, forever, with no ties to the world. Crazy, and yet...

"Penny for your thoughts, Lar." Chance's breath felt warm and welcome as he nuzzled her neck. New stirrings of desire pulsated deep within her and her heartbeat quickened.

Somehow, in this uninvited interlude in my life, she thought, *this time of waiting to be free, I'm discovering some truths about myself, my strengths, my weaknesses, a capacity to love and be loved I never knew I possessed. Quite a change from the fragmented female I felt I was but a few short weeks ago.*

"Just glad for today, Chance," she said.

He kissed her neck, pushed a strand of her hair away from one ear, and nibbled her earlobe. "God, Lar. You are so damn tasty, so sexy," he whispered huskily. "You smell good, too."

"Plain old Ivory soap," she murmured. "Straight from our shower together, Chance." She grinned at him, eyes dancing.

Chance took her drink from her, set it on a nearby glass table, and pulled her to her feet just as Frank—carrying a pan of marinated steaks in one hand and some plates in the other—came out of the adobe house. As Lara remembered from her introduction to him at the Bracken's ranch, Frank wore a perpetually tight, thin-lipped, somber expression on his gaunt, tanned face. Did the guy ever smile? How could he and Chance, so different, be such solid friends? Frank nodded a silent "hello" at her.

"I'm taking Lar in for a tour of the house, Frank. Grill's good and hot," said Chance.

So is the girl, thought Lara, bemusedly. "Need any help, Frank?" she asked him as he speared the meat from the pan with a long-handled fork, setting each fillet on the grill.

"No. You're company. Thanks anyway," Frank mumbled. He peered at Chance intently. "Should be ready in eight minutes or less. Pick up the salad Igor left in the fridge on your way back, Chance."

"Will do." Chance led Lara by the hand through one of two sets of mammoth French doors and into the vast, white-walled living room of the Wheeler's ranch house. The cathedral log-poled ceiling, two stories high, was flanked on opposite sides halfway up with burnished, balustraded balconies, each reachable by matching stairwells. "The balcony doors up there lead to all the bedrooms. Off limits to us, I'm sorry to say," Chance laughed.

Lara noticed several huge, gilt-framed oil paintings of horse and cattle roundups decorating the walls of the massive room. She was especially fascinated by a drawing of a rodeo that hung, framed under glass, over a red lacquered Oriental cabinet set against one wall. "That looks like a Raoul Dufy, the French artist," she said, recalling her art history at Syracuse. "Is it an original?"

"Wouldn't doubt it. A.K. and his wife went to Paris before the war broke out and met the artist there, I think."

"But this is a Western scene."

"Yeah. Well, I dunno... oh now I remember. A.K. said the artist was in Arizona for a while. That was the connection, and why the Wheelers bought his work. There's another one by the same guy, hanging in the dining room."

Between each set of French doors facing the patio was a great stone fireplace as high as the ceiling. The large head of a moose hung above the enormous wrought iron grate.

"Along with art collecting, A.K. is a big-game hunting enthusiast," said Chance. "Bagged that one up in the wilds of Wyoming."

"Poor moose," Lara said, glad Mr. Wheeler wasn't there to see her reaction. "I thought A.K. loved horses. How could he possibly shoot down another innocent four-legged creature?"

"I just work for the guy, Lar. He does love horses, as I do, and he pays me well. That doesn't mean I agree with everything he does." Chance, his tone tense, lit a cigarette with a quick snap of his lighter.

"Whoa. I didn't mean... I'm sorry, Chance," she said. Why was Chance suddenly so defensive? "It just seems cruel, that's all."

"Cruel world, Lar. Which you find out when... " He paused as he looked away from her. "Like a lot of guys, I helped fight a war. Men died right next to me, all around me. Shot, blown up, whatever... human beings, good people. Ask any marine worth his salt who lived through Guadalcanal and he'll say, what's a damn moose, for chrissakes?" He left her standing alone as he moved to turn on a few floor and table lamps in the heavily furnished room, long on dark leather and colorful Indian rugs.

Lara stood stock-still, unsure how to react. She'd touched a sore spot in his soul and she felt awful about it. "Maybe we should go outside again. I have to be getting back before long."

She turned from in front of the hearth, thinking she'd ask Frank to drive her back to Desert Lake, when Chance suddenly grabbed her almost savagely and kissed her hard on the mouth. "I'm sorry, Lar," he said, releasing her for a moment then hugging her close to his chest. "I'm a damn fool about stuff sometimes. Please forgive me." He kissed her softly, lovingly. "The hell with the moose. It's A.K.'s sport, not mine. It's just what happened in the war. I was fortunate, some weren't."

Melting, Lara kissed him back with an open mouth and a contrite heart. "Oh, Chance, Chance. You beautiful man. I wouldn't hurt your feelings for the world," she said between kisses, sure if they gave in again to the rampant passion so easily generated by their closeness, they'd end up on one of A.K.'s rugs, copulating into oblivion. "Maybe we'd better ..." She drew back from him, breathing rapidly. "I mean, Frank might ..."

"Right." He let her go and looked at his watch. "Uh, oh. Chow time." He grinned at her. "I'll take *you* over steak anytime, Lar."

Turning to go outside, Lara noticed a black baby grand piano in a corner by the French doors. There was an array of silver-framed photographs, randomly arranged on top of the instrument's polished ebony surface.

"Oh, is this A.K.?" she asked, pointing to a large framed color image of a tall, stocky, ruddy-cheeked, white-haired man standing in front of a handsome racehorse. The man, debonair and distinguished-looking, was dressed in a white suit and was smiling from ear to ear. His pride was obvious, crinkly eyes glittering, as he held up in triumph what appeared to be a great silver trophy cup.

"Yeah, that's him when Kane's Able won at Del Mar," said Chance.

Other shots showed a gregarious A.K. Wheeler with numerous celebrities: Bing Crosby, Gene Autry, Roy Rogers, Jimmy Durante, Clark Gable, and Carole Lombard among them. "Mr. Wheeler certainly gets around," said Lara, also noting a photo of A.K. shaking the hand of President Truman.

"Who is this?" Lara touched a smaller, black-and-white shot of a lovely woman with silver hair styled in a long pageboy. She was posed in low-cut black, obviously a professional glamour photo. Lara couldn't decide if the woman was a platinum blonde or just the possessor of prematurely silver tresses. "Whoever she is, she's gorgeous."

"That's Zoe, A.K.'s present wife, his fourth. She's a former cover girl. Major magazine stuff. Zoe is twenty years A.K.'s junior. Originally from Terre Haute, Indiana. Great gal."

"She looks like a fun person. I like her dimples." Lara kissed Chance's cheek. "I love yours."

"I love everything about you, lady," he said, lighting a cigarette, offering her one. "C'mon. I'll show you the most modern kitchen in Nevada."

Everything was black, white, and gleaming, including the check-ered-tiled floor. The black refrigerator was the largest Lara had ever seen. Chance opened one of its three-paneled, many-shelved doors and grabbed a copious glass salad bowl filled with crispy greens and delectable-looking raw vegetables. "Good ol' Igor," said Chance. "Let's see, salad dressing?"

Lara found a cruet of oil and vinegar already mixed. "Just needs a good shaking up," she said.

"Oh, and some of Nadia's home-baked rye bread. The best. In the breadbox on the counter, Lar. Thanks."

They joined an impatient Frank on the patio. "If these cow slabs get grilled anymore they won't be fit to eat," Frank said. "Pass your damn plate, Chance." Frank looked at Lara, murmuring sheepishly. "Oh, sorry, ladies first."

"Nag, nag, nag," Chance said and laughed at his buddy. "At least you remembered your manners, pal."

Awaking abruptly, Vince Caparelli was startled to see two Indian kids, a girl in her teens and a small boy, both staring down at
him propped against the tree. Vince rubbed his eyes and pushed his
Panama hat back from his forehead, aware of a sharp, annoying crick
in his neck.

"Mrs. Bracken wants to be sure you don't miss supper, mister,"
said the girl. "She sent me and my brother to find you."

"You wasn't in your cabin, mister," said the boy. "Billy 'n Bip
said to look by th' lake."

"Oh, yeah." Vince struggled to get to his feet. "Whew. Boy-oh-
boy. I was zonked." He consulted his watch and figured he was snooz-
ing against the damn tree for maybe …"Wow. Six o'clock already.
Well, thanks, kids."

As he walked with them up towards the lodge, he thought he'd
interrogate the two while he had the opportunity. "Say, young lady,
ah,... what's your name?"

"Nita. And this is Jimmy. Our mom's the cook for the ranch."

"Well, Nita. A pretty name for a pretty girl. I need to speak to
a Mrs. Treadwell. You seen her around lately?" He hoped he wasn't
coming on too strong. Maybe they knew something, maybe not, but
so far his batting average wasn't as good as usual, so any info would
help, however minimal.

Jimmy stopped walking, his coal-black eyes alive with excitement. "Missus Treadwell? That's Billy's mom. Billy said she went to
see some horses."

"Here at the ranch or somewhere else?" Vince asked.

"No, ah …"

Before the boy could finish, his sister quickly took him by his
little brown hand, giving him a stern look of admonishment. "Come
on, Jimmy. We have to help Mom in the kitchen," she said, her striking, liquid brown eyes piercing Vince with traces of suspicion.

A sense of dismay clutched at Vince as he watched the kids run
ahead of him, bound for the lodge's kitchen. At least, he rationalized,
the Indian boy was about to spout a clue, so maybe he would again.
It was obvious the kid's mom had taught them to be cautious with
strangers. *Good for them, unlucky for me, except now I know the Treadwell*

*dame's off at another ranch somewhere. Maybe unlucky for her, too, if she
doesn't make the curfew.*

A quick clean-up and shirt change in his cabin got Vince to the
dining hall in time for a serving of his favorite: Lasagna Bolognese.
Ah. How appropriate. Italian cuisine night. He scanned the room for
Maria and spotted her sitting with the Gorman guy, another couple,
and a classy-looking dame. No sign of the boys or Pidge.

"This place taken?" asked Vince. He pulled out a chair next to
Maria and Stan, and across from the others.

"Free country." Maria mustered a smile and introduced him to
the couple, the guy a balding, dark-haired, intellectual type, and his
tall, freckly-faced, auburn-haired wife. "Mr. Vincent, meet Nick and
Claire Janus. Oh, and this is Harriet Renquist. She's from the East
Coast, too. Where in Connecticut was that again, Harriet?"

"Greenwich. Lovely to meet you, Mr. Vincent. Are you here for
the usual reasons?" asked the dark-haired gal, taking a sip from her
cup of coffee.

A bell rang in Vince's head. "Greenwich. I used to go out near
there to sail on the Sound." *I did sail on the Sound once*, he thought, *in
a police patrol boat, but that was from another life.*

"Oh, you're a sailor. A yachtsman, perhaps?" said Harriet.

Fat chance. "No, actually... I write. Love this dish," he said as he
savored another bite of the lasagna.

"What do you write, Mr. Vincent?"

Vince broke a crisp dinner roll in two. "I'm working on a detective story." Some truth there.

"I'd love to read it when you finish it."

Is this dame coming on to me? he wondered. "Yeah, well, it'll be
awhile." The bell in his head clanged louder. "Hmm... Connecticut.
Mrs. Bracken said she had several guests lately from the East." He
nodded at Maria and Stan. "Includes us, of course." Then, smiling, he
asked the Janus couple, "Where are you folks from?"

"The West Coast, California," the redhead answered. "But someone else,... oh, yes, Lara, Lara Treadwell. She's from Connecticut, like
Harriet here."

"Oh? Yeah. Met her son Billy today. Delightful kid." Vince stopped chewing, swallowed, and peered at Maria. "Where's Billy? And Pidge?"

"They ate earlier. Pidge is reading to Bip and Billy."

"And Billy's mom?" Vince asked nonchalantly.

"She had to go to Reno." A strange, slow smile crept over Maria's face as her dark eyes met his. "You ask more damn questions, Mr. Vincent."

"Do I? Must be 'cause I'm a writer." He scraped remaining tomato and meat sauce from his plate with a piece of the dinner roll.

"Mr. Vincent," said the auburn-haired Claire Janus. "Like Harriet, I want to hear all about your book. Would you join all of us for after-dinner drinks at The Trading Post?"

Vince wasn't sure, but he thought he saw Maria and the Janus dame exchange meaningful glances. Oh, well. He had to stay connected to these people, all of whom knew the Treadwell gal. Maybe they were protecting her. If so, he needed to find out why.

"Sure," he said as he pushed his plate away, wiped his mouth with his napkin, and refused dessert from the German waitress. "Sounds great." He fished a cigar from his pocket and lit it, thinking, *I have to figure out a fake plot, and fast, for my so-called "book."*

As he followed everyone out of the dining hall, Vince thought of a title for his bogus detective story: "The Big Search." *Not bad, and not far from the truth. I always loved a mystery.*

CHAPTER 22

Imparadis'd in one another's arms.

—— *John Milton,* Paradise Lost

At the glass patio table by the Wheeler's lighted swimming pool, the dinner conversation centered mainly around horses, but Lara didn't care. Occasionally she contributed positive comments regarding the foaling she felt privileged to have attended. It was enough, she thought, just to be sitting there, partaking of a meal under a starlit sky with Chance. *Just as long as I get back in time...*

"Moon's about full," said Chance, gazing skyward.

"So am I," laughed Lara. "That steak was amazingly tender. Thanks so much, Frank. Can I help clean up?"

"Not a problem," said Frank in his usual taciturn way.

"Not if we all take stuff back to the kitchen," said Chance. "We can set the dishes to soak and Nadia and Igor'll finish up tomorrow."

Bidding goodnight to Frank, who said he had to work on some racecourse contracts for A.K., Lara and Chance strolled in the moonlight past pastures and white-fenced paddocks to Chance's cabin. The sweet scent of clover and hay filled the soft night air as crickets chirped and an owl hooted in the shadow of a cottonwood tree. As they neared the cabin, Lara asked, "Who lives in the other cabins near yours, Chance?"

"Nobody now. A.K. keeps them handy for extra guests. Especially the ones who like to rough it. Why, Lar? Worried about spies again?" He offered her a Chesterfield, took one for himself, and lit both as they sat themselves down on the porch steps.

"'Course not. But it's good to know no one's around to bother us." She smiled, looking at him sideways, flirting while puffing on her cigarette.

"Why, Lar, sounds like you're cooking up some nefarious scheme to get me all to your delectable self again. If so, I confess... I'm a goner," said Chance, his fingers playing with the tendrils of hair around her ear.

Lara felt her face flush, despite the cool, nocturnal breeze. A now familiar rush of desire washed over and through her, pulsating, throbbing. "Chance, I ..." His kisses stopped her. "Again, Chance? I can't believe it," she said, coming up for air.

"Again, Lar. Over and over," he whispered softly.

"Right here? On your porch?" She managed a nervous giggle in between kisses, flicking her cigarette out on the grass, feeling a mosquito buzz annoyingly past her ear. "I'd rather the 'lovebug' got me than the damn mosquitoes," she said. "But, seriously, Chance, I do have to think about getting back."

"Not to worry, Lar. Still time before we have to hit the road." He touched her face, looking deep into her eyes. "Y'know, you never told me why you're getting a divorce. The guy must be out of his mind to let you go."

Lara twisted the gold band still on her finger. "You have a right to know, Chance, but all I can say is... I haven't sorted it all out for myself yet. Until I came to Reno, I was an emotional wreck. I feel stronger now, thanks to you." She sighed. "Can we talk about this some other time? Today was so special."

"Of course, Lar. Just want you to know I admire your not cussing the guy out even though he definitely needs his head examined." Chance put one arm around her waist and together they went inside.

"A little music?" Chance switched on a couple of lamps, turned the radio on low, then opened a kitchenette cabinet door. "Got some brandy A.K. gifted me with once, or cream sherry. What's your pleasure?"

"My pleasure, sir, is you." Lara swayed dreamily to the orchestral magic of Cole Porter's "I've Got You Under My Skin." "Oh, gosh, I love this song. Care to dance, Mr. Darwin?" She held her arms out enticingly.

"Why dance when I can stand here and drool just watching you, Lar? Keep it up and 'Mr. Darwin' may have to take matters into his own hands," he said, pouring brandy into two smoky-glass snifters.

She sipped the brandy he offered and rose on her toes to kiss him. "Goes double for me." Swaying again to the music, she sang a line or two of the lyrics.

"Good God, she sings, too." Chance grinned, grabbed her close to him and whispered in her ear, "Is there no end to your talents, you gorgeous woman?"

Her pulse beat faster. "Thanks to you, I've discovered I'm okay in bed," she teased, still swaying sexily as he held her tight and she felt him respond magically to the thrust of her hips rubbing rhythmically against him. A thrill raced through her like a powerful surge of electricity as Chance kissed her hungrily, his hands caressing her shoulders, then, cupping her breasts, moving to lower her blouse, his tongue sliding to her cleavage, then to her nipples, 'til she was on fire. "Chance, Chance... ," she gasped.

He set her brandy glass on the counter, lifted her in his arms, and deposited her on his bed. "This time," he said, his voice soothing, sexy, "I'll show you a few talents of my own, Lar."

While soft, buttery beams of moonlight shone through the window above the bed, Lara was again transported to an ecstasy she had discovered earlier this afternoon of passion's reckoning, of a self newly revealed. Chance, this delicious man so in tune with her own being, heart, body, and soul, proved himself an artist at love. His tongue and fingers were the brushes as he brought her with tender, tantalizing finesse to the edge of orgasm. Then, together, they climaxed in a conjoining so intense both were uplifted to a higher level of consciousness, another world, a space inhabited only by a fortunate few. They made love, over and over, until, exhausted, they fell asleep.

The odor of strongly brewed coffee stirred Lara from sleep, and she awoke in a daze. Where... ? She froze. What time was it? Oh no! Heart sinking, she sat up, worried, now wide awake. *How in hell,* she wondered, *can I make it back to Desert Lake without being declared missing?*

CHAPTER 23

Wild horses run unbridled or the spirit dies.
— *anonymous*

"What kind of plane is this?" Lara raised her voice above the roar of the small aircraft's engine.

"Piper Cub," shouted Frank Jensen, busy at the controls and the plane's instrument panel. "Mr. Wheeler got this one from the military. It was used for observation during the war, then rebuilt."

"You fly often, Frank?" Lara finally felt relaxed enough to unclench her teeth and release her white-knuckled grip from both sides of her seat in the two-seater cabin of the Cub whose take-off from Wheeler's ranch was shaky, but fast, zooming up easily into the dark sky before dawn's early light.

"Often enough. Had my license since '45," said Jensen.

Lara straightened up and looked around. How exciting it was to be piloted back to Desert Lake, to be flying low with a clear view of the landscape, a view now becoming more spectacular as the gray light of pre-dawn was transforming into shades of mauve, lavender, and rose pink.

The little aircraft soared out over the rugged peaks of a mountain range as the sky brightened from pink to peach, blending to a warm tangerine. Lara gazed at the peaks, crevasses, and ridges below and thought of Chance. How unexpected, how thrilling was the gift of their loving. A high point, a "peak" of experience hitherto unknown to her.

She recalled Chance getting her to the plane in record time, too, after a few gulps of coffee, a hasty throwing-on of clothes, grabbing her purse, and joining him in the convertible as he drove at breakneck speed the short distance to A.K.'s airfield. There, Frank, reliable as usual, had the plane revved up for flight. *If only I'd had more time to say goodbye to Chance*, she thought. But he had promised to see her later today, saying he had to stay behind to call A.K. and report on Diamond Lil's foaling.

From her view out the plane's window, Lara saw the peaks rapidly disappearing, and, emerging in their stead, a long, flat, dun-colored plain dotted with sagebrush. The cloudless sky was crimson now, and the rising sun sent beams of bright, blinding light glinting off the wings of the Cub. Blinking her eyes, Lara glanced below and was amazed to see a large, blurred mass of horses, running so fast they seemed to move as one entity on the flat expanse of desert.

Stunned, Lara said, "Frank! So many horses! I've never seen anything like this. Are they wild?"

"Nevada's full of herds of wild horses."

"Oh, they're so beautiful. So free! I hope... Nobody ever captures them, do they?"

"Yeah, well, mustangs bring a good price for ..."

"Please, don't tell me. I'd rather think of them the way I'm seeing them now, happy and free, the way they're meant to be." *Yes*, she thought, *the way we're* all *meant to be.*

The moment passed all too swiftly. As Lara bid a silent, reluctant farewell to the herd, a familiar feeling gripped her and she remembered again her identification with the horse on the rainy road. Tears welled in her eyes. *I, that country horse, and these beautiful free wild ones,... all of us belong together,* she thought. *We share the same spirit. I feel it so deeply. And this image of their unfettered flight will be my touchstone, whenever I need it, now and in the future. Forever. I'll never forget it.*

"Won't be long now," Frank said, interrupting Lara's reverie. "Almost to Bracken's ranch. First time I've landed here, so it might be a bit dicey." A cigarette dangling from his thin lips, he flew the Cub beyond the stretch of sage-dotted plateau and out over Desert Lake, its smooth surface shimmering misty blue-green in the early morning light.

"Thanks for doing this, Frank." It wasn't easy making conversation with this friend of Chance's, but Lara decided to ask a question that had occupied her mind since their first meeting. "I was wondering, Frank,... how long have you and Chance known each other?"

"Met in the Marines. Trained at Quantico together. Ended up in Guadalcanal. He saved my goddamned life." Frank pushed something on the plane's instrument panel. "Hold on, Lara. Got to get a bead on Bracken's landing strip, such as it is."

No wonder the two men were so close, thought Lara. She vowed to get the full story from Chance if she could. Meanwhile, she clutched the sides of her seat, her heart in her mouth as the ground whizzed nearer and she could spot the entire layout of Bracken's Desert Lake Ranch spread out below. She could even see her own cabin from aloft as she sent a silent prayer down to Billy, who, she hoped, was sleeping soundly.

Frank landed the Cub expertly on the dry, dusty, hardscrabble landing strip opposite the railroad tracks where a couple of freight trains were parked on a siding.

"Whew! You're good at this, Frank," Lara yelled over the noise from the plane's idling engine. Thank God they'd landed safely. Now, how could she get back to her cabin without being seen by early risers?

As if reading her mind, Frank shouted, "I had to land far enough from the stables so Roy's horses don't panic. Watch your footing over the tracks, Lara. Run like hell through the orchard over there and you're home free." He reached across her and unlatched the small cockpit door on her side of the plane. "Get out the way you got in," he said. "Step on the step below the cabin door, then jump to the ground."

Lara landed with both sandaled feet on the ground and took off like a blazing comet, bound for the orchard, hoping nobody—especially the Brackens and Connecticut-Harriet herself—would catch her fleeing from a plane at this ungodly hour. Slowing down only enough to pick her way cautiously across the tracks, Lara resumed running like an Olympian. She zigzagged around apple trees, keeping the distant blue shingled roof of her cabin in her sights as she heard the plane's motor fire up behind her, then take off.

Breathless and perspiring, she dared not look back. *I have to reach my cabin quickly, and safely, she told herself.* Have *to.*

Waking from a deep sleep, Vince Caparelli could swear he heard the engine of a plane. Landing? Taking off? No. Couldn't be. Away out here? But,... could be rumrunners. Nah. Those days had ended when Prohibition was repealed in '33, he told himself. Numbskull.

Speaking of which.... He swore silently, mouth twisted in a grimace. *Oh God. A helluva hangover. My skull's not numb, it's one big concrete block of pain, dammit.*

He rolled over, got no relief, and rolled back on the pillow, holding both sides of his cranium with two hands. "Havta' keep my brains from exploding into bloody bits all over the friggin' ceiling," he groaned aloud. He sat on the edge of the bed, concerned about whether he'd made a fool of himself, remembering vaguely the events of the evening before and pledging to himself to watch the booze from now on since there was too much at stake regarding the Treadwell case.

Vince found himself wondering again where the Treadwell woman had been and if she'd made it back to the ranch by midnight.

With great effort, he pulled himself up off the bed and into the john, where he splashed cold water on his face and downed a couple of aspirin. He peered in the mirror above the sink. Geez, how depressing. Droopy-dog eyes, puffy with underlying pouches peered back at him. His gray-black hair and even his goatee were scraggly and unkempt. "You," he muttered to his mirrored mug, "need a massive dose of hot java, and soon."

He brushed his teeth, shaved, and dressed slowly. Willing the aspirin to hurry and kick in, Vince looked out the cabin's window, the one facing the back of the ranch. No sign of a plane. *Did I really hear one? Can I be slipping?* He cursed himself for not checking for a possible airfield and pointed his hairbrush at his reflection. "Okay, smart guy. From now on you stick to no more than two beers. No hard liquor while on the job. Get that, Caparelli?"

Despite his mental fuzziness, Vince felt his instinct as a bloodhound begin to sit up, lick its wounds, and howl. Good. *Today*, he told himself, *I'll attempt to ascertain whether Rick Treadwell, Master Magician, has a leg to stand on, and, if so, how I, Vince Caparelli, Master Private Investigator, can deliver the proof positive.*

Armed with his Kodak, for purposes of furtive photo taking, plus a small, blue-lined spiral notepad, a workable pen, a book of matches, and several cigars, Vince locked his cabin door and set off for breakfast at the dining hall. *I'll probably be the first one there*, he thought, *but what the hell? I'm in desperate need of a major caffeine fix.*

Running through tall grass while dodging apple trees was proving daunting to Lara. She slowed down, careful not to slip on rotting fruit dotting the ground, when, without warning, she almost tripped over the form of someone curled up next to a tree trunk. "Omigosh. What... ?" Lara came to a complete halt and stared at a young woman in frayed denim shorts and a sleeveless black top who was sobbing quietly. "Oh my God! I hope I didn't hurt you. I was going so darn fast." Lara bent over, her palms resting on her knees, trying to catch her breath.

The girl's short, black-haired head was bowed low. She sat with knees drawn up and tucked under her chin, her thin arms wrapped tightly around her legs, a position which seemed to signal a desire, physically at least, to hold herself together. Slowly, she raised her face to Lara, a face pinched and stained with tears and... something else.

"Oh my God!" cried Lara. "Your eye! Oh, bless you. It must hurt like ..." One side of the girl's face was bruised, cut, and bleeding, and the eye was reddish-purple and starting to swell shut. As though embarrassed, the girl hid her injured countenance again between her knees, but not before Lara recognized her as Deb, the barmaid from The Trading Post. What, wondered Lara, was Bracken's new employee doing out here so early in the morning, and in such bad shape?

"Deb," Lara spoke softly. "What happened?"

"T... T... Tex," said the battered girl, her voice choking between sobs. "We had a fight. It's nothin'." She tried vainly to brush away her tears with one shaky hand.

"You mean Tex? The cowboy? Your brother?"

"Brother?" Deb's sad, distorted facial expression changed to one of sardonic amusement. "Hah!" she chortled. "Ain't no brother of mine. Shit. He'd be a lousy brother for anybody. He's not worth pissin' on." She leaned back wearily against the gnarled trunk of the tree. "Ya happen ta have a cigarette on ya?"

Lara dug in her purse, produced a Chesterfield from the pack Chance had given her earlier, and lit it for Deb. "You look like you could use some first-aid. I was just out for some exercise, and ..." *Perhaps it's best to fib*, thought Lara, *since I don't know if the girl can be trusted.* "My cabin's close by. Why don't you let me... ?"

"No. No. Uh... thanks anyways." Deb's one good eye, a pale shade of cobalt blue, registered alarm as she accepted the proffered cigarette and took a long drag like someone whose lungs were starved for nicotine. "I don't wanna be seen like this." The corners of her mouth turned downward. Her over-painted, brick red lips trembled. "That's why I ran over here to hide out 'til I pulled myself together," she moaned, putting her hand to her face. "Damn, it hurts. Bet I look like shit, too." She commenced crying softly again.

"Look," said Lara, "I can run over to my place and bring back a wet towel and some bandages, Deb. Please let me help you."

Deb shook her poodle-cut head back and forth as she sobbed, "That damn Tex. He's so stuck on ballin' that rich-bitch-whatser-name so's he kin grab all her cash. Meanwhile, he's ballin' *me*. I let him 'cause he keeps bringin' up how he got me this job 'n all and how we're gonna high-tail it to Mexico soon. I dunno. I told him last night I don't wanna go along with his shitty scams, an' he hit me... real hard. Threw me outta his truck right on th' damn highway, drove off, left me there, an' I kept walkin' in th' dark and ended up out here." She pulled up one tip of her shirt and winced as she used the cloth to dab at her blackened eye. "Tex likes ta dance with you and make the bitch jealous. How come you weren't at th' Post last night, Lara?"

So, thought Lara, *we've never been formally introduced, and here this poor, tough, strange person knows my name and who knows what else about me? Better not get too friendly with this girl.*

Deciding to ignore Deb's question, she said instead, "Sounds like Tex wants to control you and you let him, so he's used to it. Believe me, Deb. I understand. I'm just learning myself. Somehow you have to find a way to stand up to him without getting beat up."

"Hell, don't I know that? But that no-count cowboy knocked me up. What th' hell am I gonna do about that? I don't have th' dough ta get rid of it an' he won't pay. He's mad at me. That's mainly what we was fightin' about, that and his damn scams he's got cooked up. Which I ain't gonna do no matter what." She started crying again.. "Tex sez he'll get rid of me *and* th' kid if I don't stick with him all th' way. I'd rather stay here 'cause this is th' best job I ever had. 'Sides,... I'm scared shitless." She bowed her head, trembling hands covering her pummeled face.

Lara knelt down, putting her arm around Deb's thin shoulders. "Bless you, Deb. I can see why you're so scared." For a moment she held the girl, hoping to calm her somewhat. Finally, feeling the pressing need to return to her cabin, see Billy again, and relieve Pidge, Lara stood up, saying, "I'll be right back with something for that eye of yours, and those cuts, too. Please wait here, Deb. Okay?"

"Okay," said the girl, staring sadly at the ground. "Ya got one more cigarette, Lara?"

Lara gave her the pack of Chesterfields and a book of matches and resumed her run to her cabin. At the same time, she marveled at the ability of one human being to lord it over another for their own selfish purposes. Puffing hard, Lara reached her gate, aware of how much she was learning in the short time she'd been at the ranch and how she could apply the lessons to her own life in the future, whatever that might be.

Unlocking her cabin door, she slipped silently into the room to find Billy still sleeping and Pidge on the opposite bed snoring softly while cocooned in her favorite red, black, and gray Indian blanket. As silently as she could, so as not to wake them, Lara found a towel and wet a corner of it. Then, armed with iodine, gauze, and Red Cross tape she'd borrowed from Duke after Billy's rope injury, she crept from the cabin and headed for the orchard.

The profusion of trees momentarily threw her concentration off as she stepped over the many apples hidden in the weeds. Which one was the tree with Deb curled next to it? She tried to retrace her earlier steps, searching from tree to tree. But it soon became obvious. Deb had vanished.

Discouraged, Lara trudged back to her cabin, thinking that perhaps she should tell June of Deb's plight. June was the girl's employer, after all. *No. Better not*, she reasoned, *because, in the telling, how could I explain how I, Lara Treadwell, a responsible parent and resident of Desert Lake Ranch, happened to be out in that part of the property around sunup? Trouble sleeping? Wanted to see the sunrise? No. Lying is risky. Besides, it goes against my grain. Always has. On the other hand, I know I missed curfew. If that's discovered, it might not go well with me in court.*

Overwhelmed with a burgeoning feeling of guilt and concern, she opened her front door. All her negative feelings evaporated as soon as Billy saw her and leapt from his bed.

"Mommy, Mommy! You're back! I missed you." He ran to her, wrapping his small arms around her neck as she knelt to hug and kiss him, appreciating anew what a sweet child he was and how much she loved him.

"I missed you, too, Billy. Oh, so much." She held him tight.

"Did you see the horses, Mommy?"

"Yes, and I saw a beautiful baby horse, too, Billy. I'll tell you about it at breakfast." Lara looked up at Pidge, who, arrayed in a long, sleeveless, shapeless, sky-blue cotton nightshirt, stood barefoot by her bed, stretching and yawning. "Bless you, Pidge. I can't thank you enough. I've got to do something to return the favor."

"My pleasure, Larie-love. No return required."

"How did it go last night?" asked Lara.

"Mr. Billy is a veritable little prince. Best child in this whole desert kingdom." Pidge's tanned, wrinkled visage beamed at both mother and son as she gathered her special blanket around her, saying grandly, "I shall depart now to dress for breakfast, dear ones." She patted Billy on his blonde head. "Take care of your mommy, Sir Billy. She looks a bit weary." To Lara she said, "Hope all went well, Larie-love. Can't wait to hear. And, I have much to impart. Maria does, too. See you at breakfast." Wrapped in her Indian blanket like the squaw of a chieftain, Pidge blew a kiss and left.

I wonder what Pidge meant by "much to impart," thought Lara as she directed Billy to wash up and get dressed. Quickly she applied a rosy shade of lipstick, brushed her hair, and changed into white shorts and a dusty-pink, lightweight, sleeveless summer sweater. She helped her son double-tie the shoelaces on his sneakers, and soon they set off for breakfast at the lodge.

As she walked to the dining hall, hand in hand with Billy, Lara's heartbeat quickened at the possibility of seeing Chance again. *I miss him already*, she thought. Meanwhile, there was the problem of Deb. *What is my responsibility to the girl? Darn that Tex. What a sad excuse for a human being, causing trouble wherever he goes.* Were June and Roy aware of Tex's insidious involvement with Kat Kavanaugh, and his lies and cruelty towards their new barmaid?

As Lara entered the dining hall in a state of apprehension, such feelings became magnified when she spied a portly fellow with a goatee and a shock of salt-and-pepper hair chatting with the Januses, Harriet, and Maria. *Who is that?* she wondered. *I don't feel like meeting anyone new right now.*

Somehow managing the semblance of a smile and accompanied by her sunny-faced young son, Lara approached the table of her friends with a palpitating heart and an increased sense of trepidation.

CHAPTER 24

*To convert a setback into a success should be like
riding a horse to the edge of a precipice.
Be not so careless as to whip it even once.*

—— *Chinese epigram*

Before she and Billy could reach the table, Lara saw Maria rise from her seat and run toward them. Instantly, Lara felt herself embraced by Maria, who whispered breathlessly in her ear, "Ixnay, kiddo. Watch me for signals. Remember this. You went to Reno to see your lawyer, ran into old friends, and stayed late for dinner." Out loud for all to hear, Maria exclaimed, "We missed you yesterday, Lara. Welcome back."

Does Maria's nutty behavior, wondered Lara, *have something to do with the stranger sitting at the end of the table?* She was acutely aware of his staring at her since she entered the room.

The Januses waved and Harriet smiled in greeting. "Good morning," Lara said cheerily. She and Billy sat down next to Maria and across from Stan and Bip. All were served a breakfast of scrambled eggs, bacon, and cook Wanda's special blueberry muffins, along with honeydew melon slices and freshly squeezed orange juice.

"You just missed a major event," Maria said as she buttered a muffin. "Vida Zembrowski left the dining room here to take a call from New York, came back and announced that her husband dropped dead of a heart attack while 'getting it on' with his mistress. So now Vida is a widow. No reason to hang around Reno anymore. Tomorrow she flies the coop. We should all be so lucky," Maria snickered as she stirred a spoonful of sugar into her coffee. "You should've seen how Kat Kavanaugh reacted to the news. She had a royal fit. You know Vida's been like a mother to her. The Brackens escorted Krazy Kat out of the room to calm her down. And all this before our eggs arrived. Talk about scrambled. 'S wonder our *brains* aren't scrambled!"

"Well, I can see how this solves the problem for Vida." said Lara, wondering how much Billy understood of the conversation. "Poor Kat. She's so emotionally dependent, not only on Vida, but in other ways, too. I'm concerned for her." No reason to divulge what she'd overheard between Kat and Tex, especially not to Maria, who would only launch into another diatribe. But Lara knew she was equipped with special information about Tex and Kat, *and* Tex's threats aimed at Deb. What to do? And how to do it? *Maybe Chance can help solve my dilemma*, she thought. *I can hardly wait for him to call.*

"I swear, kiddo," said Maria, "You're too good to be true. Ever the chaplain's daughter. Which reminds me ..." She winked at Lara. "How'd everything go yesterday? I can't wait to hear, and ..." She paused, diverted by Pidge's sudden entrance into the dining hall.

As Maria indicated for Pidge to take a seat, Lara noticed the Januses deep in conversation with the stranger. *Why*, thought Lara, *does that man keep glancing in my direction?*

She whispered to Maria. "Do you know who the new guy is? He gives me the creeps. And why in heck were you trying to warn me when I came in?" She munched on a slice of melon. "By the way, that was some greeting you gave me. I love you, too!" she laughed as she poured cream in her coffee. "I mean, seriously,... do you know anything about that guy?"

"All I can say is, something about him didn't sit well with me from the start," said Maria, smiling at Pidge who took a seat across from her and Lara. "He got here yesterday after you left. Says he's a writer. Asked where you were, so, natch, Pidge 'n I got suspicious. Why would he care where you went, for pete's sake? He never met you. " She exchanged meaningful glances with Pidge. "We all came up with a plan. And it worked. Right, Pidge?"

Pidge answered, "I wasn't witness to the final chapters of the plan, since I was guarding Prince Billy here." She smiled at the boy, saluting him with a blue-veined, jewelry-bedecked hand. He grinned happily back at her, a fragment of egg adorning his small, round chin as he attacked his meal with enthusiasm.

"Billy and I were lost in storybook land," Pidge continued. "So I don't know what befell the illustrious writer, Mister Vincent." She leaned over her plate, beady eyes glistening with glee as she peered intently at Lara and Maria. "But of this I am sure. United we stand, m'dears. Just like in the war." She put a twisted finger against her mouth. "Loose lips sink ships."

"But why do you call him 'Mister Vincent'? Why so formal?" asked Lara. "Is he here for a divorce, or what?"

Before Maria or Pidge could answer, June Bracken's strong voice was heard making an announcement. "Sorry to interrupt your meal, everyone, but Roy and I have decided to hold our monthly birthday party for guests a week early. This month we celebrate the Leo birthdates among us. Mrs. Zembrowski, who happens to be a Leo, could use some cheer. So come one, come all, at five thirty in the recreation room next to the lodge. Beer and wine will be served, along with soft drinks and a buffet supper. For dessert, ice cream and a special cake our cook, Wanda Big Horn, is baking. You are all invited." The tall, blonde proprietress of the ranch started to leave, then, turning back, added, "Oh, yes. One more thing. Roy wanted me to tell you The Trading Post will be closed due to the party and will re-open at nine tonight. Thank you." She smiled at all assembled, then exited the dining hall with her usual grace and poise.

Maria turned to Lara. "Well, I'm gonna have to wrap my present for you, kiddo. It's been sitting in my cabin for days now. You're a Leo, right?"

"Yes, but... you don't have to give me anything, Maria. Your friendship is enough, believe me," said Lara, thinking she'd invite Chance to the party, when and if he called her. The thought of him made her pulse flutter wildly. What delicious passion they shared. She ached to see him, feel his closeness, his strength, the dizzying touch of his skin against hers, to lose herself in his warm, loving embrace, to...

Lara sighed inwardly and ate in silence. As she and Billy were finishing the meal, she was dismayed to see the stranger, Mister Vincent, greet Pidge, who, in turn, bid him a pleasant good morning. His heavy-lidded eyes were focused across the table directly on Lara. She felt an immediate rush of hot blood course through her veins as she attempted to avoid his gaze, lowering her eyes and drinking her coffee. *Maria is right*, she thought. *Something about him is weird.*

"I don't think I've had the pleasure," said the stranger as Pidge, a pasted-on smile creasing her wrinkled physiognomy, introduced him to Lara.

"Nor I," Lara's smile was cool and polite. "Nice to meet you, Mr. Vincent." She helped Billy up from his chair and took the boy by the hand. "Please excuse us," she said, as much to Maria and Pidge as to the stranger. "We have to go to our cabin."

"But Mommy," Billy said, casting a disappointed glance at Bip. "Can't we play?"

"Of course, Billy," Lara answered gently. "After we go to our cabin. Mommy doesn't feel well." She looked at Maria with an expression of quiet entreaty. "Could you come with us, Maria? Thanks." Giving Pidge, Stan, and the others a friendly wave, she and Billy left the dining hall, accompanied by Maria.

"I know you think I'm nuts, Maria," Lara said as they walked briskly along the path outside the lodge. "But, if I hadn't left right then I would've upchucked. In fact, I still may. Too much is happening, and that man staring at me didn't help." Lara inhaled several deep gulps of fresh morning air, trying to quiet herself. "I... I have so much on my mind."

"It's okay, toots." Maria took hold of Billy's other small hand as they neared Lara's cabin. "Don't sweat it. Did I ever tell ya I graduated high school from a convent in Brooklyn? They don't call me 'Mother Maria' for nothin'. I'm all ears, kiddo."

Tex Otis finished breakfast in the mess hall adjacent to the bunkhouse. *Why the hell don't the Brackens hire a better cook fer us ranch hands?* he opined to himself as he lit a weed and walked out in the sunshine toward the horse barn. *Goddamn grease in them ham 'n eggs could keep my truck runnin' fer a week.*

His thoughts were interrupted by a cheery "Hi, Tex," from Duke. The old wrangler came toward him, leading a handsome chestnut stallion he'd saddled up for a prospective rider soon to arrive. "Hey, damndest thing," said Duke. "Jes' talked to Roy. Y'know thet big-titty blonde Vida? Her ol' man keeled over havin' sex, so now she's a goddamn widder. Don't thet beat all?" He spat in the dirt. "There's gonna be a farewell party tonight fer her at the 'rec' room. Say, ain't she tight with thet Kat whatzer-name? The one ya been seein' so much of?"

"Yeah. So?"

"Oh, hell, I dunno. Well, anyways, because of the party, the Post closes at five an' don't open again 'til nine tonight." Duke chuckled and winked at Tex. "Miz Bracken ast me ta bring my ghee-tar an' harmonica to play at th' shindig. Ya don't wanna miss *thet*, now do ya?" The old cowboy laughed heartily and strode over to the corral to hitch the horse to a post.

So, thought Tex, *The Trading Post will be unattended for a good four hours, at least three.* He felt his pulse gallop as fast as a racehorse on a winning streak. *Damn! Jes' what I've been waitin' fer*, he told himself. He stomped his cigarette out with the sole of one boot and half-walked, half-ran to his truck parked behind the barn. He knew in his gut Deb would be cowering there. *Shit. Where could she go? She couldn't hide out in th' hills with them damn coyotes 'n all. 'Sides, she's afraid of th' dark. Mebbe I shouldn't of pushed her outta th' truck thet way, but she's gotta learn. Gotta lissen to ol' Tex. Don't I give her hot sex? An' a good job, three squares, an' a place to hang her hat? Who th' hell ever did thet fer her, fer chrissakes?*

As if he willed it, Tex found Deb curled up in a ball on his truck's front seat, shivering and scared. "Hey, Deb. It's me," he said through the open window on the driver's side. He reached in to touch her short, curly hair and she shifted and stared up at him, one eye red-purple and swollen shut, the other filled with hate and fright.

"You touch me, Tex, I'll scream bloody-murder," she hissed.

"Hell. You look like shit. I didn't do thet to ya. C'mon."

"Yes you did, you shithead. But you ain't gonna do it again. Lara made me promise."

"Lara? Y'mean, th' filly? Where did ya... ?"

"This mornin'. When I hid by th' apple trees. I was hurtin' bad an' all cuz-a you, you shithead."

"Okay, okay!" Tex untied his red-checkered neckerchief and handed it to Deb. "Look, babe," he said, leaning through the car window. "I wanna ask you. This is important, so, *think*. Those times at th' Post when you saw Roy or June open th' safe. You told me you caught th' combination. You remember it now?"

Deb dabbed shakily at her swollen eye. "Uh... I dunno. Can't remember."

"C'mon, c'mon, dammit-ta-hell, THINK!"

"It was somethin' like ..."

"No, no. You gotta get it straight. See. Tonight's th' night. You 'n me. Grab th' cash an' split." Tex opened the truck's door. "Okay. Sit up, dammit." He pulled at her, propping her up like a rag doll on a shelf against the truck's seat back. "I'll getcha some coffee to clear thet excuse you got fer a brain. An' sumpin' to eat from that bum of a cowboy cook. While I'm gone, ya think, *hard*, dammit!"

"But I look so godawful. Besides, it hurts," Deb whimpered softly.

"Geezus fuck. Here." Tex reached across her to open the truck's glove compartment and threw a pair of sunglasses on Deb's lap. "Put these on. Nobody'll see us. We'll split wit' the cash straight to the border. Now shut up and think."

Tex loped off at a half-run toward the mess hall, cursing the cunts of the world. *Can't live with 'em, can't do wit'out 'em*, he thought. *But ol' Deb'll come through or I'll beat it outta her. She's goddamn better'n thet bitch, Kat.* The typed letters he'd sent to Kat's father still hadn't turned the trick in his favor. *Didn't even get an answer. Don't he give a fuck fer his daughter? Ol' bullshit moneybags. But I don't need his dough. The Brackens ain't been to the bank fer 'most a week now. I know fer a fact they go every Friday. This here's Thursday. Should be a helluva stash in thet safe right now an' I aim to grab it, goddammit.*

But a new thought, like the buzz of a pesky horsefly, made Tex pause by the mess hall door. *Wait a minute. What th' hell was thet filly, Lara, doin' talkin' to Deb? I don't like her messin' in my business. Not one fuckin' bit. Mebbe I oughta trip up thet kid of hers again with thet goddamn rope. Teach her to stick her fancy nose in where she ain't wanted, once 'n fer all.*

At the drink table, Vince sipped on a foaming libation of draft beer and surveyed the party scene. Music for dancing blasted from a phonograph player in one corner of the rectangular, pine-paneled rec room. Streamers of red, blue, and yellow hung from the room's log-pole beams. A few couples two-stepped their way around the beige linoleum floor to a country music rendition of "On Top Of Old Smoky," while others sat together at round tables covered in red gingham tablecloths. In a corner by a picture window stood an old upright piano. Nearby was a green, felt-covered pool table. As some guests competed in a game, others looked on, drinking and kibitzing.

Standing there, Vince recalled viewing the Treadwell woman from a distance all day prior to tonight's party; first, as she and Maria left Lara's cabin to pick up the morning mail, and later, as Lara took a few phone calls in June Bracken's office.

Vince felt comfortably certain he had been successful in his attempts at non-detection as he shot photos of Lara relaxing by the pool with Maria. He even managed a few close-ups of Lara interacting with Billy as she toweled him off, hugged him, and gave him a drink from a bottle of orange-colored soda.

Geez, thought Vince, *this Treadwell dame seems like any other good mom I've ever seen, even-tempered, loving, concerned. Damn obvious the rapport she has with her son. Why would anyone in their right mind want to upset something so special? And Lara's a looker. Not that it matters. But she does seem outgoing and cheerful, and people appear to respond positively to her.*

He watched her over the rim of his mug of beer. She was sitting with Billy, Maria, Stan Gorman, and Bip at one of the round tables, eating barbecued chicken and potato salad from a paper plate and sharing it with Billy.

It was then Vince saw her jump up quickly, say something to Maria, pat Billy on the head, and run to the entrance of the rec room. He took immediate note of the object of her excitement as a tall, blonde fellow in a denim shirt, jeans, and cowboy boots came through the door. From the way Lara Treadwell greeted him it was obvious the two had a hot thing going. Maybe Rick Treadwell had something to pin on his wife after all.

CHAPTER 25

A wise gamester ought to take the dice
Even as they fall, and pay down quietly,
Rather than grumble at his luck.

—— *Sophocles*

Lara and Chance sat on the front seat of the black Ford convertible, top up, windows down, parked on a graveled area facing the lake, not far from The Trading Post. The sun, soon to set, hung low on the horizon where far-off magenta mountains met the placid, azure lake. No one was around as far as both could see. It would be another forty minutes before the Post opened for business.

"Still early yet," breathed Chance as he nuzzled Lara's neck.

"Keep that up and I'll get too hot to handle," Lara said softly. "You've spoiled me, Chance. All I can think of since last night is how much I want to make love with you, over and over." She gazed into his golden green eyes and touched his face, her fingers tenderly tracing the strong line of his handsome, tanned jaw.

He took her hand, held it tightly, and kissed her lips, his other hand moving slowly, tantalizingly up her thigh and coming to rest at the edge of her white shorts. "I know, I know. But where can we go? You never seem to be able to get away for long without a lot of planning. Nothing against Billy, of course. I'm glad I finally got to meet him. He's a great little kid." Chance sighed, removed his hand from her leg, and lit a Chesterfield, offering it to Lara as he lit one for himself. "By the way, Lar,... how much more time do you have here at the ranch?"

"About another week. I heard from my lawyer today. My court date's the end of this month." As she smoked, Lara watched the sun fast becoming a flame-colored ball, accompanied in its inevitable descent by varying hues of saffron, vermillion, apricot, and rose. *How*, she thought, *can I keep my personal sun from setting on these moments with Chance, moments so precious they've become a part of me?*

She smiled at Chance, her heart warming. He smiled back.

"Where were you planning on going after this?" he asked.

"Denver. A family named Garner, good people my husband befriended when he was stationed at Lowry Air Force Base during the war. They promised to help me get settled there."

"Why Denver?"

"Never been there. I thought it would be a good place to start a new life and raise my kids. Going back to Connecticut wouldn't work. Too many reminders." She turned her face up to Chance's and changed the subject, saying, "Thanks for making it to the party today, Chance. Wasn't Pidge a kick playing 'Happy Birthday'? I didn't know she could play the piano. Or, Duke, the guitar, for that matter. And Roy was a surprise, too, when he dragged out that big tin wash bucket with the broom handle attached and thumped away like a bass player. Everybody loved that, 'specially the kids." Lara cuddled close to Chance. "I'll never forget this place," she said, feeling a familiar flush of hot, titillating desire rush through her like a runaway train. "Oh, Chance, I wish I didn't have to leave here. I'll miss you so much."

He drew her closer. "I'll miss you like crazy, too, Lar." He took her cigarette, and, with his, extinguished both in the ashtray. "Let's make the most of things with the time we have left." His voice was husky as he played with the wisps of hair at the nape of her neck with his fingers. "You're so damn beautiful." His lips felt warm and moist as he nibbled on her earlobe. "Oh, Lar, Lar ..."

"Oh my God, Chance." She wanted desperately to melt into him, to give of herself completely once again, and yet again. The feeling was irresistible, though she knew she didn't have much time to spend with him alone tonight. Maria had agreed to take Billy to play with Bip at her cabin, and Lara had promised Maria to have only one drink with Chance. Then she'd pick up Billy so Bip could be put to bed. *But Chance is right*, thought Lara. *Why not make the most of what little time we have together? Maria will understand.*

Heartbeat quickening, she eased herself down on the cool, tan leather seat, smiling invitingly up at Chance.

"I'm sure of one thing, Lar." Chance was on top of her, at least as best he could given the limited space in the front seat of the Ford. "If I don't make love to you right now ..."

For one bizarre moment Lara felt like laughing out loud at the sheer physical awkwardness of the situation, but, driven by her insatiable need to couple with Chance, she ignored the impulse, instead wrapping her arms around his broad shoulders to help pull him closer to her.

"Oh God, Lar, I want you so much," he whispered.

"I want you, too, Chance." It was true. Nothing seemed to matter to her but this glorious, uninhibited desire, this seemingly unquenchable hunger she and this man had for each other. And nothing, nobody, could ever take it away. *It will always be a part of my life,* she thought, *like the horses I saw from the plane, running wild, their spirits forever free as their Creator surely must have intended.*

She felt Chance's hand cup her sweater-clad breast as, lost in pulsating passion, she kissed the top of his blonde head. Their lips joined together sweetly, sensuously, tongues engaging, and Lara felt immediately transported in a delirium of sexual longing as her lover's other hand traveled up her inner thigh to ..."Chance," she whispered. "Wait. I hear something." It was definitely someone shouting a command.

A rough voice shouted louder this time. It seemed to be coming from The Trading Post. "I said, hold it right there or I'll shoot!"

"Oh my God." Lara struggled to sit up, bumping her head on Chance's forehead. "Ouch! Did you hear that? Omigosh, who... ?"

Chance, frowning, one hand to his head, looked in the car's rearview mirror. "I can't see through that window in back." He opened the driver's door, got out, and squinted in the gathering twilight. "Something's going on at the Post. Stay down. I'll be right back."

As she watched Chance cautiously tread in a circuitous route in the general direction of The Trading Post, Lara slid off the car's front seat through the open door, and, peeking from a bent position saw three figures on the portico of the Post, one obviously holding two others at bay. Bravery, new to her, combined with curiosity, caused her to step beyond the car for a better vantage point.

She heard what sounded like a familiar voice. "Hey, bud. Who th' hell d'ya think you are? Put down the damn piece, will ya? We ain't done nothin', ya jerk."

Lara crept closer to hear, but not so she could be seen, she hoped. Her pulse was racing like a speeded-up metronome.

"The hell you haven't." The rough voice she heard shouting earlier was now tinged with a straightforward, no-nonsense tone of steely calm. Lara saw Chance, just ahead of her, stand stock-still and, turning, signal her to keep back as he continued edging off into a nearby clump of trees.

"You're in big trouble, cowboy," growled the owner of the rough voice. To Lara's amazement the voice sounded like that of... yes, as she recognized the man's physical bulk she was sure the voice was that of none other than Mister Vincent. What in the world was he doing? He appeared to be pointing a gun at... Her heart jumped. Tex Otis! The cowboy was carrying what looked like a black satchel in one hand while strong-arming a girl who was straining vainly to break free of his grip on her. Lara realized with dismay the girl must be Deb, as much as she could see of her. Poor Deb. Never able to free herself from Tex's evil hold on her.

Horrified, Lara saw Tex suddenly whip Deb around so the girl, directly in front of him in his grasp, could serve as a human shield. "Hey, blubberface," Tex yelled at Vincent. "Shoot me, ya shoot her, too. Ha! Some gun ya got there. Probably fake. Like yer stupid name."

Out of the corner of her eye, Lara noticed Chance slowly ease his way behind a nearby shed sheltered by a weeping willow tree. She felt certain Tex hadn't seen Chance, so involved was the cowboy in taunting Vincent. She prayed she also remained undetected, as, hunched over, she backed up to the car and crouched down by the Ford's rear left fender. In this position she had an overall view of the tableau, which now included Roy Bracken, unseen by Tex whose back was turned. Roy, sneaking carefully around the shadowed corner of the Post, was holding a rifle at the ready. Lara saw Roy signal to Chance and heard Deb's high, plaintive voice pleading, "Damn you, Tex. Lemme go! I won't tell, honest." The girl was frantically attempting to free herself from Tex's stranglehold across her chest by pulling down hard on his arm and biting it. She kicked back against his shin with one foot again and again. "I hate you, ya damn shithead. Lemme go!" she cried.

With one powerful motion Tex swung the satchel he was holding in his right hand and aimed it at Deb's head. It hit her directly in the face, causing the dark glasses she wore to flip off as she wailed in pain and sank to the ground. Now, holding the satchel against himself as a shield, Tex screeched at Vincent. "See what ya made me do, motherfucker? You ain't got no right to stick me up in th' first place. Hey, we kin share the stash. I'll give you half if you drop th' piece. Deal?"

"No deal," Vincent's voice was steady and strong. "I wasn't a New York cop for twenty years for nothing, cowboy. Drop the bag."

"Ha! I already did!" Tex laughed. "See?" He spit on Deb's inert body. "Like most dames, she ain't worth shit." He kicked at her with the tip of his boot as he fumbled for something in his jeans jacket, and Lara, feeling as though she might faint on the spot, saw the unmistakable gleam of metal rise in Tex's hand, aimed directly at Vincent.

Lara let an involuntary scream escape from somewhere deep within her. "Look out!"

Both Vincent and Tex jerked their heads to look in Lara's direction as, at precisely the same moment, Chance, having stealthily managed to join Roy, made a running tackle at Tex's back, wrestling the cowboy to the ground. As Chance pinned Tex's gun arm down so he couldn't move it, Roy Bracken and Vincent pointed their firearms at the surprised cowboy, now cursing and sputtering. "Goddammit, you fuckers. Gimme a break. It was all Deb's idea, fer chrissake. I was only tryin' to help her 'til thet fruit stopped us. Our mom's dyin' an'... "

"Tell it to the judge, Otis. You're fired," said Roy as he retrieved the moneybag from Tex's grasp and handed it to June, who at that moment had arrived on the scene. "Call the sheriff," Roy said to her. "And get an ambulance out here quick."

As Lara shakily approached the portico, Chance pulled Tex up to a standing position. Vincent handcuffed the now subdued cowboy while Roy stood guard with his rifle. Lara, avoiding looking at Tex, knelt beside Deb. "Deb, Deb. You're safe now. It's Lara." She shuddered at the sight of the girl's bloodied features and was grateful to see Deb slowly regain consciousness as June appeared with a wet cloth and some towels.

"Thank God she's still alive and those sunglasses she was wearing are shatterproof. She could've been blinded," whispered Lara to June as June placed the wet cloth on Deb's forehead and dabbed at her battered face. "I was going to tell you earlier, June. I saw Deb this morning. She was hiding from Tex after he beat her up. I wish I told you then, 'cause... ." Lara felt tears sting her eyes. "Maybe this wouldn't have happened. "

"Forget it, Lara," June said. "I've been having my suspicions about Tex for years." She glanced over at the cowboy slumped on the portico's bench, docile now, but still cursing under his breath while intermittently begging his captors for a smoke, to no avail. "That guy's been trouble since the get-go, Lara. I'm sorry you and Chance had to be bothered with this." She checked her watch and stood up, smiling at Chance who sauntered over next to Lara. "We thank you both so much. Help is on the way. Why don't you two go into the Post? Marge has the bar open and drinks are on the house."

"Now, where were we, Lar?" Chance beamed, dimples dancing. "Before we were so ..."

"Rudely interrupted?" She laughed quietly and took his hand. "Let's walk first, Chance. I'm still kind of shaky."

"What? No free drinks? I could use a beer."

"I'll wait in the car. I need to calm down." She gave his hand a squeeze. "You're a hero, Chance. You deserve a free drink... and lots more." She smiled beguilingly at him and blew him a kiss. He saluted her with mock seriousness, grinned, and strode back to the Post.

The silence of the car's cool interior was comforting. Lara leaned her head against the seat's back and closed her eyes, trying to make sense of what just happened. So... Mr. Vincent was a cop. *What is a big city policeman doing away out here? And why the interest in me, for heaven's sake? Oh no.* Lara dismissed what occurred to her as,... but no, it was preposterous. *Rick wouldn't, or would he? What if he actually hired some guy to spy on me? No. He wouldn't stoop so low, unless... .* She remembered his words on that dreadful day. Was it really only eight weeks or so ago? *I've lost count*, she thought, blanking out. *It seems like a century ago since I heard Rick say if he and I split up each "could get a kid."* But her lawyer, Sylvester McDermott, had assured her she'd get custody of both children.

"Got you a Moscow Mule Deluxe made especially by Marge," said Chance, a bottle of beer in one hand as he leaned through the car window and handed Lara the frosted mug. "The Post is filling up, and the sheriff's arrived. Roy said the ambulance is on its way." Chance opened the car door and set his beer on the floor of the driver's side. "Think I'll put the top down so we can enjoy the stars," he said. He uncoupled the heavy canvas from the metal hooks securing it to the top bar of the windshield, folded it like an accordion, and fastened it back to set neatly against the trunk of the car. Mission accomplished, he took a swig of beer, placed the bottle back on the floor, and lit two Chesterfields, giving one to Lara.

"Thank you." She exhaled slowly. "You're so special, Chance. Such a heroic person, jumping in to right a wrong, regardless of your own safety. Frank told me you saved his life in the war. Would you tell me about it?"

Chance picked up his bottle of beer and slid into the driver's seat. "I will if you tell me what's eating you, Lar. I can tell something's bothering you."

"What do you mean?"

"That Vincent guy. I know you were aware of his watching you at the party. And now you know what he really is, so ..." Chance paused, taking a sip of beer. "He told me he was here on a case. He's an ex-cop, working now as a private investigator. Which is why the gun and handcuffs. Didn't say who he was watching, but it's kind of obvious it's you. Also, he had a strong bead on Tex."

Lara shivered. "I hate to think it, but maybe my husband hired him to see if I'm behaving myself. And if it's found I'm not, well, Rick might fight me for Billy and my baby girl. Oh, Chance. Don't you see? I've got to be really careful from now on. I can't, I mean, we can't ..."

"See each other? Make love? Hell, Lar. What we have together isn't wrong, dammit. It's beautiful... like you." Chance squashed his cigarette out in the car's ashtray. "Wait a damn minute. Can it be?" He tipped her face gently but firmly up to meet his. "You still love him, don't you?" He released his hand from her chin and lit another cigarette. "I should've known."

Lara shook her head. "Oh no, Chance, I don't think so. Especially now since ..."

"You don't have to explain, Lar."

"Yes, yes I do." She shifted forward in the car's seat and turned toward him, looking him in the eye. "This is the honest-to-God truth, Chance. I've never been as crazy about any man as I am about you. Not ever. Even Rick, though I fell for him enough to marry him and have two kids by him." Carefully, gently, she touched Chance's arm. "I'm thinking I... I must love you. I mean, I haven't said it in so many words."

"Sometimes it's better not to say it, Lar, unless you're sure."

"I know, I know, but,... oh God, Chance. I'm so damned confused right now. Can you understand that?" She stubbed out her half-smoked cigarette.

"Hell, yes." He laughed, then turning serious, said, "But one fact remains, Lar, set in stone, rock-solid for eternity like those amazing formations out in Desert Lake. It's simply that we can't keep away from each other, you and I. Call it whatever stupid thing you want... love, sex, sheer idiocy. Who knows? What's more, I don't give a damn why your sap of a husband sent you out here except to be grateful to the man 'cause I never would've met you otherwise. And that would've been my loss. Forever, dammit."

"My loss, too, Chance," Lara sighed. "It's just... I'm scared, I guess. I thought I loved Rick, truly. And loving him, before I came out here, of course I trusted him. Ha! So much for that." She sank against the car's seat, head tipped back, and stared up at the late August night sky. "And now that I've found out what Mister Vincent's real mission was all along, well... it shakes my confidence in everything. I have to watch my step from now on, for my kid's sakes especially, and for my own need to be strong and carry on, no matter what." *What a relief it is*, she thought, *to put my feelings into words*. She took a long sip from the mug of refreshing, gingery Moscow Mule.

"You'll do fine, Lar. You're one helluva woman." Chance reached for her hand and gave it a squeeze. "You're like a Thoroughbred at the starting gate, ready to run. You're a winner. Maybe not the first time out, but you've got what it takes for the long haul." He smiled his heart-stopping smile. "When things get tough, just remember I said that... and meant it."

The vision, viewed from a Piper Cub, of wild horses streaking en masse across a sagebrush-dotted plain at sunrise filled her heart anew. She held Chance's hand tightly. "Thanks. But I feel more like a mustang. In spirit, that is. I need to taste my freedom, get my head straight and figure things out." She smiled at him. "But I appreciate your vote of confidence, Chance... so much. I jumped into marriage too fast this first time. Next time, if there is a next time, I want to be sure." She kissed him tenderly on his cheek. "Does that make sense?"

"As much as anything in this screwed-up world, Lar."

"You're a wise man, Chance Darwin. The best." She drank the last of the Mule. "And if what we have together is meant to be, well, this sounds trite, I know, but... time will tell. Oops!" she said. "That does sound trite."

"Yeah." Chance swallowed the last of his beer. "Funny thing, time. Too bad it doesn't whiz right by in the worst of times and stand still so we can savor the best of times, like being here with you."

"Omigosh. Speaking of time, I promised Maria I'd pick Billy up at her cabin way before this. I've got to go, Chance." Her eyes locked with his and held his golden-green gaze for one timeless, hypnotic moment. She wished she could stay like this, always at his side... never leave... his woman, his Thoroughbred, as he called her... forever. But she could not.

"I'll walk you back, Lar."

"No." She smiled wistfully, patting his arm. "Thanks, Chance. It's not too dark. I'll be okay." She slipped out of the car's passenger door, closed it, and leaned in to blow him a kiss. "If I get too close to you again, well, we both know ..."

Chance straightened in his seat and started the car, engine idling. "Damn good thing A.K.'s keeping me busy this next week, Lar." He raised his voice, saying, "Or, like a dog in heat, I'd be camping out on your doorstep every damn night. You'd have to throw rocks at me to fend me off. Hell, I might follow you to Denver. Then what would you do?" He flashed his dimpled smile at her.

"You know I'd love it!" Lara laughed. "Oh, Chance." She reached across to grasp his hand firmly, warmly. "Will you call me in Denver? I'll leave the number with June and Roy."

"Better yet, Lar. I'll fly out when you least expect me and scoop you up on my trusty steed. Then I'll carry you off to some high Rocky Mountain cave and have you all to my greedy self." He made a funny face, licking his lips lasciviously.

"Oh? Won't I have anything to say about it?" Lara feigned innocence.

"Nope. I'm a selfish bastard. Time you knew that about me." He let go of her hand and gave her a friendly, fake-military salute. "Happy landings, beautiful. See you in Denver."

Chance revved up the Ford's engine and slowly traveled down the gravelly dirt drive. In the next moment Lara saw him stop the car. She watched as he turned his handsome blonde head to look at her and shout, loud and clear, "I love you, Lar!" In the next second he was off again, racing toward the main road by Desert Lake in a moonlit cloud of dust.

Her heart thumping wildly, Lara stood frozen as the taillights of the black convertible disappeared into the night. "I love you, too, Chance," she whispered, wishing now she'd said it to him in person. But where would that lead? *No. Too much work ahead of me yet*, she thought. *Maybe... after I get settled in Denver.*

Reluctantly, she headed for the Post where she dropped off her empty copper-colored mug, then hurried through the sultry night to Maria's cabin to pick up Billy.

One week later, as the Woodie raced towards Reno, once again piloted by Roy at speeds nearing ninety, Lara felt a strange sense of regret. She couldn't understand exactly why. Today was the day she should feel the elation all who spent the required six weeks out here were supposed to feel, shouldn't she? Certainly most guests she met at the ranch, the female ones at least, would celebrate the attainment of a divorce decree by tossing their connubial rings off the Truckee River Bridge or leaving a red-lipsticked kiss print on the columns of the courthouse.

"You look pensive, Larie-love. Can I help?" Pidge was sitting on the Woodie's back seat with Lara. She leaned closer to be heard over the car's engine but not by Roy or Uta Crouse and son Axel in the front seat. "I'm your cheering section, m'dear, which is why I came along today. That, and to watch Axel while Uta sees her lawyer." Pidge stuck a Kool in her ebony cigarette holder and lit it.

"Thanks for the kind thoughts, Pidge. You're a true friend." Lara held up her left hand and shook her head. "Look at this. I haven't taken off my wedding ring yet. Somehow, everything's so final. And, for all I know, I may have lost Chance, too." She sighed, letting her mind wander.

I wish Maria were still at the ranch, she thought. I *valued her no-nonsense comebacks. She helped me put things in perspective.* But Maria, along with Stan and Bip, had left this past week. So had the Januses. Harriet Renquist, of course, was still there, taking Vida's place in Kat's troubled life. And Harriet, with her caretaking skills, had persuaded Kat to stay on at Desert Lake and attend regular counseling sessions in Reno. *Good for her. After I get my decree today*, Lara told herself, *our cabin will be occupied by new guests, and Billy and I will be flying to Denver. I'm so glad Billy's in the care of Nita Big Horn today and gets to play one more time with Jimmy. No point in our son being exposed to the official dissolution of his parent's marriage. But I'll make a sincere effort to explain things to him when he asks questions.*

She gazed out the window, fiddling with her wedding ring as the Woodie zoomed along the highway like a fire truck on the way to a major disaster... an apt metaphor for what was about to take place in her life. Was this really happening?

She heard Pidge say, "You haven't lost Chance, Larie-love. He's steady and dependable like the hero he's proved himself to be, helping catch that nasty cowboy Tex. Chance'll pop up again."

"How can you be so sure, Pidge?"

"Because I'm psychic, m'dear." She laughed. "What branch of the service was he in?"

"Marines. "

"Semper Fidelis, Larie-love. If he's a true Marine he'll follow that motto, even in love. And I know he loves you. He just got scared off 'cause he sensed you weren't as sure of your feelings for him. Not 'til you get your 'diploma,' that is."

"What makes you so wise, Pidge?" Lara smiled at her friend.

Pidge blew out a plume of smoke and watched it curl up to the roof of the Woodie. "Age, m'dear. That and observing cowboys 'n divorcees romance each other over the years. Some work out, some don't, but I'd gamble on you and Chance any ol' day. 'Course, I'm a cockeyed optimist, as the song goes."

Pidge chuckled and reached out to give Lara's hand a reassuring pat when, BAM! Without warning, the Woodie was rocked by a tremendous shudder and the impact of something huge hitting the windshield.

"Oh my God!" Lara saw glass spraying into the front seat of the vehicle. "Uta! Axel! Are you okay?" she shouted as the car screeched to a halt and Roy jumped out onto the highway to inspect the damage. It was then Lara viewed the ugly head and bloodied beak of a vulture half-embedded in the shattered windshield of the Woodie.

"Yah, tanks. Ve are fine. No cuts on Axel, praise Gott," answered Uta, clutching Axel close as she brushed tiny pieces of glass from herself and her frightened young son, who, amazingly, didn't utter a sound.

Pidge shook her head. "Poor ugly bird," she sighed. "Too greedy for roadkill and it ends up the same way. Tsk, tsk. I'm sure there's a lesson there somewhere."

They all watched as Roy, the crusty old cowboy, seemingly capable of dealing calmly with any emergency, removed the mammoth, feathered creature from its prison in the windshield, tossed the carcass to the side of the road, wiped blood from the car's hood, and, firing up the Woodie's motor, sped off again as if nothing unusual had happened. But, Lara wondered, could the bird's violent death be an omen of some kind? Or just signifying the death of a marriage?

After a surprisingly speedy procedure in the courtroom where Roy testified he'd seen Mrs. Lara Treadwell every day at Bracken's Desert Lake Ranch and Lara took the stand, answering the few questions for which Sylvester T. McDermott prepared her, she was legally divorced.

Five years of a union I foolishly thought was fine, all wiped out with the bang of a gavel, thought Lara. *Now what?*

CHAPTER 26

God forbid that I should go to any
heaven in which there are no horses.

——*Robert Bontine Cunninghame Graham*

"Look, Mommy! It's Daddy's plane!" Billy directed Lara's attention to the lights of a large aircraft about to land onto the tarmac of Denver's Stapleton Airport late one balmy September evening.

"Yes, sweetheart. I see it. Daddy's bringing us your baby sister."

Lara smiled at Grams and Dad Garner standing with her at the gate. *What a dear couple*, she thought. Grams was a tiny, feisty bird of a woman, and Dad was quiet and thoughtful. More like family than just friends. They were good people, with hearts as big and wide-open as the Rocky Mountain country surrounding this mile-high city.

The huge plane rolled to a stop, and as its doors opened and passengers started to disembark, Billy cried out, "I see him, Mommy! See? He's coming down the steps."

Lara held Billy's hand as they went through the gate and stood waiting to greet Rick. The man she was married to for five years walked toward her carrying a pink bundle in his arms. Lara restrained herself from running and embracing him, thinking, *how strange to feel this way. Yet it does seem a natural impulse. After all, he is the father of my children*, she reasoned. Somehow, the six weeks away from him didn't add up in her brain. Were they really divorced?

Billy rushed to wrap his arms around his father's legs. Rick set a carry-on bag down with his free hand to pat his son on the head. Then, followed by Billy, he approached Lara, cradling the tiny pink bundle in the crook of his arm.

Lara felt her eyes flood with tears as she grasped a wee hand escaping from the soft bundle and feasted on the sight of Candace's pink cheeks and a charming tuft of angel-like blonde hair. "Oh, she's darling! And so much bigger!" said Lara.

"She's a good baby," Rick said. "No trouble at all on the flight. The stewardesses hated to see her go."

Lara could see Rick struggling with his emotions as he handed their baby daughter over to her. For a moment she felt a flash of sympathy for him. At the same time she was glad she had been awarded custody and he visitation rights, and she vowed to herself that—even though he'd been cruel to her—for the children's sake she would always speak highly of him to them. No need for negativity, she'd decided, and far better for the children in the long run.

"Thank you, Rick," she said quietly, hugging the warm, precious bundle to her breast.

The Garners welcomed Rick pleasantly. Soon all were driven by Dad back to the Garner's comfortable, tidy brick home in the suburbs of Denver.

As Lara fed Candace her bottle and changed her, Rick and Billy got re-acquainted. Both children were then tucked into bed, Candace first in the borrowed crib set up in the Garner's tiny attic bedroom where Lara and Billy shared a double bed. *How wonderful it is*, thought Lara, *to pick up where I left off as a mom with my beautiful baby girl.* As she settled Billy in bed and kissed him goodnight, the Desert Lake Ranch seemed like something she'd experienced in a dream.

Even Chance seemed unreal, but not quite. It was no dream, the gift he'd given her of a better sense of herself, no dream the fact he imbued her womanhood with the boost she needed to travel on and be strong, no matter what. When she first arrived in Denver, he had called her, promising, if possible, to fly out to see her around Thanksgiving during a trip to Wyoming with A.K. and Frank. *So much to look forward to*, she told herself. A thrill flashed through her just thinking about it.

When Lara came downstairs, Rick was chatting with the Garners and enjoying a tuna sandwich Grams had fixed for him along with some of her home-baked oatmeal cookies. Lara, feeling slightly detached, sat with all three of them in the cozy, diminutive living room. Grams and Dad left the room to go to the kitchen, ostensibly to make coffee, but Lara felt it was really so she and Rick could talk alone. In the strained interim, Lara asked Rick how things were going with him and his work. As he caught her up on several recent television appearances of his, her mind wandered. She was tempted to question him regarding Vincent Caparelli, but since she'd no proof Rick had hired the detective to watch her, she kept silent.

Relieved when the time came for Rick to catch his flight back to LaGuardia, Lara wished him a safe trip. To her, he seemed a bit sad. It felt awkward for both of them as they stood facing one another. "Please say hello to your parents for me and tell Gladys to expect a most sincere letter of thanks for taking such good care of Candace."

"Well,... goodbye, Lara," Rick said as he reached for his briefcase propped near the Garner's front door. "Looks like the ranch I sent you to did you some good. Billy, too. I'll be calling him soon." With that, he turned quickly and headed out the door toward Dad Garner waiting for him in the car.

Lara stood with Grams, both waving goodbye as Dad backed the car out of the driveway for the trip back to the airport. As the vehicle disappeared into the night, Lara felt Grams pat her affectionately on the shoulder. "Now you've got your babies together, you can start a new life, Lara," the wise little lady said. "It's clear to me Rick already realizes what he's lost." She gave Lara a hug. "You know we'll help you all we can."

True to their word, the Garners encouraged and participated in Lara's scanning the local ads for a rental. Soon, four blocks away from where Grams and Dad lived, Lara found a trim ranch-style house with two bedrooms and a large fenced back yard. As part of the divorce settlement, Rick sent the furniture out, and, to Billy's delight, Lara enrolled the youngster in kindergarten a convenient two blocks from home. She herself made friends through a local church, and, when both Billy and Candace were tucked in bed, spent many evenings working on her art and writing a poem dedicated to Pidge, entitled "Edge Of Tranquility." This she hoped to show to Chance around Thanksgiving.

The holiday was but a few weeks away when Lara received a letter, postmarked London. There was no return address. At first she thought it might be from Chance, as the address on the envelope had been typed, perhaps by Frank. Could Chance be in London on business for A.K. and that's why she hadn't yet heard from him? With quivering fingers, she ripped open the envelope.

It was from Claire Janus. "Dear Lara," wrote Claire, "Sinatra is right. Love is definitely better 'the second time around'. Nick and I married (finally) and are temporarily in England preparing to return to Greece, Nick's homeland, where his father is the premier of the present government. I'm not at liberty to give you details. All very hush-hush and a bit unsettled due to the political environment. Suffice it to say, Nick's real moniker is Janusopolus. Perhaps you've heard the name? In the near future, you may be reading in *Time* or *Life* about his political endeavors as he leaves academia behind and follows in his esteemed father's footsteps. Naturally, I will support him in all his ambitions, and we look forward to starting a family."

Claire went on to wish Lara and her children the best. "And please keep performing, Lara. I loved watching you dance. You've real talent. Hope you see Chance soon. Didn't he say he planned to meet you in Denver? You two make such a beautiful couple. I know you'll find true happiness in love as we have. Fondly, Claire and Nicholas Janus(opolus)."

How intriguing, thought Lara. It was fascinating to finally get some insight into the mystery she'd felt about them. *I wonder which of the two of them was getting unhitched? Surely that was the real reason for their stay at the ranch. How clever of them to hide their identities while at Desert Lake. I wonder if the Brackens knew. But, of course, they were good at keeping secrets.*

But where was Chance? *Maybe*, she pondered,... *maybe he's not comfortable communicating on paper. Surely he'll call, at least before Thanksgiving as we planned.*

But Thanksgiving came and went.

Sometime between Thanksgiving and Christmas, Colorado and its neighboring Western states experienced a blizzard of epic proportions. When the snow stopped swirling, the sun eventually came out, shining with blinding brilliance on huge drifts of the white stuff six feet high in spots. Soon the roads were cleared enough for Lara to feel safe in venturing out to the grocery store for some much-needed items. No car, but she was slowly saving for one with some extra money she'd earned babysitting a neighbor's child in her home. She was watching for used vehicle ads in the paper while taking driving lessons from Dad Garner.

"Let's walk to the store, Billy," said Lara. "It's cold out, but if we walk fast we'll keep warm." She bundled Billy into his blue snowsuit and boots and tucked a wool-bonneted, mittened Candace under warm blankets in her carriage.

Wearing a ski jacket and pants, a fur-lined parka, and stadium boots herself, Lara and her little party set out for the store several blocks away. Biting cold wind whipped her face and stung her nose and eyes as she pushed the carriage, followed by a red-cheeked Billy bravely trudging behind like a sturdy little snowman.

Finally, as they pushed through the doors of the store and savored its warmth, Lara exclaimed, "Oh, that feels good, doesn't it, Billy?" She kissed him on his frosty cheek and helped him remove his mittens and tuck them in the pockets of his snowsuit.

"Can I help you, miss?" the friendly storekeeper asked as he finished waiting on an elderly customer.

"Yes, thank you." Lara took her list from her purse in Candace's carriage. As she did so, her eyes drifted to the headline of a copy of The Denver Post lying on a stack of newspapers on the counter: PRIVATE PLANE CRASH IN WYOMING.

"Excuse me," she said to the grocer, handing him her list, as, her heart beginning to pump alarmingly, she read further. "The bodies of famed racehorse breeder, former U. S. Senator from Nevada and big-game hunter, A.K. Wheeler, 64, his pilot, Frank Jensen, 29, and his co-pilot and ranch foreman, Chance Darwin, 28, were discovered in their plane on a snow-covered peak in the Sawtooth Mountains early today. The nose of Wheeler's twin-engine Cessna 310 was found buried in deep snow by Barney Blankenship, a helicopter pilot for the National Park Service. The A.K. Wheeler plane had been missing since before Thanksgiving and Zoe Wheeler, well-known fashion model and wife of Sen. Wheeler, offered a substantial reward to anyone spotting the Cessna. A.K. Wheeler, Jensen, and Darwin were heading for the horse ranch of a friend of Wheeler's when ..."

Lara could read no more. She clung to the counter in a numbed state of shock, feeling faint, staring into space.

"Miss, miss, are you okay?" asked the grocer.

Lara felt hot tears well up and roll down her cheeks. She was breathing so fast even Billy became alarmed, about to cry himself. "Mommy?" he said. "Mommy,... are you sick?"

"No, no, I'm just ..." Absently, she patted Billy's rosy cheek. "Don't worry, sweetheart." She felt herself recover enough to say to the grocer, "Could you,... would you call a number for me, please? I don't know it offhand. It would be in the phone book. Garner. On East Floral." There was no way she could walk the five blocks to her home and she knew she could count on Dad to drive them back. *Dear God*, she prayed, *have him be at home.*

The storekeeper, along with a pleasant-faced woman customer, led Lara and Billy to the back room of the store, pushing Candace in her carriage there as well. Lara sat on a spindly chair and hugged Billy, as she rocked back and forth in despair. "Oh, Billy, Billy, I love you and Candace so much. We're on our own now. We'll be fine... we'll be fine."

Maybe this is what heaven looks like, thought Lara. The view from the window of the plane revealed nothing but a billowy carpet of clouds stretching interminably to meet the horizon of bright, cerulean-blue sky. A magnificent sight, powerful, yet peaceful. She could imagine, yes, out there in that endless stretch of whiteness, the "White Knight" of her dreams, handsome, blonde, smiling his tantalizing, dimpled grin, beckoning her to join him. "Goodbye, my Chance," she whispered. "My beautiful chance for a new love." She sighed softly. "Never to be, dear Chance,... never to be."

For here she was, six months later, flying to Los Angeles to join her sister Janelle in a house they had rented in Santa Monica. Lara's eyes moved from the window to her children, lulled to sleep by the plane's droning engines. *Thank God for them*, she thought.

Gaze shifting again to the window, she envisioned far out on the horizon a herd of heavenly horses, wild as the ones she'd viewed before, flying with winged hooves. I will live, she told herself, live proudly, for Chance, his memory, and all the wild horses running free.

EPILOGUE

Fortune may have yet a better success for you,
and they who lose today may win tomorrow.

— *Miguel de Cervantes,* Don Quixote

Standing in the wings, Lara Treadwell listened as the band's brass section rose to a raucous, show-bizzy crescendo. Her heart beat crazily, as usual. "Okay, okay. You're a pro," she whispered to herself. "Just wait for your intro and watch for the light cue."

To Lara, Reno seemed different this time. Same city, of course, but now it was October of '54, the backdrop ring of mountains was snow-capped, and the air downright brisk. She missed her kids. At least she knew they were being cared for by Mrs. Davis, a motherly, trustworthy sitter both children loved. She knew this gig was something her agent arranged as just a test to see if it was a job she wanted to pursue at this point in her career.

Gee, thought Lara, *three shows a night, the last one at two in the morning. Might not get to bed sometimes 'til four. What kind of a life is that? If I move my little family from L. A. to Reno, how could I get up in the morning to see Billy and Candace off to school? I'd be wiped out. Sure, the money's tempting, which is why I took the gig in the first place. Alimony and child support only go so far.*

The velvety voice of the show's announcer boomed from backstage. "Ladies and gentlemen! Reno's Hotel Riverside is proud to present, direct from Hollywood, California, the lovely Miss Lari Wells, performing for your pleasure with the fabulous Hal Gaines Orchestra and the dynamic Don Dragon Dancers."

Applause, applause. The band settled down to a low, pulsating tempo, teeming with tension. Lara, nee Lari Wells, thrilled to the music as she waited in the wings, primed to step into the spotlight. Eight chorus girls in blue-sequined net-and-feathers slithered by her. Bathed in a glow of cobalt, they swayed and sizzled downstage in sexy syncopation, then swooped upstage to form a sinewy line in front of the bandstand as Lara made her entrance, glittering in peach-colored, sequined capri pants and a matching, strapless, pushup bra giving her instant cleavage.

All was illusion, and she reveled in it. She loved the perky, peach-colored pillbox hat and gold-sprinkled, three inch, ankle-strapped heels with which she was costumed, loved the spotlight hiding the faceless crowd watching her every move.

The baby spotlight followed her like a second skin as she gracefully, sensuously, circled the proscenium back and forth—traveling mic in hand—singing to the smoke-filled darkness the sultry message of "Blues in the Night," all about how a man could speak out of two sides of his face at the same time when it came to lovin'. God knew she could relate to that one. But hope had become a steady presence in her life, and she felt stronger now.

Between shows, Lara heard a knock on her dressing room door and a familiar voice inquiring, "Are ya decent, kiddo?"

Flinging open the door, Lara gasped, "Oh my God! Maria! What are you doing here? Did you see the show? Come in, come in. You look terrific," she exclaimed, admiring Maria's mink coat, smartly coiffed dark hair, glowing complexion, and shining amber eyes. "Looks like life is treating you well."

"You, too, toots. You're as gorgeous as ever," Maria said as she and Lara hugged, "And Burt and I loved your singing. We didn't know ahead of time you were the headliner here."

"Burt? Who's that? What happened to Stan?"

"Went back to his wife. Can you believe it? Mainly for Bip's sake, but Stan wanted to give her a second chance when she joined AA." Maria lit a Pall Mall. "I read about Chance's crash. Geez, kiddo, I'm so sorry. I didn't have your Denver number and I'm just no good at writing. But I've thought of you so often. What's new? Besides the fact you're a goddamn star."

"No star. Just a hard-working single mom trying to put a little extra 'bread' on the table. But these crazy hours are too much. I'll be back in L. A. soon. Thank God, 'cause I miss my kids. My agent works hard for me, though. Gets me radio spots, television commercials, and, I'm crossing my fingers, a possible recording contract with Capitol Records, if I'm lucky. How about you, Maria?"

"I run my own detective agency! 'Member how I used to talk about that? And Burt was my first client. He's in insurance." She glanced at her watch. "Burt's waiting upstairs for me. He's short, bald, and true-blue. Not bad in bed, either. We have a lotta laughs. What's up with you in that department, kiddo?"

Lara felt her face flush under her stage makeup. "I have a new man, too. Only known him a few months, but,... oh, Maria."

"Tell me, tell me." Maria's dark eyes danced.

"He's, ah,... fun to be with, intelligent, tall, handsome, and works as a counselor at UCLA. My kids like him, too."

"You're in love. I can tell, toots. Congrats! And, what of your ex?"

"Eloped with the teen. Six months after our divorce. She's a really nice girl and good for Rick. They've come out to L. A. to visit the kids often. When Candace gets a bit older she and Billy can fly back East to visit for a month in the summer. It all works out fine." Lara switched gears. "You know, Maria, Desert Lake was a turning point for me and you were so much a part of it. I'm indebted to you... eternally." She gave Maria's mink-clad arm an affectionate squeeze. "Oh! Got a card from Pidge. It's off-season at the ranch so she went back to Philadelphia to take care of family business and Roy and June are up at their cabin in the mountains above here, deer hunting, and ..."

The stage manager's gravelly voice interrupted, blasting over the intercom. "Five minutes, Miss Wells."

Lara checked her reflection in the mirror. "Oh, gosh, Maria. I wish we had more time to talk."

"Don't 'spose you're ever in New York?" Maria flashed a white-toothed, ruby-red smile.

"Only if my agent gets me a job there. Because of my kids I stay in or near L. A. most of the time. Even way out here in the 'Wild West' is too far."

"Here's my card, toots, so you won't forget me." Maria fished a professional-looking business card from her purse and handed it to Lara. "Oh, meant to tell you. Burt and I go to the track a lot. One time at Belmont I bet on a horse with a name I thought you'd get a kick out of. And the damn thing came in a winner! Boy, we really raked in the dough that day."

"What was the horse's name?"

"'Lar's Chance'. Too coincidental, I thought. Ever hear of it?"

Lara felt her heart leap up to her eyeballs, like that of a bronco being broken to the saddle. "No." She gulped and sat down hard on the chair by her makeup mirror. "Oh my God, Maria. Do you suppose that could be the same horse I watched being born at the ranch where Chance worked? I never knew that he... ."

"A last gift from him to you, maybe? Naming a Thoroughbred after you and him? Ye gods! What a fabulous thing to do!" Maria said, leaning to kiss Lara airily on the cheek. "Well, gotta go. Burt 'n I hafta catch the red eye to LaGuardia. Break a leg, kiddo."

Lara rose and hugged her friend goodbye, promising to write and call often. Maria left, leaving a trail of "Tigress" perfume wafting in her wake.

A last minute glance in the mirror and "the lovely Miss Lari Wells" left her dressing room and climbed up the iron spiral staircase to stage right to wait for her musical entrance cue.

Aware of a special kinship with "Lar's Chance," Lara felt a thrill rush through her. *If I hadn't spent those six weeks at Desert Lake*, she told herself, *I'd never have met Chance Darwin. He'd dubbed me a Thoroughbred, like himself, even naming a racehorse to commemorate our love.* Now, like Lar's Chance, she was waiting at the starting gate, waiting to run the race of life like all the horses—humans, too—yearning to be free.

At her cue, she stepped onstage, traveling microphone in hand, warmed by the spotlight, certain tonight's performance would be one of her best. Life was good.

EDGE OF TRANQUILITY

High on the craggy cliff of time
As rays of dawn turn cadmium red
And purple sagebrush dots the desert plain below,
A golden horse stands, silent and alert,
Listening, listening,
Straining to catch the vibration of a sound,
Far away yet fast approaching,
Not one sound, it seems, but two,
One from the sky, one from below.
Melding together, as in the rumbling din
Of distant thunder.
Soon a sturdy colt and his frisky baby sister
Scramble up to join their mother
High on the rocky ledge of time.
"Shh," the mare cautions her young ones.
"Listen. Listen. Something is coming."
On guard, they stand as one,
Dark velvet eyes searching the sky
And the vast plain below,
Equine senses attuned to the sounds,
Almost upon them, drawing closer,
Ever closer, until...
The sounds converge
With cataclysmic force,
And hundreds of horses' hooves rumble relentlessly
Beating down on the desert floor in mad momentum,
A wild, hard-charging mass of mustangs
Whipping across the plain
In a fluid stream of horseflesh,
Hell-bent towards the horizon,
Desert dust rising in their wake, as...
Simultaneously,
In fierce choral coordination,
A small, yellow-bodied airplane,
Black wings glistening, shimmering

In the blinding flash of rising sun,
Roars deafeningly over the ledge of time,
Dips a wing to the equine trio,
Startled as they stand there,
And flies on, disappearing
Into a swirl of morning mist
Mirrored in the desert lake beyond.
And all is quiet again.

With the sun up and the sounds gone,
The golden mare nudges her young ones
And draws them to her.
"Soon, my children," she whispers.
"Soon we will join the herd
And fly with wings of gold
To the edge of tranquility.
We will splash in the desert lake,
Then race with hearts aflame,
Liberated, unbridled,
And forever free."

Lara Treadwell
Denver, 1951
(For Pidge, keeper of the password.)

Marilu Norden lives on the "Edge of Tranquility" in the Sonoran Desert east of Tucson, Arizona. Readers are invited to visit her Web site at www.MariluNorden.com.